SUNRISE
on
MONARCH BAY

PATRICIA YAGER DELAGRANGE

Alameda, California

Printed in the U.S.A.

Digital ISBN: 978-1-954395-14-5
Print ISBN: 978-1-954395-15-2

Dedication

In memory of our Rhodesian Ridgeback Jackson, and our chocolate labs Mocha, Java, Annabella, and Jack. And a special part of my heart belongs to my Friesian horse Maximus who died after seventeen years.
I'll miss you all forever.

Chapter One

Stella slid the last tray of chocolate croissants into the display case, took a step back and gazed out the front window of Patti's Pastries. When was the last time she'd stopped to smell the roses, to use an overly worn cliché?

Since she'd moved to Monarch Bay almost seven years ago, the weather had proved to be even more perfect than her sister Kat had told her. Blue skies were almost a daily occurrence on the Central Coast of California. White clouds formed undeniable pictures of ice cream cones, frolicking dogs, and any number of recognizable entities, if one took the time to sit (or lie down) on the beach or the grass and look at the sky. Something Stella hadn't done since the first year she'd moved here. Or, she should say, since she'd *escaped* to Monarch Bay, which would be a more appropriate description.

But she didn't feel like reminiscing right now. The thermometer she tacked up on the outside wall of Patti's Pastries read 74 degrees. How perfect was that? And here she was, same as every other day, Monday through Sunday, seven days a week, schlepping croissants, pies, cakes, cookies, and donuts from the bakery in the back of the building to the front of the shop, where anyone who entered this quaint establishment could see the artwork David and Sunny created for the people of Monarch Bay.

A bright orange and black monarch butterfly fluttered near the rose bush outside the window, wings floating gracefully up and down as it flew from one rose to the next, yellow pollen covering the delicate edges of its wings like shaved chocolate on the almond tort cakes David and Sunny created each morning.

Which reminded her how many hours she'd been up and at 'em, like every day of the week. Four or five a.m. seemed to come quicker than in the past, when she'd started working at Patti's Pastries. So much had happened since then. But that was for another day of thought-gathering. She didn't have time right now.

Their assistant, Sunny, scuttled to the front of the shop and checked the coffee canisters. At twenty-five years old and slender, he looked more like a high school student. His cropped, white-blond hair stuck straight up in a military-short cut, and his jeans hung low on his hips, as was the style, especially here in California. "Full to the brim and steaming hot." He turned to Stella and tilted his head. "Everything all right, boss?"

Stella leaned on the top of the glass case, eyes wide. "I think this is one of the most beautiful places I've ever lived." She turned to him. "And I don't take advantage of that very often, you know? Neither of us, David or I. All we do is work."

Sunny walked toward Stella and stood in front of her, blocking her view. "That could easily be changed, boss. I can handle it here while you and David take some time off for yourselves. David taught me all the baking I need to know. And if your daughter can sub for you like she does when you have a doctor's appointment or whatever, you'd be all set to go whenever you want. Just name the date, and Loreen and I can run this place while you and David are gone."

Stella pushed a stray strand of hair behind her ear. "Loreen's my accountant, Sunny. She doesn't have time to do both my job and her job every day. She'd never be able to leave this place."

Sunny smirked. "Sounds like someone I know. But, hey, boss, she got her bachelor's degree in accounting from San Luis Obispo College. She can do that number stuff in her sleep. And what? We're talking about a week, maybe two weeks, you and David would be gone?" He shrugged. "Piece of cake." He chuckled. "Apropos in this case."

Stella blinked, reverting her view to the drifting clouds dotting the sky. "A week would do. Two weeks would be pushing it."

Sunny patted Stella's arm. "Start small, if that'll make you feel more comfortable. Start planning now. Talk to Lo too. Feel her out."

A wide smile lit up Stella's face. "I'll run it by David when he gets in. See what he thinks." She glanced at the clock on the wall behind her. "Where is he anyway? He should have been here by now."

"Was wondering the same thing," Sunny murmured, wiping off a nearby table. "I'll finish up here and take an early lunch, if you don't mind."

"Fine by me. It's always slow after the morning rush. I'm going to go in the back and talk to Loreen. I'll hear the bell if someone comes in."

She lifted the apron over her head and slung it across her arm as she walked through the swinging double doors marking the entrance to the bakery in the back. She paused in front of a dark wooden door marked "Accountant at Work" in bright white letters. She smiled and knocked lightly. "Loreen?"

"Come in, Mom."

Stella entered the sunny office, the wall of windows brightening the rooms that ran along that side of the building. "Have time to talk, Lo?"

Loreen swiveled her chair to face her mother, wide pouty lips lifting up at the edges in an easy smile. "Wassup?"

Stella sat in the chair in front of Loreen's desk, leaned back, hands cupping the arm rests. "I need your opinion about something."

Loreen reached up and adjusted the scrunchy holding her long, blonde ponytail in place, looking much like she could be Sunny's twin sister instead of Gabriel's. "I'm all ears."

Stella recalled her ex-husband Robert ranting and raving that Stella must have had sex with another man to have given birth to a blonde baby. Robert was classically tall, dark, and handsome. Stella's auburn hair, which lightly grazed her shoulders, hung free and wavy, flattering her naturally pale skin. Robert could have had a DNA test done, so Stella could prove he was the father. But the enjoyment he got from his emotional hammering outweighed his need for physical proof of the fact. But again, no more walking down that lane of broken glass. He was long gone and out of their lives forever.

"I was just talking to Sunny about how David and I… well, all we do is work. We never take the time to play and have fun. I was thinking we might go on a short vacation. The only way we could pull it off is if you subbed for me. Sunny would do all the baking, and the accounting would have to be put aside for a short while. Otherwise, you'd be working into the night, every night. I don't want to burden either you or Sunny." She paused, lifting her gaze to the tree swaying in the breeze outside the window. "I want your honest opinion about my plan."

Loreen placed her elbows on the arms of her chair and put her hands together, interlacing her fingers. "Totally doable, Mom. Where are you gonna go? And when?"

"Hold your horses, young lady." Stella shook her head and chuckled. "I haven't even decided yet whether it's, as you call it, doable or not. What about Charlie? You usually pick him up every afternoon from school. You'd be too busy here to leave, working as cashier, dealing with all the customers."

"I can pick up my little brother from the Academy in about five minutes, bring him here, set him up at a table with a bunch of Star Wars Legos or something. He's easily entertained, Mom." She rolled her eyes. "He's only five."

"But what about after the bakery closes? You always walk to your Aunt Kat's house and visit Peter, almost every day. It's your special time with him. I don't want to interfere with that either."

Loreen swiveled back and forth in her office chair, shaking her head. "Seems to me you're just looking for excuses *not* to go. It's only gonna be for a week, Mom. Not a month." She paused. "I see my son almost every day. And I can take Charlie with me. They're best buds anyway."

Stella jerked her head back. "You said your son? Does he know already? Does Peter know you're his—"

"His mom? No, not yet. But Aunt Kat and I have been talking about that lately. Originally we thought when Peter entered first grade, that might be a good time to introduce the fact I'm not his auntie but his birth mom. We don't want him to hear some gossipy crap from one of the other kids who heard from their mothers and fathers that Aunt Kat adopted my baby."

"Sounds like a good idea to me, honey. A preemptive strike. Take control of the situation before it blossoms into something you never wanted. Not that you asked my opinion."

Loreen tilted her head to the side. "Mom, you know damn well I value your opinion. Above all others, for sure. As much as I love living in Monarch Bay, we all know it's a small town. People talk. Not in any malicious way, but kids overhear stuff. And one day that 'stuff' is gonna be who Peter's real mommy is, and Aunt Kat and I don't want him finding out that way."

Stella nodded. "Exactly. No disagreement from me on that one. But…" She stared out the window, chewing on her bottom lip. "What about Harley? Doesn't he want to be with you when you explain to Peter who his birth parents are?"

Loreen took in a deep breath, letting it out slowly through her lips. "He said he did. I mean, in the beginning."

"What's wrong, Lo? You're acting weird. I thought you two were on the same page about this whole thing."

Loreen flicked her eyes toward the ceiling, then stared at her mom. "We aren't really doing all that well together, you know?"

Stella's eyebrows drew together. "No, I didn't know. Last time we were all together he—" Stella paused. "Actually I don't remember the last time he came to a family dinner at our house or Aunt Kat's place."

Loreen pursed her lips. "He's not doing all that good. In my opinion at least. He dropped out of school. Doesn't wanna be a psychologist any more. He's fixing motorcycles out of his aunt and uncle's garage, making shit for money."

"I'm so sorry, Lo. I had no idea. So did you actually break up?"

Loreen shrugged. "Not yet, but I have a feeling it's inevitable. I mean, Mom, he's going nowhere. I don't blame him for not knowing what he wants to do with his life, but he's gotta pick a direction and walk down that road, and if it's the wrong road, then pick another road to walk down. But fixing motorcycles? Most of the time it ends up him hangin' with his bros and not doing much of anything but fixing their bikes for free. They always say they'll pay him and that he, quote unquote, knows they're good for it. He never gets that money. So we can't move in together like we planned. He can't afford the rent." She paused. "And I feel bad saying it, but he's not a shining example of a dad who I want my son to follow in his footsteps, ya know?"

"I can relate to that part, Lo." Stella sighed. "Which is why I took you away from your father. I didn't want you and Gabriel to think that's what all marriages were like. Hitting, yelling, cursing—that's no way to grow up, thinking that's what marriage is all about. That sickened me."

"I know, Mom. And Gabe and I are forever grateful you got us out of there when you did."

Stella stood. "Luckily all that is water under the bridge, honey. Robert's in jail, and we never have to see him ever again." She leaned over Loreen's desk and kissed her on the forehead. "Thank you, Lo. For telling me about Harley and also talking about your plan to tell Peter about his birth parents. Either way, Peter will eventually want to know who his father is. But you'll figure that out with Harley. I'm sure of it."

"Thanks, Mom. You know... for your faith in me." She swiveled back to her computer, then quickly turned around again to face her mom. "Where's David anyway? He's never *not* here."

Stella's cell phone played a rap song she'd always been fond of, "Ayo," by Chris Brown and Tyga. She pulled the phone out of her pocket, glanced down, smiled, and answered. "Hi, Kat." She held the phone pressed to her ear, nodding. "What?" Her brows squinched together. "But how…?" She dropped into the chair, frowning. "But how could that be? David wasn't going anywhere this morning. He…" She paused, stared at her daughter, eyes glistening. "I forgot. He had to go to San Luis Obispo to pick up a piece of equipment for the oven." She stood abruptly. "I'll head there right now. I'll call you as soon as I know anything." Stella shoved the cell phone into her pocket.

Loreen rounded the desk and stood in front of her mom. "What happened? Did something happen to David?"

Stella stared into her daughter's eyes and it was as if she was looking at herself, albeit a blonde version, back when she was twenty-four years old. "Kat said she was watching the news, and there's been a terrible accident on the 101 North. She swears it's David's van lying on its side, smashed up against the concrete barrier between the two sides of the freeway. She saw the Patti's Pastries logo."

Loreen grabbed her hoodie and took hold of her mom's elbow. "Let's go. I'm sure they'll take him to our hospital. It's the closest one in the area. Just down the street. Come on, Mom."

Sirens blared in the distance. Loreen and Stella halted, turned toward each other.

A solitary tear slid down Stella's cheek. "It can't be David. It can't."

Loreen slid her purse onto her shoulder and headed toward the back of the bakery. "Come on, Mom." She clicked the remote, and a small chirp pierced the silence behind the building. "Get in the car. I'll tell Sunny what's going on."

Stella ran out the back door and bolted for Loreen's Jeep. As she slammed the door shut behind her, Loreen rushed out of the back of the bakery and slid into the driver's seat.

"Please don't let it be him," Stella whispered.

Loreen jammed the gear shift into reverse, glanced behind her, and screeched backward, then shifted into drive and flew out of the parking lot. "Don't go there, Mom. We'll find out everything in a few minutes."

Chapter Two

In fewer than five minutes they reached Monarch Bay Hospital. Loreen parked in the adjacent lot, and they both ran to the entrance, not stopping until they reached the reception desk.

Stella could hardly catch her breath, the mix of running and adrenaline causing her to feel as if she'd just completed a marathon. She reached up and wiped her forehead, finding her hair net still in place. Ripping it away with one hand, she covered her trembling lips. "I'd like to know if David Crockett was admitted to the hospital?"

The young woman raised one finger as she picked up the phone, answered several questions, then smiled at Stella. "What was the last name again?"

Stella shut her eyes, drew in a deep breath.

Loreen nudged Stella over a few inches and took charge. "We think a David Crockett was just in a car accident on the 101 and may have been admitted within the last few minutes. Can you give us any information?"

The receptionist stared at her computer screen. "Are you related to Mr. Crockett?"

Stella's words came out a bit too loud. The slowness in which time passed irritated the heck out of her. "I'm his wife. Could you please check for us?"

The young woman nodded, picked up the phone, pressed several buttons. "Do you have a David Crockett who--" She nodded. "I understand. It's just that his--" She set the phone back in the cradle and looked at Stella. "They're working on him right now. There's no information available yet."

"Where can we wait then?" Loreen asked.

"Third floor. ICU."

Stella pressed her hand to her chest. "ICU? What? Is he okay? What--"

"Ma'am, they couldn't tell me any more than that, but if you take the elevators behind me to the third floor, there's a waiting area for relatives of patients in the Intensive Care Unit. Coffee and drinks are provided. We also have a cafeteria on the fifth floor."

By the time the word cafeteria exited the receptionist's mouth, Loreen had already grabbed Stella by the arm, and they ran to the bank of elevators.

Loreen slammed her hand on the Up button and glanced at her mom. "I'm sure he'll be okay. David's a strong man."

Stella's face felt hot, her breathing rapid—all signs her stress level had risen to an uncomfortable point. "We don't know anything, Lo. He could be dead by now."

Stella grasped her mother's shoulders. "He's not dead, Mom. They don't turn on the sirens of an ambulance if a person has already passed away. Calm down." She took her mom's hand. "Here's the elevator."

To Stella, the ride to the third floor took forever, and by the time the doors opened, her heart was pounding so fast, she was hyperventilating.

A U-shaped reception area dominated the room, the quietude almost unwelcome to the ears. No one spoke above a whisper, and it seemed as peaceful as a library. But Stella knew the silence only masked the near-death experiences hidden inside the rooms surrounding the nursing station.

Loreen rushed to the counter. "Could someone help us?"

One of the nurses, a young man of about thirty years old, backed away from his computer and greeted them. "Who are you looking for?"

"Crockett. David Crocket. This is my mother, Stella Crockett. He was brought here in an ambulance a few minutes ago."

The young man met Stella's eyes. "They're bringing him up right now, Mrs. Crockett." He pointed behind Stella. "You may sit in the waiting area, and I'll talk to the doctor as soon as he's available. Make yourselves as comfortable as possible. I know that sounds impossible right now. But I'm sure tests are going to be run and perhaps specialists notified. I'll be with you as soon as I can."

Loreen nodded and pulled her mom toward the waiting area. They sat on the couch. Loreen placed her arm around Stella's shoulders. "Let's both take a breath, Mom. We don't know anything right now. It may be nothing big."

"He said they're working on him in the ER, Loreen. So it's not nothing." Stella's voice quivered, and a lone tear escaped down her cheek. "I'm scared, Lo."

Loreen squeezed her mom's hand. "Of course you are. But, hell, he's alive, right?" She stood. "Let's just hold it down a little. Take a breath. Hey, there's a mini-fridge." She bent over and opened the small door. "I'm gonna have a cola. Want one?"

Stella shook her head. "I feel like I'm going to throw up." She placed a hand on her throat.

Loreen knelt in front of her mom, placed the can of cola on her mom's knees and flipped open the tab. "Drink this, Mom. Your energy is probably totally zapped right now. Take a few sips."

Stella brought the can to her mouth and guzzled half. "Thanks." She gasped. "Charlie. Oh, my God. Charlie's waiting for us at school. And I've got to tell Gabriel and Kat."

Loreen glanced at the clock. "School bell just rang. I'll call Aunt Kat and explain everything to her. She can pick up Charlie and take Peter with her. He's homeschooled, so Kat can do whatever she wants. No problem. I'll call Gabe too."

Stella nodded, and Loreen walked around the corner to talk in private.

Stella played with the tab on the can, then shut her eyes. If something happened to David, what would she do? She'd be all alone. Yes, she had Loreen and Gabriel and her young son, Charlie. After all those years with Robert, David was the first man in her entire life she could count on. He was solid; understood the world around him; knew what he wanted out of life; held her up; made her feel necessary, needed, important; loved her unconditionally. Without him, she was nothing but a mom. With him, she was a wife, a lover, an important part of his world and the world around her because of his gentle guidance and support.

After the hell she'd endured for ten years with Robert, it was a life-changing relief to be with David. Robert was gone. Those days were over. Had been over for five years. But her life with David still felt new and secure, and she'd finally gotten her confidence back. She was surely and wholly loved and madly in love with her husband.

Loreen rounded the corner. "Aunt Kat's gonna pick up Charlie and take him to her house. We have nothing to worry about. He'll have a blast with Peter. He'll probably spend the night, too, she said. If you want." Loreen sat next to her mom. "You feeling a little better?"

"I'm trying not to go down the doomsday road—something I always seem to do, no matter what negative thing happens."

"Of course, Mom. But you're no longer with… uh… Dad." She took in a quick breath. "Sorry. I never talk about… him. But you're safe now, Mom. Not everything that happens is gonna turn out to be bad. Please, please let's wait for the doctor or the nurse to give us more information before we jump ahead a thousand feet and start planning David's funeral. Okay?"

Stella nodded. "I'll try, Loreen. I promise, I'll try."

A young man wearing blue scrubs who looked to be in his twenties entered the room, a file in his hand. "Mrs. Crockett?"

Stella stood. "Yes?"

"I'm Dr. Hamilton. I'll be Mr. Crockett's neurosurgeon."

"Neurosurgeon?" Stella and Loreen said at the same time.

He gestured toward the couch. "Let's talk."

Chapter Three

Stella lowered himself slowly to the couch, never taking her eyes off Dr. Hamilton. He was so young. How on earth could he be—how could she say it—that experienced? But she was getting ahead of herself as usual, plotting the future. She had to let him talk.

He pulled up a chair in front of Stella and Loreen. He had piercing blue eyes, almost like those of a few-weeks-old puppy. He opened the file in front of him, placing it on his lap.

"As I understand, your husband, David Crockett, was in an accident on the 101 freeway. A truck coming from the other direction jumped the meridian and broadsided Mr. Crockett's van." He glanced up. "Another gentleman stopped his car on the side of the freeway and pulled your husband from the wreckage, only seconds before the van burst into flames. It was undeniably quite a miracle. If that man hadn't done so, your husband would surely have died in the flames." He reached out and covered Stella's hand with his. "Your husband's alive. But he's suffered a serious concussion."

Stella's throat felt as if it had closed, and she nodded. "That does sound like a miracle," she croaked. "I mean, that he was saved by a complete stranger. Do you know who he was, so we can thank him?"

"He's probably talking with the CHP officers right now. I'm sure they can get you in touch with him. But, Mrs. Crockett… do you know much about concussions?"

Stella shook her head.

"A concussion is a traumatic brain injury, or TBI, that affects your brain function. Effects are usually temporary, depending on the level of severity of the TBI, but I have to do several tests before I'm able to know the extent of the damage to Mr. Crockett's brain. TBIs are usually caused by a blow to the head, and, in his case, it looks as if he sustained a massive TBI due to the speed at which he was driving. It was a freeway, after all, and the truck that hit him was probably going at an equal or higher speed. The combination could be life-threatening, but, again, your husband has just arrived, and I have more tests to run. I won't know much more for awhile."

Stella couldn't take her eyes off him, each word exiting his mouth striking her like the tip of a tattoo gun. "What's awhile, doctor? Minutes, hours, days?"

"Hard to tell, Mrs. Crockett. A mild TBI is usually not life-threatening, but a serious TBI? These things take time. Sometimes a lot of time. Weeks, perhaps months to heal… if ever. But I'll know a bit more by tomorrow, I hope. There are closed brain injuries, which means nothing actually penetrated his brain, and in your husband's case, there doesn't seem to be a break in his skull. Even a mild TBI can cause headaches and problems with concentration, memory, balance, coordination.

"As I said, it looks to me on initial exam that this is not just a mild TBI, Mrs. Crockett. There could be seizures, dizziness, visual changes, paralysis, balance problems, memory loss. A full and functional TBI recovery is possible, but it's way too early to tell." He stood. "I have to get back to your husband. I'm sorry I don't have any definitive information. This type of brain injury not only takes time to evaluate. It takes time, often a lot of time, to heal. And sometimes total recovery just isn't possible. But waiting is always necessary. Each individual's TBI functions differently. There are no set rules or timelines." He turned toward Loreen. "I'm sorry. I neglected to ask your name and relationship. Are you Mr. Crockett's daughter?"

Loreen shook her head. "My birth father's in jail."

Stella placed a hand on Loreen's forearm. "Loreen! Sorry, Dr. Hamilton. Too much information."

The doctor nodded. "It's a generational thing."

Stella stood. "Mr. Crockett… David… he's my second husband." She tried to smile, but knew it was more of a grimace than anything else. "Thank you for taking the time to explain all this to us, Dr. Hamilton."

"You're welcome. Feel free to stay and wait to see what we plan to do for your husband. If it gets too late you might want to rest at home, if you live close by."

"Our home is about five minutes from here, but we'll wait to see if you have more information before leaving the hospital. It doesn't feel right to leave him here alone. Can I see him?"

He shook his head. "I'm sorry, Mrs. Crockett. Right now is a highly sensitive time for a patient in his condition. A lot needs to be done for him and to him before we feel it's wise to introduce his condition to you or your daughter. We feel it's best to get more of a handle on this before allowing visitors. It can be disturbing for him and we must be very watchful of the impact it could have at such an early stage. " He took a step back. "But I promise to keep in touch, and either I or one of our nurses will be back here to give you an update."

"Thank you, doctor."

Loreen stood and took hold of her mother's hand. "Yeah, thank you."

Dr. Hamilton nodded and left the room.

Stella and Loreen turned toward each other. Stella put her arms around her daughter and burst into tears.

Loreen patted her mother's back, murmuring words of comfort. "He's gonna be okay, Mom. I can just feel it."

"We don't know much of anything, Loreen. He could be a vegetable for the rest of his life. Or die." Her cries grew into gasping hiccups of sorrow, and she dropped down onto the couch. "If he dies, I'll—"

"Don't, Mom. You heard the doctor. They haven't even figured much out yet. They haven't finished the intake evaluation or done all the tests they need to do. We don't know that much, Mom. But he's alive. There's every chance in the world he'll pull through this and be just fine. Don't get ahead of yourself. Have some faith, Mom."

Stella drew in a huge breath. "Okay. All right. I have to get myself under control."

"Do you want to go to the cafeteria and get something to eat?"

Stella glanced at the clock on the wall. "Oh, my God. It's almost three o'clock. Charlie has to have dinner at five and—"

"Don't worry about him. He's at Aunt Kat's place. Let's go to the cafeteria. I have a feeling we might be sitting here for awhile. Let's take a few minutes to collect ourselves."

"You're right. I'll let the nurse know where we're going first. Just in case."

They took the elevator to the fifth floor. Windows surrounded them on all sides, the views of the sky and trees comforting in their colors and the closeness of nature. Stella found the place soothing. They each got a hot cafe latte and a croissant and sat at a table facing the ocean located a few blocks away.

Stella played with her coffee cup, turning it round and round while staring into the foam gracing the top of the steaming brown liquid. "What are the chances of a truck careening over the meridian on the freeway and David's van being the one it struck?"

Loreen reached out and covered Stella's hand with her own. "Mom, life is unpredictable. We both know that. Did you ever think we'd be here, in Monarch Bay, living the dream, after everything that happened with, uh… Dad in Oregon?"

"You're right. Of course. But this is just unfair, Loreen."

"And so was what happened to you and me and Gabe in Oregon."

"You're right. Your father was a mean man, Loreen. You didn't deserve how he treated you and Gabe."

"And you didn't deserve how he treated *you* either. Hitting and pushing and forcing himself on you…"

"Let's not go there, honey, okay? Not today. That's over. Forever. I don't even like to think about it. Which is why this is so very, very horrible. David and I have only been together a bit over five years. Charlie's just a little kid. There are so many happy years to look forward to and now this happens? It's unbelievable."

"Mom. Bad things happen to good people. Look at you. Your life with Dad was awful. You didn't deserve any of it. But you do deserve to have David in your life. And shit happens. Sorry, but it's true. You know how I look at it? If we hadn't escaped from Oregon like we did and come here, you never would have met David, and Charlie wouldn't exist. In fact, then I wouldn't have met Harley, and Peter wouldn't exist either. So look on the bright side. Whatever this is that happened to David, I believe it'll have a positive outcome in life. Don't ask me how or even why, but I believe that. Good stuff can come out of the worst shit that happens, ya know?"

"You're pretty darn philosophical for someone your age. You know that, Lo?"

"The way the world is today, my generation is almost forced to be. There's so much negative crap happening today, you gotta have a positive outlook. Otherwise, you'd be depressed every day of your life."

"That *is* depressing, honey."

Loreen nodded. "Yeah, it is, Mom."

"You called Gabe, right?"

Loreen nodded. "Both Gabe and Aunt Kat. They said they'd wait to hear from us. I told them they didn't need to come to the hospital. They can't go in and visit David anyway."

Stella nodded. "Plus Kat has the two boys, and Gabe is probably in class."

"He was," Loreen said. "But he's gonna keep his phone on. He said he'd drive up here from San Luis Obispo."

"Let's wait until we talk to the doctor again, Lo."

"Stella!"

Stella turned in her chair to see who had called out her name. She stood abruptly, bumped the table with her thighs, and knocked over her coffee cup. She grasped the edge of the table, wetting her fingers with foam and coffee and glared at the man who had called out her name. "What the hell are you doing here?"

"I don't fucking believe this," Loreen mumbled.

Chapter Four

Loreen stood and threw her arm out in front of Stella. "I don't know why you're here, and I don't care. We're leaving." Loreen slid over, blocking Robert's view of Stella. "Move or I'll fucking scream so loud, they'll call the cops."

Robert jutted his arms out in front of him, hands splayed. "No. Please. Just give me a moment. I don't want anything from you. I don't want to argue or fight. I just need a few seconds to talk to your mom."

Stella automatically, without thinking, backed away from her ex-husband, heart hammering in her chest, stumbling into a chair.

Loreen grasped her mom's elbow and pulled her further away from the table, away from Robert. "Don't come anywhere near us. I swear to God, I'll scream bloody murder. Now move the hell out of our way. We're leaving." She pulled her cell phone out of her back pocket. "I'm calling the police, and you'll go back to where you belong."

Stella swallowed and swallowed again, feeling the croissant and espresso inching its way up her throat. She opened her mouth, about to say something, afraid all that would come out would be vomit, and she would not give this man the satisfaction of knowing he could make her feel anything… anything at all.

He'd been sentenced to ten years in prison. He couldn't possibly be standing in front of her in this hospital. It was impossible. Unless he'd escaped. She shook her head.

Flaming red splotches crawled up Loreen's neck onto her face. "How the hell did you get out of jail already?"

Robert bent his head, took a deep breath, then glanced at his daughter then Stella. "Got out for good behavior."

Loreen snorted. "It's only been five years. Are you kidding me? You were in for ten."

Robert nodded, pursed his lips. "I'm not the same man I was,

Loreen. Stella, please. Can I just have a moment? Then, if you want, I'll leave you alone. Forever. Just please, give me two minutes."

Stella's eyes widened. She was seeing a ghost. That had to be it. She was so emotionally distraught, she'd hallucinated Robert's appearance. This could not really be her ex-husband. The stress over David's accident was causing her to see something that was not really there. But, no. Loreen was right by her side. She could hear her talking to Robert. This was not a dream. It was real.

And it was her worst nightmare.

She never thought she'd ever, ever see her ex-husband again. And here he was, in the same hospital as her husband, who right now was lying in a bed, likely hooked up to tubes and machines. And he might die. She couldn't care less about Robert or his lies and machinations and tales of woe in prison.

He'd brought a gun into her and David's home on Thanksgiving Day five years ago, threatening David's life, as well as those of the two babies, Charlie and Peter, and of anyone else who got in his way. He wanted revenge for Stella kidnapping "his" kids, Loreen and Gabriel, from their home in Oregon and hiding away in Monarch Bay with her sister Katrina.

He was insane. And she was sure he hadn't morphed into someone entirely different just because he'd been in prison, obviously pretending to be a model prisoner, if he'd gotten out five years earlier than he was supposed to. He must have lied his way through his parole hearing or possibly paid someone off to vouch for his "good behavior." How else could he have gotten out after serving only half his sentence? He must have escaped. That was the only plausible explanation.

"Stella, please. I don't want to cause a scene," Robert whispered, all the while walking slowly toward Stella and Loreen.

Stella gasped, air finally entering her lungs, feeling as if she'd just broken through the surface. She couldn't allow this man, of all people, to drown her in bad memories that had only recently begun to subside. "You're a liar," she said loudly. "I don't believe a word coming out of your mouth." She grabbed Loreen's hand, yanking her further away from Robert. "Don't come any closer, or I'll make the biggest scene you could ever imagine. Don't follow us. Leave us alone."

Loreen pulled her hand out of her mother's grasp and took several steps toward her father, stopping right in front of him. "I hate you. Mom hates you. You got a lotta balls coming here when Mom's husband's in the ICU, fighting for his life," she spit out.

Robert shuffled back several steps. "I went to the bakery first. The young man working there told me about the accident. I came here looking for your mom, Loreen. I only need a few minutes to explain."

Stella's face contorted into an angry mask of murderous proportions. If she had a knife, she'd stab him in the gut, hoping he'd bleed out onto the brightly polished cafeteria floor. "You went to our bakery? Looking for me?" She inched a bit closer to Robert, hands clenched into fists, nails biting into the palms of her hands. "How dare you! How dare you!"

He turned toward Stella. "I'm sorry. I don't know where you live, and I just wanted to talk to you for a few minutes. He told me you were at the hospital because your husband had been in an accident, so I came here. We don't have to talk now, Stella. I know this is a bad time. It can be any time you want."

Stella cleared her throat, the words stuck so far down inside her, she didn't know if she could speak. "No time is a good time, Robert." She took one step closer to her ex. "Now we're leaving, and don't you dare follow us or try to contact me or I swear I'll call the police and have your ass back in jail."

Loreen sneered at Robert. "Get the fuck away from us."

Robert shook his head, staring at Stella. "I'm sorry about your husband."

"Stop! Stop!" Stella covered her ears with her hands and squeezed her eyes shut. Tears flowed like rain down her cheeks. As she was feeling Robert's presence, thoughts of the past whirled round in her head. All the times he'd smacked her. All the times he'd yelled at her and the twins for absolutely no reason. All the bruises that covered her arms and face that Loreen and Gabe saw the morning after his rantings and ravings about dinner not ready at exactly six o'clock or the noodles being soggy or the meat too tough.

He'd been a horrible father and an even more horrendous husband. He'd never turned his physical abuse onto Loreen and Gabe—until the time he'd head-butted Gabe, knocking him to the floor. All because Gabe had defended Stella when Robert called her "dumb". Gabe had told Robert he couldn't treat his mother that way anymore. Gabe stood up for Stella the only way he knew how, but Robert couldn't allow anyone to usurp his authority over "his" household.

Stella opened her eyes and swiped at her tears. "I don't want to hear my husband's name come out of your mouth. He's a good man. You're a horrible man. And you… you… you're nothing to me."

Loreen curled her arm around Stella's shoulders. "Let's go." She paused. "Right now, Mom."

Stella edged further away, staring at Robert's face. He hadn't changed a bit in appearance, tall, dark hair cut short, a few grey hairs at his temples, but he looked fit and, surprising her to no end, handsome as ever. All things that initially drew her to him in the first place, only to let her down the moment they left the altar as a married couple. It was shortly after that, when he'd changed into an emotionally and physically abusive monster.

Robert shook his head over and over. "After the way I treated you and Loreen and Gabriel, you owe me nothing, Stella. I know that."

Loreen smirked. "You're right. She doesn't owe you shit."

"I agree," he whispered.

The elevator pinged, and Stella and her daughter rushed toward it, turned and faced the doors as they closed.

Stella was positive she'd seen tears roll down Robert's cheeks. She glanced at her daughter. Loreen's sneer hadn't left her mouth.

Loreen hated her father.

So did Stella.

Chapter Five

They rode the elevator in silence to the ICU, then walked to the waiting room. Stella sat on the couch, Loreen, in the chair opposite.

Loreen tapped her fingers on her knees in a nervous twitch. "I can't believe he came here looking for you. What the hell was he thinking? I wanted to puke."

Stella stared at the wall, trying to calm her racing heart. She could feel her pulse in her ears, like a drum banging inside her head. "He tried to kill David. And he would have killed me… and the two boys… and maybe the rest of the family." She paused, placing a hand over her heart. "I feel sick to my stomach."

Loreen took hold of her mom's hand. "Let's take some deep breaths, Mom. Together." She squeezed Stella's fingers. "Close your eyes. Breathe in, one, two, three. Breath out, one, two, three."

They breathed together for several minutes.

Stella's heartbeat slowed, and she unclenched her hands, relaxed her face and neck. She opened her eyes and turned to Loreen. "I think I'm okay now."

Loreen nodded. "Me too. I've seen you meditate so often, but I've never tried it myself." She smiled. "It works."

Stella leaned over and hugged her daughter. "Thanks for taking care of your old mom."

Loreen pulled back. "You're not old, Mom. You look like you're in your late twenties."

"Why did they let him out early, Lo?"

"All I can think is that he lied his way out. Somehow. Some way. But he obviously pulled it off."

"It should have been him in that car crash. Not David."

"For real."

"I don't want to have to deal with Robert right now."

Loreen stood and walked to the window overlooking Main Street. "You shouldn't have to, Mom." She turned around. "So don't."

"What if he comes to the bakery? Or to the house?"

"Then call the police."

"Maybe I should take out a restraining order."

"Again, you shouldn't have to, Mom. He shouldn't be allowed anywhere near you." Loreen tapped her bottom lip with her finger. "Wait a minute." She paused. "You and David… both of you… should have been notified of his release. Isn't that the law or something? Maybe you should get in touch with your attorney. See why you weren't told about it, ya know? I bet Dad… Robert… whatever… I bet he's not even allowed to contact you, Mom. I mean, maybe your attorney can call his parole officer. He's gotta have one. I bet that would keep his ass away from you."

Stella leaned back into the cushions of the couch and sighed. "I don't know why we weren't notified, honey. Maybe somebody screwed up. We're talking the prison system, Lo. What can you expect? Or, given the fact David takes care of all the bills and mail, maybe he missed reading it? Maybe he put it in the 'to be read' file?" A sole tear slid down her cheek. "I don't want to deal with this, Lo. All I care about is Dav—"

"Mrs. Crockett?"

Stella leaped off the couch. "Dr. Hamilton. How is he?"

The doctor sat in the nearest chair and let out a breath. "He's not awake and probably won't be for awhile. What's miraculous is, he's breathing on his own, but he's not responding to manual stimulation of his feet or his hands. I don't think he's paralyzed. We did a full MRI, and he has a small brain bleed, which we'll continue to observe since it's not actively leaking any longer. But we don't know what effect it will have until or if David wakes up."

"*If* he wakes up?" Stella whispered.

"Sometimes patients with severe TBIs don't ever wake up, Mrs. Crockett. As I explained before, it's far too early for us to make assumptions on when he'll awaken or what will have been affected after he awakens. There are so many ways this could go and I'm sorry I don't have anything definitive to tell you."

Stella nodded slowly. "So he may or may not be able to talk or walk or—"

"Mrs. Crockett. I always advise the family of patients with this type of TBI to hope for the best and just wait it out. There's nothing we can do to hurry the process. Mr. Crockett's body will do what it's going to do, and if he wakes up and cannot talk or walk but he's capable of learning, then he'll eventually be able to do some of those things. But, as I said, every patient is different. But we're doing our best to keep him safe and stable and comfortable, and he'll be monitored every second of the day." He covered Stella's hand with his. "Keep the faith, Mrs. Crockett."

"Can we see him?" Loreen said.

Dr. Hamilton pursed his lips. "For a few minutes."

"Should we talk to him? Would that help?" Stella said.

"You can surely talk to him," Dr. Hamilton replied. "Studies have found those patients who do wake up often tell us they heard words being spoken, stories being read, their hands being held. So, on the chance that Mr. Crockett is one of those people, then I would encourage you to talk to him. But for today, just take a couple of minutes, then I suggest you go home, and we'll just take it day by day."

Stella nodded. "Thank you, Dr. Hamilton."

"Come with me," he said.

They followed him to a room directly across from the nurses' station in the center of the ICU floor. Glass walls allowed David to be observed by the staff. A nurse exited his room and nodded as she passed them.

Dr. Hamilton gestured for Stella and Loreen to enter. "I'll see you tomorrow."

Stella thanked him, and she and Loreen walked tentatively into David's room.

"I've never seen so many tubes coming in and out of a person," Loreen whispered.

Stella couldn't take her eyes off David's face. His cheeks and nose were badly bruised, and the top of his head bandaged completely in white gauze. He lay as still as a corpse and that image seemed to pull all the breath from Stella's lungs. She placed her hand on her chest and opened her mouth to speak, but nothing came out. Her lips moved, but she'd lost her voice.

Loreen grasped her mother's forearm. "Mom. Mom. Are you all right? Mom!"

Stella's eyes shifted in the direction of her daughter's face, tears rolling down her cheeks. "He… he… looks dead," she whispered.

Loreen hugged her mom, while Stella stood like a statue, unmoving, not speaking. Loreen took a step back and lightly pressed her mom's back, guiding her toward the head of David's bed.

Stella inched her way to her husband's side, never taking her eyes off his bruised and swollen face. The beeps of the monitors broke the silence of the room. Stella glanced around at the lines and squiggles on the faces of the monitors that showed David's pulse, heart rate, temperature, and other things she didn't understand.

She placed a hand lightly on a spot of his forearm that wasn't bruised and to which nothing was attached and leaned down several inches. "David. It's me. Stella." She shut her eyes. "I'm here, honey. Loreen is here with me too. We love you. We're waiting for you to wake up, so we can talk to you. I… I love you, David. So very, very much. We'll let you rest now. The doctor told us we can only see you for a few minutes today, but I'll be back tomorrow, babe. Okay?" She smiled, swiped at the tears covering her cheeks, then glanced at Loreen.

Loreen shook her head. "I can't do this."

Stella walked toward her daughter, grasped her hand, and slowly led her out of the room. "That's okay, Lo. It's shocking. I know."

Loreen turned into her mother's arms, and Stella held her as they both cried. After several minutes they walked to the elevator bank, both silent until they reached Loreen's car.

They climbed in and sat there for several minutes. Stella tilted her head back and breathed in and out slowly.

Loreen stared out the driver's side window.

"He's going to wake up, Lo. I just know it."

"How can you be so sure?"

"Because he's a good, strong man, and he'll pull through this." Stella turned to her daughter. "Believe it, Lo. With all your heart, believe it. Send that out to the universe, and, maybe, like some sort of karmic force, it'll come true."

Loreen's glassy eyes met those of her mother's. "I'll try, Mom. I promise. He's been more of a dad to me than my real dad ever was, and I love him."

Stella smiled. "So do I. More than you'll ever know."

Chapter Six

After Loreen graduated and received her degree, she'd moved into the extra bedroom in Stella and David's house. Her living there made it easier on her budget, since she was repaying her student loans. It also allowed her to babysit Charlie when the need arose, which was a big help to Stella and David.

Now as Loreen and her mom entered the house, Stella hovered in the doorway, wondering if she'd ever see David's face again, greeting her when she arrived home. His hours were earlier than hers, since he did all the baking and got to work at 3 a.m. Stella arrived around four or five in the morning. Patti's Pastries opened at 8 a.m. Loreen arrived soon after, stayed until it was time to pick up Charlie from school then either dropped him off at Aunt Kat's house for a playdate and went back to the bakery or stayed and visited with her son Peter.

"What's wrong, Mom? Why're you just standing there? Did you forget something in the car?"

Stella stood near the front door, scanning the house from the foyer, eyes flitting from the pictures lining the walls to the front room furniture, letting it all sink in. This was their house, hers and David's. "I was just picturing all the times David greeted me after work and was wondering if he would ever do that again." She walked around the corner into the kitchen and rummaged through the refrigerator. "Do you want something to drink, honey?"

Loreen appeared at Stella's side. "Mom, go in the front room and sit down. Put your feet up and I'll bring *you* a drink and start dinner. You've gotta be starving. I know I am."

Stella smiled at her daughter. "I'll take you up on your offer. I'm exhausted. It's late, and I never had lunch. What're you planning on cooking?"

Loreen gestured for Stella to leave the room. "Don't worry about it.

You'll love whatever I fix. You always do. I'm thinking… maybe an omelet. It's quick and full of protein, and I'll add all sorts of veggies."

Stella trudged out of the room, feeling a hundred years old. "Thank you, Lo. I'll just relax in the front room. Take your time. I'll watch a little TV."

"I'll call Aunt Kat and explain the situation, that we're kind of in a holding pattern, and that you'll talk to her tomorrow, after you've seen David's doctor."

"Can you talk to Gabe, too, honey? I just don't think I have the energy to do it right now. I'm doing my best to hold it together, and there's really nothing more to say, but I want Kat to know it means a lot that she's taking care of Charlie. And tell Gabe I love him and I'll speak with him tomorrow, okay?"

Within fifteen minutes Loreen brought Stella a dinner tray with two plates, sodas, utensils, and napkins. She placed the tray on the coffee table and glanced at her mom whose eyes were fixed on the television. Loreen glanced at the screen, saw it was the local news, and sat on the couch.

"An accident occurred this afternoon involving local businessman David Crockett, owner of the well-known Monarch Bay bakery, Patti's Pastries, ending in Mr. Crockett being taken to Monarch Bay Hospital, his condition unknown, although we've reached out to the hospital staff, who have yet to return our calls. What we do know can be seen on the following footage, taken by a man whose car was sitting on the side of the freeway at the time with a flat tire. We interviewed him, and you can hear his recollection of the events right here on Channel 21. Listen in."

"This is April Langley, Channel 21 news, and I have with me a Mr. Carl Nuhfer. Mr. Nuhfer, can you tell us what happened today, before we watch the video you took of Mr. Crockett's accident on the 101 Freeway?"

"I was sitting in my car and had just called the CHP about a flat tire I had while driving down the freeway. They were going to send out a tow truck, and I was just sitting there watching the cars go by when I heard a terrible sound, like a huge crash and screeching brakes and metal scraping against metal. Hard to describe, but I glanced up, and a big truck had jumped over the meridian separating the sides of the freeway, and here it comes, flying toward the cars going in my direction. I'd been looking at my phone, and I pressed the camera icon and began shooting a video. That truck smashed into this van, just ripping it in half,

and one of the cars behind the van pulled over, and this guy jumped out of his car and ran over to the van, which was already on fire. You can see in my video. Flames were bursting out of the engine in the front, and the guy who was driving the van was slumped over the steering wheel. And there was no way that other guy was gonna be able to save the dude in the van before the entire van blew up like a bomb hit it. But anyway, this guy runs to the passenger side of the van, climbs in, and I guess pulls the dude out of the van, and as he's dragging him into the bushes along the side of the freeway, that damn van explodes. And I mean, it exploded like a bomb hit it, parts flying up in the air, all over the freeway, flames shooting into the sky, and the smoke was so bad I couldn't see the guy or the dude from the van after that. I called the CHP again, even though they were already on their way. I wanted them to know what happened so they'd send an ambulance."

"Mr. Nuhfer, we're going to play the video you shot of the accident so our viewers can see it. Here is our exclusive coverage of the horrific accident that happened in Monarch Bay on the 101 Freeway today, folks."

Stella and Loreen watched as the scene Mr. Nuhfer explained revealed itself on the TV screen. Stella covered her cheeks with the palms of her hands, fingertips underneath her eyes, brows scrunched downward, lips trembling. Loreen stared at the television and reached out her hand to hold onto her mom's trembling knee.

When the video ended, Loreen turned the volume down. "That man's a freaking hero. He risked his life to save David. It's a miracle they both weren't killed in the explosion."

With Stella's glance riveted to the tabletop in front of her, silent tears flowed over her fingertips, dripping over her wrists to the floor. "I want to thank that man who saved David."

"I'm sure if you contact the CHP, they can put you in touch with him."

"I'll have to do that. Though saying thank you doesn't seem enough, you know?"

"I know, right? Maybe we can do something for him. Wait until you know more about the guy. If he has kids or something, you could, I don't know, do something special for his family." Loreen shrugged.

"Good idea." Stella slumped further into the cushions and leaned her head back and shut her eyes. "What do you think your father wanted to say, Lo?"

Loreen mimicked her mother and leaned back and closed her eyes. "You know that old expression, 'a leopard doesn't change its spots'? I'm sure whatever he wants to say to you, it's all a bunch of bullshit, Mom. You don't wanna hear it. He might wanna say it, but that doesn't mean you have to listen."

"They say a lot of men change in prison. They often find God, and when they're released, they become useful members of society."

Loreen let out a sigh. "And you think that might have happened with… with my father?"

Stella sat up straight. "I don't know, Loreen. It was just something that popped into my head."

"Believe me, Mom. I'm sure he hasn't morphed into a caring and loving and changed man in five freaking years."

"You're probably right."

Loreen leaned forward and turned her head sideways to look at her mom. "Knowing him, when he was in prison he probably was somebody's pimp, making lots of money pairing up dudes with other dudes for sex."

Stella frowned. "Well, Loreen, we really don't know what happened while he was inside that awful place."

"And you don't know that what I'm saying isn't true either, Mom."

Stella covered Loreen's hand with her own. "There's a part of me that would love to know how the heck he got out so early. Something happened in there. Why else would the parole board have let him out in such a short time?"

Loreen twisted toward her mother and leaned her arm across the back of the couch. "Are you gonna listen to what he has to say?" She stared into her mother's eyes. "Are you telling me you're willing to see him? Talk to him? Let him try to convince you he's not the asshole he's always been?"

"No. I didn't mean that, Lo." Stella stood. "I'm exhausted, honey. I don't know what I'm saying." She scrubbed at her face and stared at her daughter. "I probably will never see him again anyway."

Loreen stood, reached above her head, and stretched her arms. "Oh, he'll be back. I know it. He always gets his way."

Stella nodded. "He always did, *back then*. But this is now, Lo. He didn't seem all that pushy when we saw him in the hospital cafeteria."

"Mom, what do you mean back then? It's only been five freaking years. Not enough time to do a complete 180 and turn into Mr. Rogers. Sounds to me like you're almost defending him. I swear to God, he'll try to see you again, believe me. And you've got to be ready to deal with that."

"I know that, Loreen. I'll call the attorney. I'm not defending him."

"Sounds to me like you are, wondering why he's trying to contact you, saying shit about how some men change when they're in prison cause they found God or some crap. Promise me you won't do anything weird, Mom."

Stella frowned. "What do you mean by that? I'm not going to do anything weird, Lo."

Loreen slapped her hand against her leg. "Dammit, Mom. You know what I mean. You let him walk all over you for ten fucking years. Why should I believe it'll be any different now? He'll try and weasel his way into your life, ask you to give him another chance."

Stella's jawed dropped open. "Loreen, don't be ridiculous. You're acting as if in five years I've totally forgotten what kind of man your father truly is. Remember, *I'm* the one he beat up. *I'm* the one he raped over and over. *I'm* the one…" Stella began to cry in earnest, sobs racking her rib cage, tears engulfing her cheeks and chin.

Loreen encircled her mom in her arms. "Shit. I'm sorry, Mom. I didn't mean to bring up all that crap. I just don't want you to forget."

Stella pulled away. "As if I ever could. It was horrible, Loreen. It's a nightmare I still have sometimes. After five years I wake up drenched in sweat and tears and have to face David and explain to him what I was reliving in my dreams."

"Just promise me, if you see him again, you won't be sucked in by his lies and his total bullshit."

Stella shut her eyes for a second. "I won't, Loreen. I promise."

Loreen gazed into her mother's face. "I'm not trying to treat you like a little kid or pretend I'm the adult and you're the child. But we both know how persuasive he can be in order to get his way, then he pounces when you least expect it. I don't wanna see you hurt again."

"I promise, Loreen." She kissed her daughter's forehead. "I hope we don't see your father again for another five years… or ever."

"Hopefully not, Mom. I mean, he doesn't live in Monarch Bay. We didn't even know he got out of prison. Somebody should have told you."

"I agree, Lo. You talked to Aunt Kat, right? And Gabriel?"

Loreen nodded. "I told them everything the doctor told us. Gabe's gonna leave the university tomorrow morning since it'll be Saturday anyway. He asked if he could stay here. I told him it was okay."

"Of course. And Kat?"

"Charlie was really excited to spend the night at Aunt Kat's house with Peter tonight. Oh, and I forgot. She told me she and Uncle Marcus will come by tomorrow morning. She couldn't bring everyone to the hospital since children aren't allowed. Plus Marcus just got back from a three-week haul, and the boys were playing well together. Both Gabe and Aunt Kat said they love you and hope David bounces back from this."

"Did you say anything about your father?"

Loreen pursed her lips, shook her head. "No, I did not. I would have been on the phone forever with Aunt Kat, if I'd said anything."

"Thank you for that. I'll explain it all tomorrow." Stella stared out the window overlooking the backyard where the nightlights twinkled in the trees, their limbs and leaves swaying in the breeze coming off the Pacific Ocean. She sighed. "It's so peaceful here. But my mind is going in a thousand directions." She turned and walked toward the hallway. "I was thinking. Our medical insurance won't cover all of David's hospital costs. We can't just close down the bakery. This isn't the time to close up shop. The last thing I want to do is talk on the phone to Sunny about all this and then ask him to work a double shift, if I'm not there."

"Mom, Sunny would do anything for you. I'll call him now, and I can go in tomorrow early and work the front register. I can put the accounting part on hold for a few days. It's not as crucial as keeping the bakery open. The customers are, as you say, our bread and butter. The books can wait."

"I agree. Thank you for talking to Gabe and Kat and for calling Sunny. I feel bad about not talking to Gabriel and Kat personally, and I neglected Charlie. I always put him to bed and read him his favorite nighttime story. I—"

"Mom! You've had a horrible day. Everyone will forgive you, that you didn't get on your phone and call them. I already phoned Gabe and Kat, and I'll text Sunny. He'll handle closing up today if he hasn't already, and I'll call him tonight to tell him when to come in tomorrow morning. I'll handle all that, Mom. Don't trip, chocolate chip."

Stella leaned in and gave Loreen another hug. "Thank you, honey. What would I do without you?"

Loreen gave Stella a crooked smile. "Probably go bankrupt, since you don't know squat about cash flow and numbers and all that important stuff I learned at college."

The edges of Stella's lips curved up a bit. "You always make me happy I had kids, Lo. You're the light of my life. You know that?"

"I heard you tell Gabe the same thing the other day on the phone."

"Did I? Well, so I have two lights. Is that so wrong?"

"Not at all. You wouldn't wanna play favorites. I learned in my psych class that it can fuck up kids forever."

Stella shook her head. "Such language."

Loreen snickered. "My language, as you call it, can't compare to Aunt Kat's garbage mouth, and you know it."

"You're right about that." Stella walked away slowly, then stopped at the hallway, glanced back at her daughter. "Thank you for today."

"For what?"

"For being there with me. I don't think I could have stayed sane without you by my side."

"What are daughters for? I'll support you no matter what, Mom. Don't you know that by now?"

"I do indeed. Goodnight, Lo. See you in the morning." Stella stared at her beautiful and ever-efficient daughter. Loreen grabbed her computer, open it, and started typing. What would everyone do without computers and the internet and the swiftness of social media and cell phones?

Sometimes she wondered if it was a good thing or not. Hard to tell.

Chapter Seven

Stella woke to her cell phone ringing. Eyes still closed, she felt as if someone had drugged her. She sat up and grabbed her cell. "Hello."

"I have you on speaker," Kat said. "We're coming over with the two boys."

Stella opened her eyes and glanced at the clock at her bedside. It read 7 a.m. "Marcus is home?"

"You poor thing. I can't imagine what you're going through right now. Remember when I called you yesterday, Marcus was on his way home?"

"Oh… right. Yes, I do remember now. I'm not quite awake yet. I need a shower or something to get me going."

"I'll bring you a latte from the bakery. Double shot of espresso. I'll be stopping there first to get the boys a pastry, then we'll head on over and you can tell me what happened."

Stella cleared her throat. "Thanks for that. I have to call the hospital right now, but you're welcome to come over. I don't know how I'm going to work this visiting thing, since kids aren't allowed. At least not yet."

"Shit, Stella. Don't worry about that crap. Between Loreen and Marcus and me, we'll figure it out. Marcus will be home for a week or two, not sure about that yet. But it's all good. See ya in a few."

Stella showered and dressed, and by the time she entered the kitchen, Loreen was already making a pot of coffee.

"You're dressed already, Lo?"

"Gotta go to work, Mom. I'll sub for you for as long as you need me, and I'll take care of the accounting stuff either during the down times or after we close. But please don't worry about that. Did you call the hospital yet?"

"I'm going to do that now. Your Aunt Kat and Marcus and the boys will be here soon with pastries and a latte for me."

"I'd like to stay and say hi to everyone, but I gotta jam." She grabbed her purse, kissed Stella's cheek, and rushed to the front door. "Call me when you know anything, okay?"

"Will do. I'll check in with them now." Stella got through to the nurse's station in the ICU and waited while it rang and rang. She wondered if David was even alive, then knew that was a silly thing to think, since someone would have called her. She was on edge and a natural born worrier. She was trying to tamp down her excessive think-the-worst thoughts when someone finally answered.

They informed her, the doctor had been in at six a.m. to evaluate David, and he would either see Stella when she got to the hospital or he'd call her soon. Her heart was beating so fast, she felt as if she'd just gotten back from a long run. And she hated running. She didn't take drugs and or drink much alcohol, but at that moment a part of her wished there was something, anything, that would calm her.

The doorbell rang and she took a deep breath before answering it.

Kat and Marcus stood side by side, the two boys in front of them.

Marcus was the first to give Stella a hug. "How're you holding up, kiddo?"

"I feel as if I'm not awake yet. That perhaps it's all a bad dream, you know?"

Kat wrapped her arms around Stella. "I can't imagine how you must feel, sweetie. Let's sit down and take a collective breath. Maybe the boys can go in Charlie's room and play with Thomas the Tank Engine?"

Stella bent down and hugged and kissed both Charlie and Peter.

"Auntie Kat told me Daddy's in the hospital," Charlie said, frowning.

"Yeah, Aunt Stella. How long does he have to stay there?" Peter said.

Stella knelt down in front of Charlie and took his face in her palms. "Honey, Daddy got hit by a truck. Aunt Kat probably told you that, right?"

Charlie nodded.

Peter put his arm around Charlie's shoulders, which made Stella want to burst into tears right then and there, but she did her best not to.

"Well, Mommy has to go to the hospital now and see how Daddy's feeling. I called and spoke with one of the nurses who is with Daddy, and she told me the doctor would talk to me when I arrived."

Peter took hold of Stella's forearm. "But when can he come home?"

Stella grasped one of Charlie's hands and one of Peter's and gently squeezed them both. "I don't know that yet, guys. I'm hoping he won't be there for too long. But he needs time to get better."

"Can I see him?" Charlie said.

"Yeah," Peter piped up. "I wanna see him too, Aunt Stella."

She looked from Charlie to Peter, then back at Charlie. "As soon as the doctor says it's okay, I'll tell you. I promise." She stood. "But right now I don't want either of you to worry. Your Daddy will be fine. It's just a matter of time. He needs his wounds to heal."

Charlie tilted his head. "But what got hurt, Mommy?"

"Well, the doctor thinks his head bumped into the steering wheel. And he has bruises and some swelling that will need time to get better and not hurt so much. Do you both understand?"

Charlie and Peter nodded.

Kat and Marcus walked to the kitchen, and the boys followed. Kat distributed the hot cocoa and pastries to the boys, then guided them into Charlie's bedroom. She joined Stella and Marcus at the kitchen table.

"I see you got your chocolate croissant, Stella. Marcus didn't forget it was your favorite. The boys and I waited in the car while he went into the bakery."

Marcus took a sip of coffee and leaned forward. "So what exactly happened, Stell? How is David really doing?"

Stella held her latte in both hands, staring into the foam. She knew this would be a difficult conversation, and, at the same time, Kat and Marcus were David's family, and they cared about him deeply. In fact, Marcus and David had been "riding" buddies for years, both having Harley Davidson motorcycles. They toured around often, or they used to, and had known each other for years before Stella appeared on the scene.

She looked from Marcus to Kat. "The doctor said David has a severe TBI, traumatic brain injury. I called this morning, and his neurosurgeon, Dr. Hamilton, wants to talk to me when I visit David today. But as of last night, David was not awake, and they can't predict when he will wake up. It sounded like they evaluate and evaluate and re-evaluate based on if they think his brain is swelling and how he responds to neurological examinations and such. They did a full MRI, and his spine is okay so he could regain use of his limbs and walk and talk. If he wakes up." She cleared her throat. "Or not."

She felt tears gathering and took a sip of her latte. "I don't know exactly what happened during the accident, since it was just the doctor telling me about David's medical situation. It's a waiting game. There's nothing I… we can do but wait to see how and if David responds and if he wakes up at all."

Marcus sat back in his chair. "We watched the news last night. Seems like a hero suddenly appeared on the scene and saved him. Is that right?"

Stella placed her cup on the table and leaned forward, elbows on the table top. "That's what the doctor told me, but he didn't elaborate. The news didn't say who it was either. I'd like to find out more. I haven't had time to think about it much, but I'd like to talk to the man or get an address so I can write a note. He pulled David out of the van before it exploded." Her eyes filled with tears. "He saved his life, and I'll forever be grateful. I just don't know how to go about getting in touch with the person."

"Don't worry about that, Stella," Marcus said. "I'll do a little investigating, talk to the local police, who will probably put us in touch with the CHP, so we can find out who the guy is."

Kat grasped Marcus's hand. "He's right, Stell. You have enough on your mind right now. We'll find out the information. You just take care of yourself and David while he's in the hospital."

Stella swiped at her eyes. "Thank you. It's been a rough time. And in reality, it's just started. We don't know what lies ahead for David. And that's scary."

Kat nodded. "It is scary. And both Marcus and I will do everything we can to make this easier on you as far as taking care of Charlie. We can drive him to school and pick him up afterward. Whatever you need."

Stella took a sip of coffee and shook her head.

"What is it?" Kat said.

Stella locked eyes with her sister. "You'll never guess who showed up at the hospital."

Marcus and Kat leaned forward, both frowning.

"Who?" Kat said.

"Robert."

Kat made a face. "Who's Robert?"

"Yeah," Marcus added. "I don't know any Robert."

Stella sighed. "My ex-husband, Robert."

Kat slammed her hands on the kitchen table. "What the fuck are you talking about? What would he be doing in Monarch Bay?"

Marcus placed his hand on Kat's arm, his eyes never leaving Stella's. "The judge sentenced him to ten years. This doesn't make any sense."

Stella shook her head. "No, it doesn't."

Kat squinted at her sister. "There's more to this story, Stella. I can tell by the look on your face."

Marcus curled his arm around Kat's shoulders. "Kat, why don't you calm down, honey. Let her talk."

Kat glanced at Marcus, then slowly leveled her gaze at her sister.

Stella puffed out a breath of air. "I was so surprised to see him, I couldn't think straight. I'm so glad Loreen was with me."

Kat spoke in a low voice. "What did he say?"

"That he just wanted a few moments of my time, so he could explain."

Kat's mouth twisted into a hateful moue. "What the fuck did he want to explain?"

Stella shrugged. "Who knows? I refused to talk to him. Loreen and I left without letting him say much of anything." She raised her index finger. "Oh, he said he got out for good behavior."

Marcus chuckled. "What a crock."

"Probably killed a guard and busted out," Kat interjected. "He's probably on the run and was coming to Monarch Bay to kill you, Stella."

"I doubt that," Stella said.

Kat screwed up her lips. "Why? That's exactly what he tried to do. That's why he's in jail, Stella. You should have told him to go fuck himself. Slapped him in the face. Kicked him in the balls." She tapped the table with her finger. "What did it feel like? Seeing him again for the first time since court, when you had to testify?"

Stella chewed on her bottom lip. "I totally freaked out. Almost vomited right there on the linoleum floor of the cafeteria." She paused. "Then Loreen and I got into a heated discussion, because I said I'm interested in knowing what it is he wants to, quote unquote, explain to me."

Kat rolled her eyes. "I agree with Loreen. Who gives a flying rat's ass what Robert wants to say. Don't give him the bloody time of day to tell you anything, Stella."

Stella shrugged. "I don't know, Kat. I've been thinking about this since he showed up. If he got out of jail five years ahead of time for good behavior… maybe he *has* changed."

"Oh… my… God. I don't believe you. You're done with him, Stella. I wanna hear you say it. You're done with the guy."

"What are you talking about?" Stella leaned back. "I feel like I'm on the witness stand here, Kat."

Kat stared into Stella's eyes. "Say it."

Stella shook her head. "I don't like where this is going, Kat. Don't tell me what to do. I simply said, I'd like to know why he got out of prison in just five years. I mean, what the heck happened to him in there. And what is it that prompted Robert to go to such lengths to find me in order to tell me something, to explain something to me. It must be pretty important. I don't know."

Kat crossed her arms over her chest, a stance Stella knew well from all the years they spent together when they were younger. Kat had a stubborn streak a mile long and knew how to push Stella's buttons. "You're doing it again, Stella."

"What is it I'm doing, Katrina?" Stella said sarcastically.

"All those years you let Robert push you around, allowing him to have his way no matter what, always backing down, giving him ten miles of rope when he should have been hung with it instead."

"I am not backing down, Kat, nor am I giving in or letting him have his way or whatever it is you're accusing me of. I told him he was a horrible person, who couldn't compare to David. I told him if I saw him around me again I'd call the police and they'd haul his ass back to prison. Loreen and I even talked about me getting a restraining order against him or at least talking to my attorney. Maybe he can get in touch with Robert's parole officer and rat him out about this or something. Plus someone somewhere messed up because both David and I should have been notified of his release.

"I called him a liar to his face. That I didn't believe a word coming out of his mouth. That if he came any closer to me in the cafeteria I'd make the biggest scene he could imagine. Told him not to follow us. To leave me alone. So, please don't tell me I'm acting the same as I did when he and I were married, Kat. It's demeaning and just… just not true."

Marcus shifted his gaze in Kat's direction and put his hand on her shoulder. When she turned to him, he raised his eyebrows.

Kat huffed out a long breath. "I'm sorry. I… I just don't want to see you hurt again, Stella. My mouth spews out shit faster than my mind can think. I apologize for saying that about you letting Robert take advantage of you like he did when you two were together. I guess I'm scared is all it is. You've been hurt so badly in the past. You don't deserve any more of Robert's shit in your life. You have David and Charlie and Loreen and Gabe and us. You don't need him in your life, in any way. And he doesn't deserve your time or your attention. You don't have to listen to a word he has to say, just like you told him. It's over. He's not a part of your life anymore."

Stella breathed in deeply and shut her eyes for several seconds. When she opened them, she took hold of Kat's hand. "I understand. And I accept your apology. Beyond that, please stop worrying about what Robert's going to do. I don't want anything to do with him, and I'm absolutely sure I made that quite clear."

Kat lifted an eyebrow. "Well, whatever you said to Loreen, it was enough to make her worry. So you can understand why I'm worried as well, Stella."

Stella nodded. "And I get that. But there's nothing wrong with me saying I'd like to know what's up his sleeve… why he took all that time to find me, to explain something he thinks I'll want to know." She shrugged. "I'm just being honest here. It's like I wish I were a fly on the wall and could listen to what this explanation is that he feels is so important." She stood. "But that's all it was. It piqued my interest. Maybe I shouldn't even have said anything. Then I wouldn't be getting all this grief from you and Loreen."

"We all care about you, Stella. It worries me," Kat said. "In my opinion, Robert wants something. That's why he went to all the trouble of hunting you down and going to the hospital to talk to you. He wants something."

Stella sat back down. "But what?"

"Kat's got a point, Stella," Marcus said. "Robert knows you and David are married, and he knows you have a child together. Maybe he does want something."

Stella shook her head over and over. "But—"

Kat waved her hand in the air. "Whatever, Stella. He wants something. And what do you think that something could be, Stell? You. He wants you back. And as soon as he's talked his way back into your life, you'll believe him again, and if David—sorry to say this—but if David doesn't make it, then you'll be able to get back with Robert and he'll start the abuse all over."

"Oh, my God, Kat. What are you talking about?" Stella said.

Kat stood and rounded the table, sat next to Stella, grasped her shoulders, and turned Stella toward her. "Don't you see? Someone like him isn't capable of unselfish deeds." She waved her hand again. "That is not in his behavioral repertoire, if you know what I mean. The guy's incapable of doing anything… anything, for nothing. He wants you back, so he can do what he does best. Control you. Have you to himself. Abuse you. Whatever."

Stella took hold of Kat's hand. "Kat, I know you care about me. And I'm the luckiest person on the earth to have such a great family who just wants the best for me. But, I'll be honest here, there's a part of me that wonders about all those guys in prison who change and when they get out, it's like they're a different person."

"I doubt that," Kat said. "Don't be a fool, Stella."

"Kat!" Marcus said strongly. Kat turned her head in his direction. "Stella's not a fool. Give it a rest, babe. She has a point too. If you take a step back, you gotta see that. Sometimes people change." He shrugged. "They do."

Stella nodded. "Thank you, Marcus."

"Fuck!" Kat yelled, glancing from Stella to Marcus and back. "I don't understand either of you. The guy's a fake, a fraud. Since the day he married you, Stella—you said so yourself—he turned into an awful man. Don't fall for this, Stella. Please. I'm begging you. Don't talk to him in person. Don't talk to him on the phone. Don't have anything to do with him."

Stella tilted her head, staring at her sister. "I'm not a fool, nor will I ever be taken in again by a man like Robert. You have to believe me. I promise you, I won't be going back with a man who beat me and raped me and abused me emotionally for years and years."

"It doesn't sound to me like you're a hundred percent convinced of that any longer, Stella, with some of the stuff you're saying," Kat pressed.

"I'll admit, there's a part of me that knows what Marcus says is true. People have the capacity to change."

"Not that guy," Kat said, shaking her head side to side. "Not that asshole."

"Well… we'll see," Stella answered.

"I don't need time to wait and see. I already know," Kat said.

Marcus stood. "You should go to the hospital, Stella. Kat and I will stay here, take care of the boys."

Stella stood, feeling a hundred and fifty years old. "You're right. I have to go, you guys. Thank you for helping me out with Charlie."

Kat hugged her sister, pulled back. "I love you. And I don't think you're stupid. I'm just angry. You know how I get. I don't want to see you hurt. Again."

Stella sniffed and tried to smile as best she could. "I know that, Kat. But you know what? Right now, all I care about is David. To use your words, I don't give a shit about Robert at this moment."

"You shouldn't give a shit about Robert *at all*. Go to the hospital. Don't worry about Charlie. Marcus and I will handle things on this end. Loreen is at the bakery with Sunny. It's all good. We'll have dinner ready for you when you get back, okay?"

Stella hugged Kat again. "Thanks." She turned to Marcus and hugged him as well. "Thank you. You're the best brother-in-law ever."

Marcus chuckled. "I'm your only brother-in-law."

Stella smiled. "I'll see you both later. I'll say goodbye to the boys first."

Chapter Eight

When Stella reached the ICU the nurse informed her Dr. Hamilton was with David and would come out shortly. Stella sat in the waiting room for a few moments before the doctor arrived.

"Good morning, Mrs. Crockett. David hasn't awakened yet, but the pressure in his cranium is subsiding, which is a good thing. We won't have to perform surgery which is what I was hoping to avoid, if possible. General anesthesia and poking around in the skull can be dangerous, no matter how good the surgeon's skills."

Dr. Hamilton seemed to be gathering his thoughts, and Stella squirmed in her seat. "I feel a 'but' coming, doctor. Is David going to get better?"

He tapped the file with a pen and met her eyes. "Still hard to tell, Mrs. Crockett. Being that he has yet to wake up, we can't evaluate his status as far as walking, talking, memory loss. As I said before, it's a waiting game with any TBI, especially if the patient is not responding to stimuli.

"Due to the unpredictable nature of consciousness in the early stages of traumatic brain injury, it is nearly impossible to predict when a patient will awaken from a coma in the first twenty-four hours. However, a coma rarely lasts over a month."

Stella let out the breath she'd been holding. David was alive. That was a good thing. No, a great thing. "So, we just wait. I understand."

Dr. Hamilton's eyes focused intently on Stella. "Time is very important when an unconscious person is not breathing. Permanent brain damage begins after four minutes without oxygen, and we don't know how long… may I call him David?"

Stella nodded.

"We don't know how long David wasn't breathing. The paramedics arrived within three minutes of receiving the 9-1-1 call, but David may have stopped breathing right when they arrived or before. We just don't know. I spoke with the CHP, and the gentleman who saved your husband told them he performed CPR immediately. But there's no telling how long David's brain was deprived of oxygen."

"Thank you, doctor. Of course all of this is completely new to me. I know nothing about TBIs."

"And we only know what we know from studies done on patients with TBIs. Let me explain a bit more. During the impact of an accident, the brain crashes back and forth inside the skull, causing bruising, bleeding, and tearing of nerve fibers. And we won't know exactly how that will affect the patient's motor skills, speech, or memory until he or she wakes up.

"I do want to tell you that while you're with him we all want to look for signs of David coming out of his coma. If he opens his eyes then his ability to keep his eyes open for longer and longer periods of time would be a positive thing. And being awakened from 'sleep' easier—at first by pain, and by that I mean a pinch test, then by touch, like gently shaking his shoulder, and finally by sound, as in calling his name. All of that is significant, because it would show us David's waking up.

"TBIs are extraordinarily difficult to predict with regard to the resultant condition of the patient. When I mentioned the brain crashing back and forth inside the skull and tearing the fibers… as the brain twists, the cerebral tissue slides back and forth until the long connecting fibers in the brain called axons tear. And right now, the MRI showed there was a tiny tear in one section, but that doesn't allow us to predict what that will actually mean for David's particular future.

"And keep in mind that, if David wakes up, the symptoms of his concussion, being that the axon has a slight tear, the recovery is usually the longest with that type of tear in the axon. It takes the longest amount of time before the symptoms would subside and also the longest amount of time it usually takes to improve. With the caveat that the symptoms may not subside and that he may not improve, or at least not improve totally, but he may improve partially. We just don't know."

Stella tried to keep her voice from wobbling, but tears slid down her cheeks and she turned this way and that, searching for a tissue. Dr. Hamilton grabbed a box of tissues next to his chair, and Stella took one, dabbing under her eyes and nose. "Thank you for explaining everything, Dr. Hamilton, and for spending so much time with me."

He stood. "Of course, Mrs. Crockett."

Stella looked up at him. "Please, call me Stella. It seems we may be seeing each other a lot in the future."

"Probably so… Stella. But keep hoping and praying, if that's something you usually do. I'll be encouraged, if I see any changes in David. And you'll be the first to know. I, or a nurse, will call you the moment we know anything. In the meantime, I encourage you to talk to David, read to him, touch his hands, face, arms. We never know what will stimulate his brain to wakefulness."

"I understand. Thank you again."

He left the waiting room, and Stella sat, staring at the wall. She had hoped for a more definitive diagnosis but understood why that was not possible. The brain was a very complicated organ, maybe the most complicated organ, and doctors only knew a portion of what they might know in the future. But for now, everything was up in the air. And Stella had to come to grips with the fact that her husband might or might not wake up, ever.

She opened her purse and took out a compact, looked at herself in the tiny mirror, tried to smile, and realized it was impossible. Her heart felt as if someone was squeezing it in their fist. Without David, her world was empty and dark. Yes, she had her family, but David's presence in her life made everything feel somehow brighter, more complete, better. Since she'd fallen in love with David, she'd been happy for the first time in years. And David had admitted, his love for her was stronger than anything he'd felt for Patti, his first wife who'd passed away from breast cancer soon after Stella met and worked for them at the bakery.

She recalled just the other day David mentioning he'd like to change the name of the bakery. He thought Patti would have wanted him to do so. They threw out different names like David's Donuts, except they served more pastries than donuts and were best known for their croissants. Then there was Stella's Delights, but both of them thought that brought to mind something almost too candy-like. David liked Stella's Sunrise Sweets, since they opened so early in the morning. Sometimes it was still dark in the winter months when they opened their doors, hence the play on the word 'sunrise'. Their pastries were hands down the best in Monarch Bay.

Stella shook her head. Why was she thinking about this nonsense? David might not ever wake up. Then what? She refused to go down that road.

She stood and walked toward David's room. The closer she got to the glass doors through which the nurses could see each patient, the slower her pace. This was Stella's first experience in an ICU, being around anyone with a TBI. But the doctor said to talk to David, touch him, read to him. She realized she didn't have anything to read, but she'd bring the book he was reading that lay on the table next to his side of the bed. She didn't even know the title, now that she thought about it. She hadn't paid much attention. In fact, she didn't even know what type of novels he enjoyed reading. Silly how her mind was going in so many different directions.

She crossed over the threshold, feeling as if she was under everyone's watchful eye, given the nurses could see her every move and probably hear her, if she spoke above a whisper. But none of that mattered.

David's position remained the same. Well, obviously, he wasn't able to move yet. His face was badly bruised, but he still looked handsome. His dark hair was a little long. He hadn't had it cut in a couple of months. The dark brown chinstrap beard and mustache reminded her of the first time she'd seen him. She'd volunteered to work the booth at the Monarch Bay Faire, held yearly on the promenade at the beach. He and his wife Patti sold pastries and coffee from Patti's Pastries, their store in the center of town, very popular and deservedly so. Their baked goods were 'to die for', as most people said. And it was true. Stella taste-tested almost every single one during the two days she helped them out at the faire.

At the time, Patti had recently been diagnosed with breast cancer. Worse than that, she was dying. She didn't have much longer to live, and soon after that weekend she'd passed away. After the funeral Stella and David had bonded, and Stella had started working for David at the bakery. They'd fallen in love, and Stella got pregnant and married David. And then they'd had Charlie.

Stella realized she'd been standing in the doorway this whole time ruminating on the past, and moved closer to David's bedside. She pulled up a chair but remained standing, taking him all in. It was so surreal, like a bad dream. Actually more of a nightmare. David could be in this coma for months, perhaps never wake up.

"Stop," she whispered to herself.

She leaned over and kissed his forehead, his skin warm to her lips. She wished she could see his eyes, one of his best features. Chocolate brown with little specks of gold in the irises. The skin surrounding his gorgeous eyes was now purple and swollen. She drew in a breath. Her thoughts wandered to the images she'd seen during her life of those she'd known who had passed away and lay in their caskets. David looked... dead. And that scared her. Goosebumps broke out on her arms, and she shivered.

She reached for his hand, making sure not to dislodge the IV taped to the back of it. She held his hand as lightly as she could, not wanting to hurt him, if that were even possible, since he was in a deep coma. Scattered patches of light purple bruises ran up and down his arms as well. Did he feel the slight pressure of her fingers holding his hand? The doctor said he didn't respond to the "pinch test". It was impossible for her to imagine the trauma his body had suffered from such a severe crash.

"David," she said faintly. Then with more feeling, "David. Honey. It's Stella." Could he hear her and, if so, would he even recognize her voice?

Nothing. No movement. No twitching. But she understood from the doctor, this was normal for a TBI patient. She hoped he wouldn't be like this forever. He had to wake up. Maybe later rather than sooner, given the severity of his brain injury, but he would wake up. She'd bring his book next time and read to him. Maybe that would help. It was possible. That's what Dr. Hamilton said. Right now, she could read a magazine to him. There was a small stack in the waiting room.

"I'll be right back, honey," she said, smiling down at his still-handsome face. Just that simple, typical gesture—smiling at him—made her realize the little things she did on a daily basis, and she already missed his response. A slight nod accompanied by a naughty grin, the feel of his hand grasping hers, not letting her go until she leaned in for a quick kiss. Oh, she would miss him terribly if he never woke up or if he didn't make it through this.

But he was lying right here beside her, and she would not give up on him. She'd do whatever she had to, to help him wake up and then reawaken all the memories of them together. Then they would continue making more memories until they were old and senile, sitting on the front porch in rockers, watching the sunrise on Monarch Bay.

She returned to the waiting room, found a *National Geographic* with a huge tiger looking straight at her from the cover page. David loved visiting the zoo. They'd gone several times since they married. Not often enough. Work always got in the way. But she promised that would change if... no, when he got better.

She picked up the magazine with the tiger on the front and flipped through a few pages.

"Stella."

She turned toward the voice. Robert stood in the hallway, looking contrite which actually he should be, given their past.

She squinted at him, wondering what he was thinking, coming here again and confronting her. "Oh, my God, Robert. What do you want?" she whispered then let out a breath, shaking her head back and forth. This was unbelievable.

"Can we talk?"

Chapter Nine

Fear gripped her stomach, and cramps squeezed her insides until she felt she might throw up. So she covered her mouth with her hand, trying to keep the bile in her throat from expelling the contents of her stomach all over the waiting room floor.

Until she remembered Robert could no longer hurt her. She was in a hospital. Nurses and doctors were just around the corner in the ICU. Plus, she wasn't in Oregon. She wasn't married to him. He wouldn't hit her, not here. He couldn't call her names. Someone would hear him and come running to Stella's aid.

But the memories were so vivid and appeared so suddenly, she gasped. His voice had grabbed her and thrown her back to their home in Oregon, to the nightmare that had been her life. But that was no longer her life. She was here. In Monarch Bay. Surrounded by people. She wasn't alone in her house in Oregon with no one to turn to and no one to hear her cries for help. That was then.

This was now.

"Stella." Robert reached out his arm.

Stella saw the tips of his fingers, the same fingers that had so many times stung her cheeks with a slap. She pulled back, almost stumbling into a chair and dropped the magazine on the floor.

"I'm not going to hurt you, Stella." He bent down, picked up the magazine, and handed it to her, then backed up to the doorway and moved to the side, giving her plenty of room. "You can leave, if you want to. It's okay. You're safe."

She was being absurd. This was the ICU waiting room, for goodness sake. Robert wasn't going to physically abuse her. She had to get hold of herself. She took a steadying breath and dropped her hand from her chest. She would no longer allow him to have any control over her. Never again. "What do you want?"

"I was hoping you'd give me the opportunity to explain what happened to me in prison. I admit, I deserved to be in prison, Stella. And I want to thank you for that. From the bottom of my heart… from my soul I thank you every day for testifying against me in court.

"Being in prison changed my life. I just want to talk to you, Stella. That's all. In a public place. Wherever you want. I just need a few minutes. Just a few minutes. Please. I'm begging you. I won't yell or scream or touch you in any way. You're safe with me now, Stella. I promise you. I won't do or say anything that will hurt you in any way. You've got to believe me. I know you don't owe me a damn thing. You don't. Of course you don't. But I'm asking you, before God and everything that's good in this world, let me tell you my story. I know you'll want to hear it. Otherwise, I would never have tried so hard to get in touch with you after I was released. Please. Please."

Stella ran her fingers through her hair while she shook her head side to side, frustrated as hell at his speech. "Why should I ever, ever feel safe with you, Robert? For God's sake, I wasn't when we were together. What's changed?"

He placed a hand over his heart. "I have, Stella. I have. I swear to God, I have. I don't expect you to believe me, because you haven't heard my story yet. And I want the chance to tell it to you. And I think it will mean something to you."

Stella looked at him with half-closed eyes. "Exactly what kind of chance do you want? I'm not going back with you, Robert. Are you crazy? I'm happily married to David. What more do you want from me? I don't owe you a damn thing."

He nodded. "I know you don't. You don't owe me anything. I owe you the most gratitude I can give anyone. You saved my life, Stella. By testifying in court and sending me to prison. Truly, you saved me. And I want to tell you why. It can be wherever you want, whenever you want. Not now. Not today. But sometime. Please. I swear before God, you'll want to hear it."

Stella closed her eyes for a few seconds, pondering whether she owed him this. No, she didn't owe him squat. But she was more than intrigued. Especially after talking with Marcus about how people change. Deep down, she believed people changed. And not just prisoners. Everyday people. She wanted to find out what Robert had to say, not only how he'd changed, but if she believed he really had changed.

For the most part, she didn't think it was possible. Words meant nothing without the actions to back them up. But she wasn't going to give him the chance to prove anything to her. She wanted nothing to do with him. Being around him made her feel sick to her stomach and scared--- again. Hatred roiled in her gut.

But would it hurt her to hear him out? Was he really a different man? And, if so, how had that happened? And something else popped into her mind. Would he want to be a part of Loreen's and Gabriel's lives? Did she have a say in that anyway, since they were now adults and could legally make their own decisions? Her mind whirled with thoughts of the past, battling questions about the present.

Robert was standing right in front of her. Right here. Right now. He'd been released from jail, unless she found out otherwise. So he must have been released for "good behavior", as he'd explained to her in the cafeteria. Though he certainly hadn't shown any good behavior while they were married. Well, maybe while they were dating, and for a short while after their marriage he was a nice man, but still…

Inquisitiveness and a need for closure won out. And she was desperate to get him to leave her alone. "All right. I'll meet you. Somewhere very public and somewhere very safe."

He breathed out a sigh. "Oh, my God, thank you. Really, Stella. Thank you so much for giving me this chance."

She smirked. "It's an opportunity to talk to me for a few minutes. I'm not giving you a chance, if you want to call it that, to get back together with you or to allow you to see your two kids. It's a couple of minutes, Robert. That's all I'm willing to give you… to say what you want to say. Then I leave. You got that?"

He nodded. "I get it. I understand."

Stella gestured toward him. "Now can you please let me by? I want to go see my husband."

Robert backed further away from the threshold and bumped up against the far wall.

"Tomorrow," Stella said. "The Blue Cat Cafe on Main Street. Ten in the morning."

He nodded. She passed him on her way to David's room. The further she got from him the quicker her breathing slowed to normal. She turned, just to make sure he wasn't following her. He stood outside the elevator, head down, staring at the floor. He swiped at his face. Was he actually crying? Just as she'd seen him do in the cafeteria when she saw him the first time?

Not her problem.

She stepped into David's room, the *National Geographic* in her hands, sat down in a chair next to his bed, and began to read aloud. She read to David for a long time. About tigers in India, bats in Central and South America, until her throat hurt and her stomach growled.

"Mrs. Crockett?"

Stella jerked in her seat and turned around.

A nurse in maroon scrubs stood beside her. Her name tag read "Nurse Maureen Ohara".

"Sorry to startle you. But can I bring you something to drink or eat? Or would you like to take a break and go to the cafeteria?"

Stella smiled. "Thank you. I have no idea what time it is." She stood. "I think I'll head home for the day. Someone will call me, if there are any changes?"

"Of course." She pointed at her name tag. "I'm Maureen Ohara. I'll be on duty until midnight. After that, the nurse on the next shift will be apprised of David's status, and there's a note in his chart to call you if anything changes, good or bad. He's well taken care of, Mrs. Crockett. I promise you that."

Stella pursed her lips, trying her best not to cry. "I know he's in good hands, Maureen. And, please, call me Stella. We may be seeing each other for weeks… or months." Stella placed the magazine on the bedside table and walked past the nurse. "See you tomorrow, Maureen. And thank you."

"You're very welcome."

It felt like her shoes were made of concrete, as she trudged to the elevator bank and pressed the down button. Maybe everything was catching up with her. Her adrenaline was waning, her energy sapped by the events of yesterday, as well as her short discussion with Robert today. She just wanted to go home and eat dinner with her family, watch some TV and go to bed.

When she arrived home, Kat greeted her from the kitchen, where she was fixing dinner. When Stella entered the room, the newest addition to their family, a chocolate lab named Uje they'd gotten from a breeder in Klamath Falls, Oregon, wiggled her butt in excitement.

Uje barked and placed her paws on Stella's chest.

"Hello, Uj. How are you, girl? Did your Aunt Kat feed you dinner yet?"

Kat was slicing radishes and laid down the knife, then turned to Stella. "Marcus fed her dinner—one cup of dry dog food, per Loreen's directions. Dinner will be ready soon. Spaghetti with a fresh salad and garlic bread."

Stella ran her fingers through her hair, grabbed a rubber band, and slid her hair into a ponytail. "I'm exhausted. Can I help with something?"

Kat gave Stella a hug and pulled back to look her sister in the eyes. "Everything's already done. How's David?"

Stella's lower lip trembled, and Kat took her by the hand, led her to the kitchen table, and guided her to a chair. "Sit. We'll talk about this over dinner or after dinner or whenever you like." She picked up a bottle of wine from the middle of the table and poured a half-glass, then held it out for Stella.

Stella grasped the stem of the glass, swirled the purple liquid several times while watching it slosh round and round, then set it down. "This'll put me right to sleep."

"Maybe that's the idea, Stell. This is a rough time. Did you sleep at all last night?"

Stella shrugged. "A little. In and out, mostly. I'll drink this with dinner though. Not on an empty stomach. Thank you. Where's Marcus?"

"He's playing with the boys out back. I'll call them in to wash up."

The boys and Marcus entered the room, and Stella hugged both kids. Kat told them to wash up, and Peter ran off down the hallway.

Charlie halted, looking up at his mom. "How's Daddy?"

"He's still sleeping. Peacefully. I read him a story about tigers in India. I think he enjoyed it."

Charlie nodded. "When can I see him? I wanna show him the picture I drew in class today."

Stella covered her lips with her fingertips. "That's so sweet, honey. The hospital doesn't allow children under eight years old, baby, so I'll give the picture to him for you. Maybe you can write a note to go with it. I'll bring it to him tomorrow. How about that?"

"Loreen could do that FaceTime thing on her phone, Mommy."

Stella grasped him by the shoulders. "That sounds like a good idea, except they don't have reception on your daddy's floor. They don't want the patients to be on their phones when they should be sleeping."

"Then when will he be home?"

"Well, honey, here's the thing. Your daddy is in such a deep sleep that he hasn't woken up yet. But when he does, I'll know more about how much longer he'll have to stay in the hospital and when he can come home. But in the meantime, keep drawing pictures for him and writing him letters. I'll bring them all to the hospital, and when he wakes up, it'll be like reading a book. And you know how much Daddy loves to read books."

Charlie stood still for several seconds, seeming to think about what Stella told him, then he nodded. "Okay."

Stella watched Charlie as he left the room, then glanced at Kat. "This is hard."

Kat laid a hand on Stella's shoulder. "I know. But he'll be fine, Stella. We're all here for you. Marcus and Peter and Loreen and Gabriel. We'll help as much as we can while this whole thing plays out."

"I know you will. And thank you for that." She stood. "I'll be right back."

Chapter Ten

"Dinner's on the table in three minutes," Kat called out.

Stella walked into the kitchen and leaned close to her sister. "I'll explain everything about David after dinner. I don't want to go into too much detail in front of the boys."

Kat nodded. "Where's Loreen?"

"Right here," Loreen called out as the front door slammed. "How's David?"

Stella hugged her daughter. "He hasn't woken up yet, but I'll explain everything after dinner, okay?"

"Sure, Mom. Be right back. Oh, and Gabe should be here soon. I invited him to dinner." She paused. "I explained everything the doctor told us yesterday."

"Did you mention your father?"

Loreen rolled her eyes. "I told Gabe he showed up and… yeah."

Stella raised her eyebrows. "And yeah would mean?"

Loreen huffed out a breath. "I'm not gonna lie, Mom. Gabe said he didn't understand why he wants to see you and explain himself, whatever that means. We both think it's just a ploy."

Stella nodded. "But a ploy for what, Lo?"

Loreen shrugged. "I don't know. Maybe he wants to slither back into your life like the snake he is."

"That's what I told her," Kat interrupted.

Stella grimaced.

Kat pointed at Stella. "See what I mean. Why'd you make that face, Stella?" She turned to Loreen. "Your mom wants to listen to what he has to say."

Loreen slammed her purse down on the counter. "What the hell? That's so much bullshit, Mom. Do you want to hang around him or something? I don't get it. Shit, man!"

Stella glanced at the floor.

"You're meeting him, aren't you?" Kat said.

Stella looked from Kat to Loreen and back. "Yes, I am."

"Oh, my God, Mom. As if you can believe a word that comes out his fucking mouth!"

There came a knock at the front door, then Gabe blew into the house like a tornado, dropped a duffel bag in the foyer, and rushed to Stella, arms spread wide. He hugged his mom. "How's David doing?"

Stella leaned back and took a good look at her son, so tall, dark, and handsome. He was totally Robert's son in looks, but nothing like him in personality. Sweet, giving, caring, polite. She couldn't have asked for a better son than Gabe. He was extremely bright and excelled at the university in all his classes.

She hoped he wouldn't be too angry with her for agreeing to talk to his father. But in reality, no one was going to tell Stella what to do in her life anymore. She had enough of that while she was married to Robert. She couldn't do a thing back then without him knowing. He'd monitored her phone calls, dictated what she bought at the store, what she ate, how she cooked, who her friends were—hence she had none.

He'd ruled her life. Because of that, Stella had times now when she felt unworthy—of David's love, her children's love, of people doing things for her out of kindness. She recalled all the times she talked herself into believing she'd done something to warrant Robert's slaps, pushes, bloody noses, broken ribs. It took years of being out from under his thumb for Stella to believe she was a worthwhile human being who deserved the best that life could offer. But there remained times when she'd backslide into negative self-talk. Kat and David were always there to talk her off the ledge, so Stella wouldn't fall into the abyss of self-recrimination and unworthiness.

So would she allow Gabe and Loreen to tell her if and when she spoke with her ex-husband? She'd listen to their opinions, since they knew Robert, and they were her children and adults. But, ultimately, she would make up her own mind with regard to what Robert told her and what she would instinctively know was bullshit. She would no longer be taken in by his words, because she quickly discovered after she married him, his actions belied those words almost one-hundred percent of the time.

Robert would say he loved her, then rape her as she begged him to stop. He'd whisper in her ear she'd never find anyone more kind and giving as he told her what to wear, how much make-up to use, if she needed to lose weight, because he was the one who bought the clothes and make-up and food. Therefore, he had the right to tell her how to use all the gifts he showered upon her. Her life had not belonged to her. She'd belonged to Robert. She'd been his possession. And if she didn't obey, she'd incur his wrath and she was stupid if she didn't see it coming.

But the two times she'd seen him now, he'd been quiet and unassuming and kind. She'd never seen him act that way before, except maybe during the short amount of time before they married. Then he'd quickly changed.

And he could be doing the same thing now. She knew that instinctively. But this time she wouldn't be taken in so easily. She knew it, but Kat and Loreen and everyone else didn't believe her. Well, that was their problem. Not hers.

She snapped back to the present and smiled at Gabe. "David's still not awake. We'll just have to wait and see. The doctor explained that's the protocol for a patient with a traumatic brain injury."

Gabe nodded then looked around at Kat and Loreen. "What's going on?"

"Mom agreed to see Robert. Listen to what he has to—" Loreen made air quotes with her fingers, "—explain."

Gabe shifted his eyes to Stella. "Are you shittin' me, Mom?"

Stella inhaled deeply and let it out in a huge sigh. "Look. All of you. Robert came to the hospital again and pleaded with me to talk to him. He said what he wanted to tell me he truly believes I'll want to hear, then he'll leave me alone, and that'll be the end of it."

"How do you know that'll be the end of it?" Gabe said, rolling his eyes. "Don't you remember how he was? I mean, don't tell me you forgot."

Blood rushed to Stella's face, heating up her cheeks and forehead. "You know what, guys? I will not let you or anyone tell me what to do. I had enough of that during my marriage to Robert. So, from now on, I'm calling the shots. I want to know what Robert has to say, and I've decided to listen to whatever he has to tell me. And no one… not even you, Kat, or you, Loreen, or you, Gabe, is going to tell me what to do. Do you all get it?" She glanced from Kat to Lo to Gabe and back, her breathing rapid, heart beating fast.

Kat looked around the room and huffed out a long sigh. "Okay. Okay." She threw up her arms. "I fucking give up. Do whatever you wanna do, Stella. It's your life. And if you're bound and determined to give that piece of shit a few moments of your time, then go for it. You're a big girl, old enough to make up your own mind. So have at it, Sis." She hugged Stella then pulled back. "And I'll be here to pick up the pieces. I, for one, won't abandon you, no matter what happens. But please don't get hurt this time."

Tears coursed down Stella's cheeks. "Thank you, Kat." She turned to her two kids.

Gabe and Loreen walked toward Stella, and she opened her arms for a group hug.

"I love you, Mom," Loreen whispered.

"Me, too, Mom," Gabe said.

"I know you do, okay? And that means more to me than anything in the world. But you have to trust me on this one. I know what I'm doing. I don't want or need your blessing, guys. But I don't want you to try to dictate my every move either."

"You promise to tell us what happens with him?" Lo said.

"Yeah, Mom," Gabe said. "Do you need us to stand guard behind you, or follow you and watch your back? Make sure you're okay?"

Stella gave them a bit of a smile. "That's not necessary, but I appreciate it. I told him to meet me at the Blue Cat Cafe tomorrow morning at ten. Nothing's going to happen in broad daylight in the middle of a restaurant. I'll be perfectly safe. Don't worry so much."

Kat smirked. "I think that worrying comes with the territory for all of us. We know what Robert's like."

"Even though he says he's changed," Loreen added.

"Yeah, right," Gabe said.

Stella nodded. "I don't have a problem with the worrying. Just don't tell me what I can and cannot do."

The three of them nodded while giving each other a "what are we gonna do?" look.

After a quiet dinner, the two boys ran into Charlie's bedroom to play, and the rest of them withdrew to the front room, each with a slice of Sunny's famous five-layer chocolate mousse cake and a cup of coffee.

Stella took a forkful of cake and stared at it for several seconds before returning the fork to the side of her plate. "Could we all please at least try to act somewhat normal? I can tell you're all judging me right now, and it's making me uncomfortable."

Marcus didn't utter a word. He didn't have to. Stella could see by the look on his face, Kat had already told him what was going on.

Stella grabbed the fork again and ate the bite of cake, swallowed, then leaned back. "I know what you all think. And I'll take it under advisement. You're not all crazy for believing my meeting Robert is just the dumbest thing on the planet. But by tomorrow afternoon, it'll all be over, and I'll never see him again. So can we just have dessert and act normal?"

Marcus nodded. "Maybe he has changed, Stella. I'm open to that being a possibility."

Kat huffed. "Are you serious right now, Marcus? Don't egg her on, man."

"He's right, Kat," Stella said. "Robert told me today that he owes me the biggest thanks in the world. That I saved his life. And he wants to explain why and how that happened."

Loreen curled the side of her lip upward. "And you believe him. Oh, shit, Mom. That's really lame."

Gabe stood, fists clenched at his sides. "After everything, you still believe not only that anything out of his mouth has the remote possibility of being the truth, but that you owe him squat after everything he did to you, Mom. What are you? His private stepping stone?" Gabe whirled around and walked toward the front of the house.

Stella rushed after him. "Gabe! Wait!"

Gabe grabbed his jacket and opened the front door. "I'll be back later."

"You just got here, Gabriel. Please don't leave mad like this.".

Gabe glanced over his shoulder at Stella. "Everything you're saying is so old and stale, Mom, I need a breath of fresh air."

"So you're coming back, I hope?"

"My duffel bag's right there," he said, pointing, then he ran down the front steps into the night.

Stella shut the door and returned to the front room. "Okay, anyone else want to tell me what an asshole I am, how stupid I am for meeting Robert tomorrow?"

Marcus spread his arms out on the top edge of the couch. "Stella, even though I don't think you owe him anything, I don't believe you think you owe him anything either. You're giving him your ear for a few minutes filled with the knowledge the guy's gonna try to make you believe he's a changed man. Honestly, I don't think you're gonna fall for that shit." He paused, staring into Stella's eyes. "Am I right?"

"Yes, you're right, Marcus," Stella said. "Out of all of you, I'm the one who had to endure his physical and emotional abuse. He fooled me over and over for more than ten years. I won't be that easily convinced of anything a second time around."

"Look," Kat said. "He fooled you day after day for ten years. Now you say you won't be that easily convinced the second time around." She stood. "That word you used? Easily? You won't be *easily* convinced? Stella, you shouldn't be convinced *at all*. As in never again. As in no way. To me, the way you said those words… leaves the door open to him convincing you, if his words somehow take root in your mind and make any kind of sense at all. You're already waffling!" Kat started walking out of the room. "I'm getting Peter and leaving. Are you coming with me or not, Marcus?" She headed down the hall.

Marcus stood and leaned over to hug Stella. "I believe in you, Stell. Don't make the same mistake twice."

"I won't, Marcus."

"Oh, and I got the name and address of the man who pulled David from the van." He grabbed a folded piece of paper from his back pocket and handed it to Stella. "He's already flown back to Missouri, but you could still write him a letter."

Stella glanced at the writing on the paper. "Thanks so much, Marcus. I'll do that. This means a lot to me. I want to acknowledge what this man did for David… and for me and the whole family."

"He's a hero, all right." He headed for the front door and pulled their jackets off the clothes tree.

Stella glanced at Loreen, the only one left. "You going to desert me as well?"

Loreen sighed. "No. I live here, Mom. I'm not going anywhere. You already know where I stand on this issue. No need for me to repeat myself." She picked up her plate and brought it to the kitchen. When she returned, she threw a kiss at her mom. "I love you, Mom. See you tomorrow."

"I love you, too, baby." Stella felt tears filling her eyes and dabbed them with her napkin. She had no plans to lose her entire family over this meeting with Robert. She'd talk to him, then be on her way to the hospital to see David. That would be the end of it. She went to the kitchen to clean up and heard the front door open then shut. Kat and Marcus and Peter had left without saying goodbye.

Charlie came in and hugged her from behind. "Read me a story, Mommy? Just like Daddy always does?"

Stella wiped her hands on the dishcloth, leaned over, and hugged her son. "Of course. But just until Daddy gets back. Then he'll read to you like he always does. Okay?"

Was she a total liar for saying those words? What if David died? What if he survived but didn't remember Charlie? Both scenarios would be devastating to the poor kid, so what was she doing telling him "until Daddy gets back"? But hope was necessary. She believed it could make a difference.

Wasn't hope just another form of prayer? Should she start going to church again, like she did after her parents were killed in that boating accident? She'd done that, and it had worked back then. She and Katrina were taken in by Fiona and Nason Dominguez, who, despite all the horror stories about foster parents, had turned out to be the best in the world. They eventually adopted both girls and gave them a loving and nurturing life until both Stella and Kat moved out. So maybe the praying Stella had done in church made the difference back then. Maybe instead of *hoping* David would wake up, remember them, walk and talk and everything else, she should get herself into church and *pray* for all that to happen. Maybe praying would answer her wishes better than simply hoping for something good to happen with David.

Stella followed her son to his bedroom for his nightly ritual. She tucked him under the covers and sat next to him, leaning back onto a pillow.

Charlie smiled up at Stella, and her heart clenched. She didn't want to raise her son without a father. He was so young and innocent. His life would be unarguably altered without David, they were so close.

Charlie would be the only one who wouldn't criticize her for meeting up with Robert. There was that. But if Charlie found out about the day Robert tried to kill David, Charlie would quickly change his tune, even though he was only five years old. He had no idea what had occurred in this house when Robert shot Charlie's father. In time, she thought. No need to interject any more drama at the moment. Everyone was already burdened enough by David's injuries and unknown future.

Stella finished reading just as Charlie dozed off. She kissed him softly on his amazingly delicate cheek and turned on the night light. When she reached his bedroom door, she turned back to look at him once more before heading off to bed herself. He looked so much like David, it hurt. Dark hair, long black lashes, brown eyes. The epitome of his father's good looks. Just as Gabriel was a veritable clone of Robert.

She shook her head, not looking forward to meeting Robert the following morning. What would he say? It wasn't enough she was stressed out about David's condition. Now she had to worry about meeting up with her ex? It was all too much. She couldn't wait for her meeting with Robert to be over and done with, so she could spend more time with David, reading to him. Hoping it would make a difference if… no, when he woke up.

She could only hope. Better yet, she promised herself she'd go to church and pray about it. Just as she'd done after her birth parents had died.

It couldn't hurt.

And before she went to sleep she'd take a few moments to write a heartfelt note to the man who'd saved David's life. That might make her feel a bit better. End the day on a positive note. She found a lovely baby blue piece of stationery with a matching envelope and shut her bedroom door, sat on David's side of the bed, and leaned back onto his fluffy down pillow.

And started to write.

Thank God you were such a brave and unselfish person to risk your life to save my husband. I will be indebted to you for the rest of my life, she began.

Chapter Eleven

Stella slept until nine the next morning, something so absolutely out of the norm, she could hardly believe the clock wasn't broken. Normally she'd be at the bakery hours ago, helping David with the baking, then working the front counter for all the customers who came to Patti's Pastries each morning.

Loreen had already left the house, and Stella had to drop Charlie off at Kat's before she met up with Robert at The Blue Cat Cafe. She took a shower, dressed, woke her son, and got him ready, then headed over to Kat's place.

Kat was mad that Stella was meeting up with Robert, so Stella waited in the car while Charlie ran to the front door. Kat opened the door and waved. Stella waved back and called out her thanks, that she'd talk to her later, then she drove to the Blue Cat Cafe and parked, let out a long whoosh of breath and headed for the cafe.

As the door shut behind her, she noticed Robert sitting by the front window toward the far side in a small booth, well away from prying eyes and curious people who might recognize Stella from Patti's Pastries. It felt as if she were walking through mud on her way to where Robert sat, and her stomach flip-flopped. She hadn't eaten or drunk anything yet this morning, but she still felt as if she could throw up. She hadn't seen her ex for five years, except for the two times she'd talked to him in the hospital. It felt awkward to be meeting another man in a coffee shop without David knowing. Almost as if she were cheating.

She ignored those niggling thoughts and slid into the booth across from him.

Robert smiled. "Thank you for agreeing to meet me. It means a lot."

"I'm not doing you any favors, Robert. If anything it's just pure curiosity on my part to know how you got out of prison five years early. Are you on the run?"

He shook his head. "No. That's the farthest thing from the truth."

She smirked. "So… what *is* the truth then? If I choose to believe anything you say anyway."

Robert took a breath. "I deserve that. I know." He paused. "Actually I deserve much more than that. I treated you and the kids horribly during our marriage. The first thing I want to do is apologize for my behavior during those years."

Stella laughed out loud. "Apologize? Are you serious, Robert? You were an abusive husband. Not only physically but emotionally. And you were a terrible father. Yes, you were a great provider, but otherwise, Loreen and Gabriel and I could have done without you in our lives."

"You're completely right. But I wanted to tell you I'm sorry anyway. I don't deserve your forgiveness, nor am I asking for it."

"Then what are you asking for?"

A waitress came to their table to refill Robert's coffee cup, and Stella ordered a latte.

When the waitress departed, Robert stirred cream into his coffee and swirled the spoon round and round for several seconds, then looked Stella in the eyes. "I'm a changed man, Stella. I want you to know that."

Stella smirked. "A leopard doesn't change its spots. That's what Loreen said. I know it. She knows it. Everyone agrees. Unless you've had a total brain replacement, you're the same man I knew five years ago."

He shook his head, eyes closed. When he opened them, they appeared glassy, as if he was close to tears again. "I've been in therapy for five years for anger management issues. I met with a psychologist three times a week for five years, Stella, and it wasn't for nothing. She helped me see why I acted the way I did. I feel terrible about the man I used to be. But at least now I understand why."

Stella leaned back and looked him in the eyes. "Please tell me, Robert. Exactly why were you such a fucking monster after you married me?"

"I didn't talk about my parents when we were together, did I?"

Stella shook her head. "You told me they died when you were in high school in a car crash. That's all I remember. That was something we had in common."

He nodded. "That's right. Your parents died in a tragic boat accident, right?"

Stella nodded.

"Then Fiona and Nason Dominguez took you in as foster children but ultimately ended up adopting you and Kat."

"I'm surprised you remember."

He took a sip of coffee. "And it was always a source of… I don't know exactly how to describe it, but… I was extremely jealous of you. Of course, it was horrible you lost your parents, but when they were alive they weren't anything like my father and mother."

He took a huge breath, and after letting it out, he looked utterly deflated. "The truth is, Stella, my father was a monster, the same words you used to describe me during our marriage. And it's true. I took after him."

"What do you mean by that? Exactly."

"He was a drunk. Something I wasn't, but he was abusive. He used to beat my mom, and I couldn't do a thing about it. I felt so helpless, so useless. I loved my mom. We were very close. She stayed home and took care of me. My father wouldn't allow her to work outside the home anyway. He brought home the bacon, he said. Typical old-fashioned behavior in those days, not that unusual. But he used his power over her to keep her under lock and key. She wasn't allowed to do anything without running it by him first, and if she disobeyed, there was hell to pay."

"Sounds familiar," Stella said.

Robert nodded. "Yes, it does." He paused. "So for most of my young life, I had absolutely no control over anything. All the way through high school. If my mom dared to side with me on anything, he beat her. I had absolutely, unequivocally no control over anything. He wouldn't let me play sports or hang out after school with my friends, because if I did anything he didn't allow me to do because I thought I'd get away with it and he'd never find out, then he'd beat my mom. Not me. Her. So it was the two of us, both Mom and I, who were completely ruled by a tyrannical king of the house, my dad. He never laid a hand on me, only her. He knew how much I loved my mom, so he controlled me by controlling her. I didn't want him to beat her, so I did whatever he told me to do.

"After they both died in that car crash, I was determined to never have anyone tell me what to do, ever again. I wanted to be in control of every single aspect of my life, from what I ate for breakfast to where I worked to who I would marry. Then I needed to control my wife and kids, just like my father. I'd get angry if you spoke your mind or wanted to do anything on your own, because then I felt as if I was losing control over *my* life, and it felt wrong. It threw me right back into my past.

"I promised myself I would never get into any situation where I wasn't in complete control of everything that happened. All those years when I controlled nothing because of my father—that haunted me, made me feel weak and useless and helpless. So when the opportunity arose to take control, I used it, because I was sick of feeling I lacked the ability to take charge of *me*. I wanted to feel strong, and, for the first time in my life, after marrying you and having kids, the opportunity to feel in control presented itself, and I jumped all over it."

"So you had to beat me up to feel better about yourself? Talk to me like I was a worthless piece of crap? Control your kids, too, in order to feel like a man?"

It took a few seconds before he answered. "In a nutshell, yes, Stella. I did anything… anything to get my way. To be in control of *my* life and *my* destiny and what happened in *my* household. Just as my dad had taken that away from me and my mother, I needed to take that control *back*. And the only way I knew how to do that was to dictate everything and everyone in my life, i.e. you and the kids."

"And if I didn't do everything exactly as you wanted it, you'd beat me? Just as your dad beat your mom? Even though you hated it when your dad beat your mom? It doesn't make sense. Why did you do it?"

"When I was hurting you, when I was talking to you the way I did, making you feel worthless and bad… it was as if it wasn't me doing it. All I could think of was, 'I'll show him. I'll show my father who's in control now.' I needed to take back my life, prove my father wrong… that I wasn't weak, and prove to myself I could have control. I'd never experienced what it was like to have control before. Having you and the kids gave me the opportunity to do so. But when I was doing it, there was a part of me that saw I was reliving the way my dad treated me and my mom, but I couldn't stop myself. That feeling of control was a heady thing to experience. It was like heroin. Thrilling. And I had to have it. I needed it to feel like a man. All the while proving to my father I was not weak. I was a man.

"It was as if this ball of rage and resentment for my past lived inside me, and the only way to get rid of it was to take it out on you and the kids. And no one, not you or the kids, was going to tell me what to do. So if you tried to exert any independence and control of your own, it made me feel insecure and brought me back to those years with my dad. I had to put you in your place, just as he'd done to me and my mom. Make you understand I was the one calling the shots. So the way I treated you… all of it… was punishment for you and the kids trying to take that control away from me."

"So you felt better afterwards?"

"That's the thing. Right after I'd act like that I'd wonder, what did you just do, Robert? You're hurting the ones you're supposed to love. But I remember vividly my dad saying the reason he punished my mom and me was to teach us a lesson. He was the father and the husband, and he deserved our respect. What he said and what he told us to do was for the best. If we disagreed we weren't being respectful and had to be punished. Just as he'd been punished, he'd say. So my therapist told me, my father obviously didn't have the best dad either."

"And so it went, right? From one generation to the next to the next?"

Robert nodded. "I guess it's unfortunately pretty typical. I learned from the worst when I was very young and then passed it onto my own wife and kids."

She chuckled. "So now you're, quote unquote, fixed?"

"Through therapy I realized how sick that was, how wrong, how demeaning to you and to the kids. I'd become the very monster my dad had been, and I hated him, then hated myself. Now I understand why I behaved the way I did, Stella. I own that. I did those things. I'm to blame for every single word I said and every single way I acted. And I still hate myself for it. My anger is now solely directed at myself and not anyone else. But I'm learning to forgive myself, with the help of my therapist, who I'm still seeing. We have Zoom calls every week, so I have the opportunity to tell her how I'm doing. It's an order by the court, concurrent with my early release from prison. Kind of like checking in with a parole officer, except it's my therapist."

"So, you're a changed man, Robert? You've morphed into an understanding and caring individual in only five years? Booyah, you."

Robert folded his napkin over and over, staring down at it. "I do not expect you to believe me, which you obviously don't. And I don't blame you, Stella. If I was in your place, I wouldn't believe me either. I was a horrible husband, a horrible human being. But I feel good about myself now—finally—after five years of intense therapy. It's taken me a long time to feel like I'm a decent human being. My therapist is proud of me, and, honestly, so am I. Not in a boastful way, but I'm happy for the first time in… maybe ever… because I feel good about the person I am *now*. I just wanted to tell you I'm sorry, Stella. That's all this is."

Stella took a sip of the latte the waitress set in front of her. "That's very nice of you, Robert. I have to go now."

"Okay. Thank you for meeting with me, Stella."

She stood, grabbed her purse, slung it over her shoulder. "Are we done here?"

"Almost."

"What's that supposed to mean?"

He glanced up at her. "I'd like to talk to Loreen and Gabriel as well. Apologize to them too."

"You have got to be kidding me."

"Just one meeting, Stella. In fact, you can come too."

"Why, Robert? What do you really want?"

"I don't want anything other than to apologize."

She huffed out a breath. "I'll tell them for you."

He shook his head while staring at the napkin that by now was folded into a tiny square. "It's part of my therapy." He looked up at her. "Like when an alcoholic returns to all the people he hurt and says he's sorry. It's part of the program."

Stella just wanted to be gone from the cafe. She couldn't stay and listen to him any longer. It brought back all the memories and scenes during their marriage that she'd shoved to the back of her mind. She wanted to forget that part of her past. All he was doing was bringing it to the forefront, in her face, and she hated how it made her feel. It swung her right back to those horrible years of living under his thumb.

"I have to go, Robert."

"Just think about it? I can tell you still hate me, Stella. And I would hate me too. For God's sake, I still hate myself for being such a horrible human being… to you and to my two kids."

"And I'm supposed to feel so sorry for you and allow you to brainwash my two kids with your psychological bullshit explanations of why you were such a fucking bastard while we were all living under the same roof?"

"I'd like your permission, yes." He stood, stared her in the eyes. "They deserve that. They both deserve an apology."

"Oh, so you're doing this for them and not for yourself?" She paused. "Right." She snickered.

"Both, Stella. I need to do it, and they need to hear it."

Stella looked into his eyes, and it was as if she'd literally been exported back in time to when she first met him. He had been so open and kind and caring and loving and more. Then he'd changed. But his face right now reminded her of the "old" Robert, the Robert she first met. The Robert who she would never in a million years have believed could or would morph into the monster she ran away from.

Her mind reeled. She needed time to think. She was incapable of making such a huge decision at the moment.

She ran a hand through her hair, lifting it off her sweaty neck, so upset and angry and confused and… more. "I've gotta go. I need time to think about all this."

"I understand. That's all I have any right to ask."

"As far as I'm concerned you have no rights, Robert."

He nodded, silent. "I know."

"Obviously, Loreen and Gabriel are old enough to make their own decisions. There is that. And I appreciate you asking me before going behind my back."

"I'd never do that, Stella."

"I'd have to believe what you say to believe that, Robert. And right now, I'm not in the headspace to make any decision, okay? David's in the hospital, fighting for his life. My son, Charlie's, staying with his aunt, because he can't visit his father in the ICU. My two kids are actually pissed off that I even agreed to meet you today. So, if you wanted to talk to them, they'd say they weren't interested anyway. So that leaves me as the one who'd have to convince them to talk to you. And right now, I can't do that."

"Understood."

"I really do have to go. I have to get to the hospital."

Robert slumped back into the booth. "I'm sorry about David, Stella. I really am."

Stella sighed. "Thank you, Robert."

"If you love David, which you obviously do, then he must be a good man. I hope he pulls through. I really do."

Stella felt a tear slide down her cheek. "I loved you once, Robert. I thought you were a good man once."

"And it's my fault I turned out not to be the man you thought you were marrying. That's all on me. David's not me."

Stella shook her head. "No, he's not. Goodbye, Robert."

"Thank you again for agreeing to meet me."

Stella turned away quickly, not wanting him to see how much this conversation had affected her. She didn't want him to know that what he told her made her very, very sad. She didn't want him to think she forgave him. Because she did not. But a part of her felt sorry for him. He had obviously had a horrible childhood, and that wasn't his fault. His father had ruined his son's life, and that was downright pitiful. Did that make it right, that he took after his father and turned his rage and need to be in control out on Stella and the kids? No, of course it wasn't "right". But it was understandable. Stella "got it". But who could she tell that to? No one. Was she too empathetic? Perhaps. Would she forgive him? There might come a day.

She just wished he'd never shown up, forcing her to have to deal with this in the middle of her family's crisis. Was she grateful he supposedly had changed? Well, of course she was. Any future relationships he'd find himself in would bear the fruit of the "new" Robert.

But what did that have to do with her?

She really wasn't sure.

At least that's what she kept telling herself as she drove to the hospital, tears falling down her cheeks.

Why was she crying? Her life with Robert was over and done with. Forever.

Or was it?

Had he really changed?

Chapter Twelve

Stella drove straight to the hospital after her discussion with Robert. She hadn't eaten a thing for breakfast and had taken a few sips of her latte at the Blue Cat Cafe. Her stomach churned, and she knew it was due to seeing Robert, sitting across from him, talking to him. But she could not and would not let that interaction color her time with David. It wouldn't be right. She needed to be strong and positive and not a "Debbie Downer" when she was so close to David in his hospital bed. It was all about positivity, and she needed to exude that each and every time she saw him.

She picked up a sweet-smelling bouquet of colorful roses at the hospital gift shop, their scent mild and comforting. It would be good to drink in their scent instead of the antiseptic odor emanating from a hospital room. When she exited the elevator she stopped by the nurse's station to ask if there were any changes in David's condition, even though they promised to get in touch with her, if there had been anything significant.

The nurse scanned David's chart on the computer, then shook her head and whispered, "I'm sorry, no change yet." Stella thanked her and inhaled deeply, then entered David's room.

She stepped to the side of his bed and gazed at his face and arms. The swelling seemed to have subsided a bit, and the bruises weren't as black and purple as before. She slid her fingers through his thick, dark hair and caressed the stubble on his cheeks.

"I brought the book you were reading, honey. I didn't know you liked Jodi Picoult. I've never read her novel *Eighteen Minutes*. I wish you could tell me what it's about. But you've only read the first couple of chapters, so maybe I'll start at the beginning, and we can read it together. How's that sound?"

She thought she'd feel silly talking to him, when she knew she'd receive no response, but she rearranged her mindset. She'd look at this as if David was in a deep sleep and at any moment he could wake up. And, if… no… when that happened, he'd be able to tell her he'd heard every word she'd said, and they'd laugh about it, make jokes that she was happy she hadn't said anything bad about him in front of someone else, thinking he couldn't hear her. Of course, that was absolutely ludicrous, because she didn't have anything negative to say about David anyway.

He was one of the kindest people she'd ever known. And compared to Robert, he was a freaking saint. David always treated her with respect; she knew he loved her dearly. He not only told her many times a day, he showed her with his actions - thoughtful cards hidden under her pillow in the morning before he left for the bakery, unexpected deliveries of her favorite flowers. Things like that were thoughtful gestures she'd never gotten from Robert in all the time they'd dated and were married. Robert always said he wasn't the romantic type, so Stella shouldn't expect such gestures. So she didn't. Which made the special treatment she got from David even more significant, because it was all so new and thrilling and romantic.

Stella drew a chair up close to his bedside, opened the book, and started reading. She understood why David enjoyed this author. She was a superb writer, who caught Stella up immediately as the drama unfolded and the characters came to life on each page. When she finished the third chapter, her eyes stung, and she closed them for a few seconds, only to feel a tap on her shoulder.

"Mrs. Crockett? Mrs. Crockett?"

Stella jerked her head up. She'd been drooling and probably snoring too. How embarrassing! She glanced to the side, and one of the nurses who she recognized smiled down at her.

"Sorry to wake you, but we're going to give David a bit of a clean-up. It's noon. Maybe you could go to the cafeteria and have some lunch. You look tired, if you don't mind my being honest."

Stella stood, and tiny stars sparkled before her eyes. She wobbled, but her vision cleared within seconds.

"You don't look too steady on your feet either, hon."

Stella nodded. "I'm exhausted actually. Maybe I'll go home and take a nap before I come back."

The nurse touched Stella's arm. "Sounds like a good idea. He's not going anywhere. He'll be right here waiting for you."

Stella sucked in her lips to stop the trembling she felt coming any second now. David hadn't moved. The expression on his face hadn't changed. Yes, she believed he'd look exactly like that when she returned. But she shouldn't think that way. Anything could happen, at any time.

She thanked the nurse and trudged to her car. Maybe she'd stop by the bakery, just to make sure everything was humming along without her. After parking the car in the back of Patti's Pastries, she entered the kitchen. There stood Sunny, pounding away at a mountain of dough, probably for a batch of his famous chocolate croissants.

"Hi, Sunny."

He startled and twisted around in her direction. "Oh, man. I wasn't expecting you. How's David doing?"

She sighed. "No change so far. But we're all hoping. It's early days yet, Sunny. But I believe he'll pull out of this. Is Loreen here?"

Sunny stared at her for a few seconds. "You don't look so hot, Stella. Maybe you should go home, rest up. This is a real hard time for you and your family."

Stella nodded. "You're right. I will. I just wanted to check to see how things are going here."

"Like a well-oiled train, as they say." He tipped his head up. "She's in her office."

"Thanks, Sunny." She knocked on Loreen's door and entered. "Hey, baby. How's it going?"

Loreen swiveled her chair around. "Hey, Mom. How's David?"

Stella slumped in the chair across from her. "No change. I just wanted to check to see if you need me here."

"We need you to go home and rest, Mom. Sunny and I have it covered. In fact, Gabe is gonna come by this afternoon and help us out in front. He knows how to work the register and what's what. Then I can do some stuff here that needs to get done."

"That's fantastic." Stella paused. "Still mad at me?"

Loreen glanced at her desk, grabbed a pen, and fiddled with it. "It's not really that I'm mad at you, Mom. It's more like… I don't want you to backslide, ya know? You've got Charlie, David, me, Gabe and Kat and Marcus and Peter. And the bakery too. Your life is full. And it's all good. You don't need Robert in it. He's toxic. You've been there, done that. You don't owe him a thing, Mom, not after suffering his abuse for so many years."

"I know that, honey. It's just, I wanted to give him a chance to explain himself."

"And?"

"And he did. I guess he's been seeing a therapist the entire time he was in prison. That's five years of psychotherapy. Sounds like an anger management program as well as intense personal counseling. He's still seeing her, even now. He explained why he was the way he was and how he's changed and…" She shrugged. "I listened. I didn't forgive him, if that's what you're wondering."

"So… that was it? He's gone?"

Stella shook her head. "He didn't say that, no. He…"

"He what?"

"He wants my permission to see both you and Gabe to explain to you, I guess, what he explained to me. And to apologize."

Loreen rolled her eyes. "You can just tell us what he said. That would be sufficient. I think Gabe feels the same way." She smiled, shaking her head. "And an apology is totally ludicrous. Sounds like a bunch of bullshit."

"I agree. And I didn't give him my blessing or anything like that. I thought he'd probably say he didn't need my permission because you're both adults, but he was kind enough to ask me and didn't push it."

"How very nice of him. Such a gentleman." Loreen smirked. "Not!"

"Honestly, Lo, I don't want to even deal with it or him right now."

"Did you tell him that?"

"Yes, I did. I told him exactly that. He's not stupid. He knows what a very stressful time this is. I said goodbye and went to the hospital to see David."

"Good for you. Don't waste any more time on him. Spend your time with David. He's worth it." She paused. "So he didn't say anything else? Like what he's going to do now that he's out of jail? Like a career or anything?"

"No, why do you ask?"

Loreen lifted one shoulder and shook her head. "No reason. Just asking."

Stella thought Loreen was acting a bit funny but shook it off and blamed it on the mental exhaustion she was feeling right now. She stood. "I read three chapters to David of the book he had started. Now I'm going home to take a nap. Would you check on Charlie for me, Lo?"

"Just got off the phone with Aunt Kat, as a matter of fact. She went by the school and picked up a few things for Charlie to work on that the class was doing today. Kat's homeschooling Peter anyway, so she'll help Charlie with all of that stuff."

"She's a gem, your aunt. Tell her thank you for me next time you call, okay?"

"Will do, Mom." Loreen came around the desk and hugged her mom. "I love you, Mom. And I'm sorry if I got mad last night but—"

"No need to explain. I totally understand." She kissed Loreen on the forehead and smiled at her. "I love you, honey."

"And I love you, Mom. Now go home and get some rest. Everything's flowing right along here. Gabe'll be here shortly too. He said the university will allow him to skip classes and do his work online. So he's not worried about that stuff, which is good."

"Thank him for me as well." Stella turned and shut the door quietly behind her, wondering what she'd ever done to have two such caring kids, having raised them in the same house as Robert.

A freaking miracle is what it was.

Once again, she wondered if she should go to church. Maybe pray for David.

She'd think about it.

Chapter Thirteen

Stella's routine followed the same path every day. She woke up, got ready to go to the hospital, and had a cup of coffee since her appetite had gone out the window the day of David's accident. She dropped Charlie off at school, then visited David. She talked to him about the bakery and Loreen and Gabriel helping out, about Charlie and how Kat was tutoring him for a few days, about their chocolate lab Uje and her most recent antics when Stella came home. She rubbed cream on his hands and arms and face. Kissed his cheeks and forehead, held his hand. She almost finished reading him the book *Nineteen Minutes*, trying to interject as much feeling and emotion into the character's words, as if she were auditioning for a part in a movie.

After entering the elevator she reached out to press the button for the fifth floor so she could get a bite to eat in the cafeteria, when she suddenly realized she just did not want to return to David's bedside. Her head just wasn't into it. She was mentally exhausted and needed a break. David's hospital room was making her so depressed she didn't feel like eating anyway, so why bother going to the cafeteria?

But how selfish was that? While her husband lay in bed in a coma, she was complaining she was sick of hanging out all day in a dreary hospital room with someone who couldn't talk to her. She found herself staring out the window and seeing the same view time after time after time. Sometimes she felt like she was losing it, all alone in his room with no one to talk to all day, except an occasional hello from a nurse or orderly. David's room was almost never bathed in sunshine, often very dreary and dark, depending on the slant of the sun's rays.

Suddenly Stella yearned to feel the sun's light striking her face, breathe in air that wasn't circulating all day within the confines of the hospital. She immediately slammed her finger onto the button for the lobby on the first floor. When the elevator opened, she rushed through the entrance doors to the hospital and stood on the sidewalk. She inhaled the air blowing in from the ocean and glanced across the street.

Monarch Bay Park stretched from the east side of the small town to the ocean boardwalk. Stella yearned to sit on a bench and watch her son play on the jungle gym and the slide and the swings.

She walked several blocks to the Academy and signed her son out, just a few hours earlier than the end of the normal school day. Stella waited for him outside the main office door, and when she saw his little face appear, she smiled and opened her arms wide.

"Mommy, what's going on? School's not out yet."

Stella hugged him, hard, then pulled away, grasping his shoulders, staring into his face. "I feel like playing hooky. Just for today. What do you say? You want to join me? Go to the park? Play on the swings?"

Charlie pressed his index finger to his lips. "Shhh, Mommy. I could get in trouble."

Stella laughed out loud. "I'm your mommy, and I signed you out in the office. It's okay for you to leave a little early today. I need a break from the hospital and wanted to spend some time with my favorite guy."

He smiled. "I'm your favorite guy? I thought that was Gabe."

Stella shook her head. "He's my favorite big guy. You're my favorite little one."

"I'm not that little." He puffed out his chest. "I'm almost six years old. Practically a first grader too."

"I know that." She reached out her hand, and he grasped it. "Let's go. Unless you don't want to."

He frowned. "Of course I wanna go, Mommy. You're being silly."

She smiled. "Indeed I am. Now let's get going while the sun's still shining and the weather's perfect."

They crossed the street and strolled through the park until they reached the playground area. Stella sat on a bench next to the swings and jungle gym. Only a few children younger than Charlie, mostly toddlers with their moms, ran around and played, but Charlie had never had a problem playing by himself. He rushed to the slide, climbed to the top and whooshed to the bottom, laughing the entire time, over and over.

Stella leaned her head back and closed her eyes, letting the sun hit her face, warming her inside and out.

"Hello."

Stella opened her eyes and lifted her hand up like a visor to keep the sun out of her face. "Robert! What're you doing here in the park at this time of day?"

"I'm staying in an Airbnb around the corner." He gestured toward the bench. "May I sit?"

"Sure," Stella said, turning in his direction, noticing his baggy Abercrombie & Fitch shorts and his soaking wet T-shirt.

He took a seat at the far end of the bench, his breathing labored. "I take a run in the afternoons, but I haven't been that consistent. Today's the day I promised myself I'd go running every single day. I'm not getting any younger." He patted his flat stomach.

Stella chuckled. "You never had a weight problem, Robert."

"No. And neither did you. We were a pretty fit couple, I'd say."

"Maybe that was the only positive thing about our relationship."

Robert nodded. "You're right there. What're you doing here?"

Stella pointed at the slide. "I took Charlie out of school a little early today so he could play. He doesn't really show it, but I know not having his father around is affecting him. A lot. He and David are very close."

"Poor kid." Robert turned his head to where the children played. "Which one is he?"

Stella looked over at Charlie, once again flying down the slide, blond hair fluffing up in the breeze as he zoomed from the top to the bottom six feet below. "He's the little boy who just reached the bottom of the slide." She waved at him, and he waved back. "White T-shirt with dark blue shorts and red tennis shoes."

"What a cute little boy. Obviously a product of David's classic good looks—and yours."

"Thank you. He has David's laid back personality. He's sweet and caring. Also just like David."

Stella and Robert faced each other.

"How's David doing?"

"Not awake yet. Which is one of the reasons I'm here today. I needed a break from being inside a hospital all day. Sort of driving me a bit crazy, you know?"

He nodded.

"But I'll be honest, I'm feeling totally guilty. While my husband lies in a coma, I'm the one complaining about not getting out enough. How self-centered is that?"

Robert shook his head. "You were never a selfish person, Stella.

Patient as the day is long. That's you. Especially for all those years you put up with my shit. Pardon my language, but that's putting it lightly anyway."

"Agreed." Stella smiled. "You seem happy, Robert."

He smiled again. "I certainly am. I feel so much better about me, about life in general, about my future."

"You've changed."

He jerked his head back. "Really? So you believe me? That I'm not the same person I was in Oregon?"

Stella rolled her eyes. "From what I've seen so far, yes, I'm guardedly optimistic that this is for real. That you're for real." She shrugged. "Unless this is all an act and you should win an Academy Award for your fabulous performance."

"No performance, Stella. What you see is what you get. I never faked any of my behavior, even in Oregon. As awful as it was, that really was me at the time. I wasn't pretending back then. Nor am I pretending now. And I feel good, you know? I have a good future ahead of me, and inside—" He pointed at his chest. "—in here I feel comfortable and healthy." He tapped his temple. "But most of all, I'm healthy inside here."

"And I congratulate you, Robert. I know it must have taken a heck of a lot of work to get to the place you are now."

"Years and years, Stella. But so worth it. I—"

"Mommeeeee!"

Stella's head jerked to the side, and she jumped off the bench. "Charlie!"

Robert ran to where Charlie lay on his back at the bottom of the slide, slapping the ground with his two hands, crying out loud. Robert knelt beside Charlie and leaned over him, blocking the sun from the child's eyes. "What happened, Charlie? Did you fall?"

Stella knelt beside her son and took his hand in hers. "Baby, what happened? Did you hurt yourself?"

Tears streamed down the sides of Charlie's face. "It's… it's my ankle. I landed hard on the ground, and it twisted. It feels really bad, Mommy."

Robert turned to Stella. "May I? I've taken a few courses on medical emergencies."

Stella nodded. "Of course."

"I'm just going to look at your ankle, Charlie. I won't touch it. I'm just going to slide your sock down a bit, so I can see if there's already a bruise. Is that okay?"

"Yeah," Charlie whispered.

"Charlie," Stella said. "This is Robert. Remember I told you I was married before I met your Daddy. This is the man I was married to in Oregon. But we're friends now. Let him take a look, then we'll decide what to do to make it better. Okay?"

Charlie sucked in his breath. "Owww. Mommy, it hurts. Bad."

Robert turned to Stella. "I think it may be a sprain, but I'm not a doctor. I'd say, let me carry him to the ER down the street. Would that be all right?"

"Yes, of course." She kissed Charlie's forehead. "Robert's going to carry you to the hospital where Daddy's staying. We'll let the doctors in the Emergency Room take a look at your ankle."

Charlie nodded, his face splotchy, tears flowing across his cheeks.

"We can be there in less than five minutes." Robert slid his arms underneath Charlie and gently lifted him up. "You okay, buddy?"

"Uh huh," Charlie said. "What're they gonna do to me?"

Robert and Stella began walking toward the hospital.

"Well, Charlie," Robert said, "one of the doctors at the hospital will take a look at your ankle. They'll be able to fix it for you. Maybe they'll fit you with one of those cool boots. Ever seen one of 'em before?"

Charlie stuck his thumb in his mouth, eyes wide, as he stared at Robert and shook his head.

Robert continued talking as he held Charlie gently in his arms. "I've seen one of those boots they put on sprained ankles. Usually you get to pick out a color you like. That's kinda cool, isn't it?"

Charlie nodded, then pulled his thumb out of his mouth. "Did you have one?"

"Yup, I sure did. I fell down some stairs when I was much older than you are. I can't remember exactly, but I think I picked out hot pink."

Charlie chuckled. "You did not. Boys don't wear pink."

Robert frowned. "They don't? I didn't know that. I think I have a hot pink tie at home that I wear with my dark blue suit. You don't think I'd look cool in hot pink?"

Charlie stared at Robert and shook his head. "You'd look silly. Everyone would laugh at you."

"Well, geez. Maybe that's why everyone I saw was talking about me and chuckling. I thought I looked really rad, but I guess I was mistaken."

"You're making up that story. Isn't he Mommy?"

Stella shared a look with Robert, and she tried her best not to smile or laugh. "If Robert says he wore a hot pink ankle boot, I believe him."

"Okay, Mommy. But I don't want a hot pink boot thingee."

Robert noticed the bright blue sign for the Emergency Room entrance and glanced down at Charlie. "You don't have to have a pink boot, Charlie. What color would you like?"

"Black. I'd want a black one. That's a boy color."

"Then I guess black it'll be." Robert winked at Stella. "Here we are."

Stella and Robert walked through the ER doors, where the nurse whisked Charlie into a private area for children. Stella and Robert followed the gurney into the room and stood off to the side while the doctor examined Charlie's ankle.

The doctor carefully palpated the ankle and asked Charlie where it hurt and where it didn't. "It's a sprain, young man." He smiled down at Charlie. "You must be a pretty brave guy, Charlie. I know this hurts a lot, and you look like you're ready to get right back out there and play some more."

Charlie shook his head. "It hurts a lot, but Daddy always says I'm big… and strong too. That's what Loreen always tells me too."

"And Loreen is who? Your big sister?" the doctor said.

Charlie nodded. "My favorite sister. But I only have one sister anyways."

The doctor chuckled. "You're lucky to have a sister like that, Charlie. She sounds very wise." He patted Charlie's hand. "I'm going to fit you with what looks like a big boot, Charlie. Then your Mommy and Daddy can take you home to rest. Then, if you're careful, you can return to school. But you have to wear the boot for at least a week. Then your parents can take you to your regular doctor to see when you can remove it. You got that?"

Charlie nodded again. "Can I pick what color of boot you put on me?"

"Sure you can. What color would you like, young man?"

"Black. It's gotta be black."

The doctor removed his gloves. "I'll see what I can do, but I'm pretty sure there won't be any problem finding a black boot in your size.

I'll be right back, okay? Your mommy and daddy can stay here with you."

Stella smiled at the doctor. "I'm his mother. This is my friend, Robert. Charlie's dad is in this hospital right now. He was in an accident. He has a TBI. David Crockett?"

"Hmm. Might have heard the name."

"Small hospital, small town," Stella said.

The doctor smiled. "Indeed." He walked away. "Be right back with that new boot, Charlie."

It took only another half hour or so to put the special orthopedic boot on her son's lower leg, then Robert carried him to Stella's car and laid him in the back seat.

"Thanks, Robert," Charlie said. "Will I see you again?"

Robert stuck out his arm and shook Charlie's hand. "We'll leave that up to your mom. Her schedule is awfully tight right now. She visits your dad in the hospital every day." He shut the back door of Stella's car and came around to the driver's side.

"Thank you so much for today, Robert. I don't know what I would have done without you there. I not only wouldn't know what a sprained ankle looks like, I couldn't have carried him four blocks to the E.R."

Robert backed away from the car. "You're very welcome, Stella." He leaned down and took a look at Charlie. "Take care now."

"Thank you again," Stella said, feeling like crying at the same time. She didn't say anything, but she'd been afraid at first that Charlie might have hit his head on the ground and had some sort of brain damage like his father. Maybe that was silly. Maybe not. But she was ever so grateful it was just an ankle sprain and nothing more.

And, of course, she was once again amazed at Robert's behavior, having never seen this caring side of him ever before. Because it didn't exist back then.

But it sure did now.

Amazing.

Chapter Fourteen

The next day Kat came over to Stella's house along with Peter. Stella picked up Charlie's class papers from school and brought it back to the house, where Kat helped both boys with their homework. She was homeschooling Peter anyway, so this was an easy and quick fix while Charlie rested in his bed with his leg propped up. Stella didn't mention anything about Robert but knew she'd have to explain Robert's involvement in Charlie's accident.

She'd have to figure out what to do for the next week or so, since Marcus had returned from another long-haul, and Stella didn't want to keep Kat and Peter away from Marcus since their time together was normally very limited. But she'd think about that and come up with a plan by the evening.

Stella visited David, then went to the cafeteria for lunch. She set her cell phone on the table and stared out the window.

"Hello, Stella."

Stella jerked out of her reverie and opened her eyes.

"Robert. What are you doing here?"

"I was supposed to have a complete physical after being released, but I never got around to it. The doctor they assigned me to is in the west wing of the hospital. I stopped by to have lunch. May I join you?"

Stella's first thought was, her kids would give her a ration of shit, if they knew she had lunch with their father. She hadn't mentioned Robert's help with Charlie's ankle yesterday. Charlie was asleep when Loreen and Gabe returned home, and both left early this morning. So there wasn't enough time. She wasn't looking forward to that conversation either.

But they weren't here, and she was the mother, and she could do as she pleased. She didn't have much, if any, interaction with adults. David was still comatose. Loreen and Sunny and Gabriel were overwhelmed running the bakery. She only saw Kat in passing. She had had few adult conversations, since David had entered the hospital. Oh, except for the dinner with her family, when Kat and Gabriel and Loreen and Marcus expressed their dismay and opposition to Stella having anything to do with Robert and their disagreement over whether people could change.

Stella hesitated for a few seconds. "Sure. Have a seat. I'll be here for a bit anyway."

Robert smiled that smile. The one that won her over back in the day. The one that disappeared shortly after they married. The one that turned into a sneer soon after saying their vows. Stella's stomach hurt. She'd always carried her stress in her gut, and right now it was rebelling, big time. Today she'd eaten a yogurt and an apple. But stress was stress, and her stomach didn't like stress, so she didn't eat much.

Robert brought his tray to the table and sat across from her, placed his napkin on his lap. "You look tired. I imagine you're spending a lot of time here with David."

"Yes, I'm here every morning and afternoon. I usually arrive early, have lunch here in the cafeteria, then go back to his room, read to him for awhile, talk to him a bit, then go by the bakery, check on Loreen and Sunny. Kat's taking care of Charlie at our house just for today. Usually I pick Charlie up from school, but Loreen's been doing that since David's accident—except yesterday. So then I go home and fall apart." She chuckled, then her chuckle turned into a sick, low laugh which morphed into a sob.

"Oh, God, Stella." He reached for her hand and held it lightly. "I'm so sorry. If there was something I could do to take this pain away from you, I would."

She glanced up at him and pulled her hand from his grasp.

"Really. I know you still hate me. I'd hate me too. But it doesn't take away from the fact, I'm not the same man, the man you knew. My heart aches for what you must be going through. And on top of everything Charlie sprains his ankle. How's he doing anyway? Is there anything I can do to help? Though it seems you've got all your bases covered."

She stared at the table for several seconds, not accustomed to having a conversation about her son and David like this with Robert. She took a deep breath and replied. "I can't have Kat taking care of Charlie for an entire week while he's laid up in bed. Her husband, Marcus, is a long-haul trucker, and he just returned, and she and their son, Peter, need to have family time. I want to keep visiting David. I need to spend time with him. The doctor explained the importance of talking to David, reading to him, touching him. When his memory returns… if it returns, that is… he might recall me staying by his side throughout this time. I need to be there. I mean, I want to be there.

"On the other hand, Loreen now has taken over my job at Patti's Pastries, and she also does all the accounting for the bakery. She doesn't have time to stay with Charlie. I can't be at two places at the same time—at the hospital with David and with Charlie at home."

She leaned her elbows on the table and covered her forehead with her palms. "I can't leave him home alone. It hurts too much for him to get around. And he's my responsibility, not Kat's or Loreen's for that matter. I'm his mother." She dropped her hand to the table and stared out the window.

Robert cleared his throat. "I could stay with him. Make sure he gets his breakfast and lunch. I could also help him with his homework. Whatever you would like me to do. I'd enjoy helping out, if you'd let me."

Stella turned away from the window to face him. Could she trust Robert with his record of past abuse? With her and David's son? "Loreen and Gabe would kill me, if I let you do that."

He shrugged. "Just thought I'd offer. I'd look after him, if you trusted me to do that. It would solve your problem, but I totally understand if you think that's too much. And I don't want Gabe and Loreen to get upset about it either."

"I know. I mean, they'd kill me."

"I completely understand. Let's just drop the subject."

Stella's mind whirled like the spin cycle of a washing machine. Should she accept his offer? Was it wrong? Foolhardy? Safe? Was she headed down a road from which there would be no egress? But she felt as if she'd been pushed into a corner with no access to get out of the room.

She closed her eyes for a few seconds to let her thoughts stop chopping away at her mind, scrambling everything into a mental salad filled with too many ingredients. After she opened them, what she saw made her heart thump - Robert's glassy eyes. He swiped at one of them with his free hand.

"What's wrong, Robert?"

He shook his head, staring at his food tray. "I never took the opportunity when we were married to spend time with the kids. Time I'll never get back. I regret that, more than I regret anything I've ever done in my entire life."

Stella's heart squeezed. She could actually feel a tightening in her chest. Robert really had changed. Or he'd taken acting lessons in prison. She knew they offered tons of learning experiences in prison these days in the hopes of lowering recidivism and allowing ex-convicts the opportunity for better jobs after their release. But she was pretty sure acting lessons were not part of that repertoire of educational offerings.

She breathed in slowly to the count of three as she'd learned to do in her meditation, letting it out to the count of three. Did she really think Robert would harm her son? No, she did not. "You'd really take care of Charlie for me?"

Robert's eyes grew wide, then a smile appeared around the edges of his lips. "Of course. I'd be honored, if you'd trust me to do that."

"I would never normally take you up on your offer, but I need to talk to David as much as possible each day. Read to him. Touch him. Act like he can hear me and pretend he's awake when he really isn't. But studies show some people recall hearing words or voices and things like that after they wake up. If that's true for David, I've got to be there for him. I can't bring Charlie here to the hospital either, because kids his age aren't allowed, and Charlie will probably be able to go back to school soon, though I'm not sure of the exact day. If I stayed home, I wouldn't be able to visit David *at all* and—"

"Stella. Stop! Honey, stop!"

Stella stared at him as if he'd called her a bitch or something equally derisive.

He shook his head. "Sorry, I didn't mean to say that. Habit, I guess. Even after five years."

Her breathing grew rapid. She was hyperventilating and didn't know how to stop. This had never happened to her before. She gripped the edges of the table with both hands as she attempted to take in a full breath. But it was as if a stone had lodged in her throat, and only little puffs of air were able to pass through into her lungs.

Robert came around to her side of the table, knelt in front of her, and twisted her chair so she was facing him. He grasped both of her hands. "Close your eyes, Stella, and breathe with me." He squeezed her hands. "Do it, okay? Shut your eyes. Good girl. Now take a big deep breath through your nostrils, as if it's coming straight from your abdomen all the way up past your belly button into your chest. That's right. Now it's passing up into your throat, you can feel it coming in, cool fresh air. Feel your chest expanding. Now let it out through your mouth, slowly. Yes, that's good. Now take another deep, deep breath. There ya' go. You're doing it, Stella."

Stella did exactly what he asked, and suddenly she could breathe normally again. She opened her eyes and met his, then slowly pulled her hands out of his grip.

Robert returned to his seat.

She moved her chair back to where it was and dabbed at her eyes with a napkin. "Thank you." She breathed in deeply several more times. "Where did you learn that technique."

"My therapist. Works every time."

Stella's eyes were still watering, and she swiped at her cheeks. "I guess that's what's called a panic attack?"

Robert nodded. "It is. They can be scary."

"You've had them?"

"Yes. But not so much now. I feel good about where I am these days. Except for… well, you know."

"Your two kids. I get it, Robert. But let's just take one day at a time here, okay?"

He smiled. "Sounds like a good plan to me." He pulled his chair closer to the table. "So how do you want to work this thing with Charlie?"

Stella pointed at his lunch tray. "You haven't eaten a thing."

"Not really hungry."

Stella squinted. "You came here specifically to see me, didn't you?"

He bent his head and stared at his plate of food. "You're right."

"You're stalking me, Robert. It feels creepy."

He shook his head. "I'm not stalking you. I really did have a doctor's appointment in the west wing. That's not a lie. I swear to you. But I admit, I thought you probably went to the cafeteria around this time, so I thought I'd stop by, and, if I saw you, I'd ask how David's doing. Is he still in a coma? Has he woken up yet?"

Stella sighed. "No, he hasn't woken up yet, and, yes, he's still in a coma. You could have texted me instead of following me here."

"I don't have your cell number, Stella. You know I don't. I've never asked you for it. I never would have either."

She glanced at the ceiling for a second. "Sorry. I don't know why I said that. Of course you don't have it." She looked him in the face. "But I guess I have to give it to you now, because we'll need to keep in touch."

"Yes, about Charlie. You're right."

Stella gave him her cell phone number, and he texted her back.

"Now you have mine," he said.

"Good. So could you come by tomorrow morning, around nine maybe? Tonight I'll tell Charlie all about our arrangement. He told me he really liked you and that you were such a nice man."

Robert laughed under his breath. "I wish you thought I was a nice man."

"I'm beginning to see that you are, Robert." She stood. "It's getting to be that time. I best get back upstairs."

He gestured toward her. "Of course. Whatever you need to do, Stella. I understand."

Stella smirked. "Oh, really? I don't think I've ever heard those words come out of your mouth before."

Their gazes locked for several seconds before he said, "You're totally right about that. But that was then. This is now."

"I know, I know," she said in a sing-song fashion. "You're a changed man, yada, yada."

"I'll prove it to you. In time." He paused. "There's got to be at least a small part of you that believes me, Stella. Otherwise why would you allow me to watch over your son?"

Stella thought about that for a bit. "You're right. Of course I see a huge change, Robert. But is it make believe? Is it real? Or is it how you were before I married you and given time, you'll revert to the Robert I knew and hated?"

Robert grabbed his chin. "Ouch! That hurt! But I deserved it." He stood in front of her, only inches from her face. "You'll see I'm for real, Stella. I promise you that."

Stella took the elevator to the ICU. Her mental meanderings segued into wondering about David and how long it would be before he woke up. If he ever did. Which was a possibility Stella refused to allow herself to contemplate for more than a few seconds. For now at least.

Gabe and Loreen knew about Charlie's accident, but Stella hadn't mentioned anything about Robert… yet. Telling them their father would be spending the next week or so with Charlie at the house was not a discussion Stella was looking forward to. And she'd have to explain to Kat as well. Kat hadn't said anything to Stella; obviously Charlie hadn't mentioned it either. That was another discussion Stella dreaded.

Life after a family tragedy was tragic in and of itself.

Chapter Fifteen

The next day, Loreen went to the bakery at five a.m. Stella left Charlie with Robert and waited for them to settle in doing homework before she drove to Patti's Pastries, where she found Sunny working the front register. He told her Loreen was in her office, so she headed to the back area, knocked on the door, and opened it.

"Hi, honey. How's it going?"

Loreen swiveled around. "What're you doing here, Mom? You left Charlie home alone? You know, you don't have to check on Sunny and me every day. Neither of us has quit and the bakery hasn't closed down."

Stella rolled her eyes, just as her daughter was prone to do. "I do not come by to see if you're doing your job. I'm simply keeping in touch. David would want me to do that. I know you and Sunny are completely capable of running the show. You've already proven that in a very short time." She sat down in the chair across from her daughter. "There's been a change of plans with regard to Charlie."

Loreen's eyebrows slid into her bangs. "Where is he?"

Stella crossed and uncrossed her legs, feeling nervous and edgy, knowing what she said would not go over well. She placed her hand on the edge of Loreen's desk and looked her straight in the eyes. "Robert is at the house, watching over Charlie. He's doing this as a favor to me."

Loreen leaned back in her chair and stared at the ceiling, her clenched fists on the papers scattered across her desk. Several seconds passed before she brought her head level with Stella's and gave her a lingering stare. "You have *got* to be kidding me."

"It's a wise decision given the fact it's imperative I see David every day. And it's just for a few days until Charlie can walk around on his own and go back to school."

Loreen tapped the desk with her index finger. "So Dad's gonna be at our house with my baby brother… alone… taking care of him."

"Robert volunteered, Loreen. Look. You can't do my job and your job and watch Charlie too. That's not an option. And since I need to be with David and this is hopefully only for a few days, having Robert watch over Charlie seems like a good option."

Loreen swiveled her chair left to right, left to right, her knuckles white from holding onto the arms of the chair in a death grip. "You call what you're doing with Robert careful? Really, Mom? It sounds to me like you've lost your fucking mind."

Stella nodded slowly. "I know you feel that way, Loreen. That I'm going to be sucked in by Robert's story or maybe you even think I'll go back with him or something equally outrageous. But that's not what's going on here. He's shown me he's changed, as far as the interactions between him and me. You don't know, because you haven't been around him. But Charlie has."

Loreen squinted. "What're you talking about?"

"When Charlie and I were at the park, Robert was jogging by and stopped to talk. Charlie screamed when he got hurt, and Robert was the one who looked at his ankle and thought it looked like a sprain. He carried Charlie four blocks to the ER, talked to him the entire way there, made him laugh, stood with me in the ER, helped me get Charlie back into the car. He and Charlie really hit it off."

Loreen let out a short laugh. "Yet you didn't want Gabe and me to have anything to do with him. Remember telling us that? You obviously had good reasons for that decision. But now… oh, *now* you expect Gabe and me to come home after work and hug him and kiss him on the cheek and sit around singing Kumbaya? Oh, it's okay *now* for him to be around my baby brother, because he's *changed*. He could say and do things to make him cross over to the dark side. Robert's side. You know exactly what I'm saying, Mom. Don't pretend that you don't."

Stella closed her eyes for a few seconds and drew in a breath. "Loreen, I hear you. I really do. But Robert really has shown me he's changed. He's not dangerous. He's been in counseling for five years while he was in prison. We talked at length about that. He's also still in therapy, even now. He's dealt with his anger management issues and continues to communicate and interact with his therapist every week."

"Well, rah, rah, rah, sis, boom, bah. Let's break out the confetti and blow a bugle."

Stella sighed. "When he was with Charlie, Loreen, I'm telling you, he was unlike anything I've ever seen during our years as a family in Oregon. He listened to Charlie, talked to him respectfully. They got along famously."

"So Robert's going to come to the house, hang out with Charlie, help him with his homework, just like he did with Gabe and me, right?" She laughed out loud. "And I'm sure you expect Gabe and me to act respectful and be ever so thankful Dad's doing all of us this huge favor by taking care of my little brother."

Stella shook her head. "No, I don't expect anything from you and Gabe, though I think if you talk to your father and let him explain about his experience in prison for five years…" She shrugged. "… you might feel different."

"Oh, come on, Mom. You believe all that shit he told you? And you trust him? After only a couple of times talking to him. An ex-con? Jesus fucking Christ—"

"Loreen, stop! Please!"

Loreen lowered her head and closed her eyes. "It just makes me feel so uncomfortable, even though I've read…" Her head jerked up, and she sucked in her lips.

Stella's brows drew together. "You read what? What did you read, Loreen?"

Loreen blew out a long breath of air. "Okay. I'm gonna be honest with you. I looked up Robert on the internet. Did a search for anything I could find on him."

"And what did you find? And why didn't you tell me about this? Was it bad? Why didn't you say something?"

"Mom!" Loreen fiddled with a pencil, twirling it between her fingers. "It wasn't bad. At all. In fact, it was impressive."

"What do you mean, impressive?"

Loreen opened a desk drawer, withdrew a piece of paper, and read it out loud. "The article's entitled *'Education in Our Prisons. The Case of Robert Walker.'*" She glanced at her mom. "I'll paraphrase. According to this article, Dad was such an exemplary model for countering recidivism that they implemented an additional educational alternative." She leaned back in her seat, met her mother's eyes. "He received his Master's degree while he was in prison, and he's a licensed family therapist."

Stella shook her head, mouth slightly open. She felt truly gob-smacked. "He's a therapist himself? I… I just can't believe this. He never said a word about it."

"I'll be honest, Mom. I thought it would be one of the first things he'd tell you, in order to endear himself to you. I have to admit, I'm impressed he didn't use it to win you over."

Stella couldn't stop shaking her head. "I'm just… there are no words. Wow. I mean, I—"

"I don't wanna hear it, Mom. Yes, it's an impressive endeavor, no doubt. And I get it. But, shit…"

"Why didn't you tell me this? Were you ever going to tell me?"

Loreen kept quiet for almost a minute before she sighed. "I'm gonna be honest. I don't know if I was ever going to say anything to you. I have such…" Her lips trembled. "I remember loving my daddy when I was really young and didn't, as they say, know no different. But as Gabe and I grew older and we saw how he treated you… the bruises… your muffled screams…" Tears flowed down her cheeks.

Stella walked around the desk and knelt in front of Loreen, cupping her daughter's cheeks in her hands. "Honey… Loreen, baby. I want you to trust me on this. He's not the same Robert. I wouldn't leave Charlie with him, if I wasn't sure of this. And now that you've told me what you found out about him, I feel even more validated. My decision is the right one.

"Lo, I can't let Patti's Pastries fail during this time when David's incapable of working here. When he wakes up, I want him to be proud of all of us for doing everything we possibly could to keep the bakery afloat, serving all those who've been our loyal customers for years. We've become one of the most popular establishments in Monarch Bay. We serve a higher number of tourists every single year too. And right now, we're keeping the bakery afloat solely because of you and Sunny and all of your efforts, because I can't help oui right now. Honey, I don't want to let David down. I have to do whatever I can to keep the bakery financially in the black. And I can't work here. Don't you understand that? Not if I'm with David all day at the hospital. So I made a decision, Lo. I wouldn't put my child in harm's way. You know me. Robert never laid a hand on either of you kids and he's not going to start now."

Loreen stared into her mother's eyes. "He head-butted Gabe once. In the kitchen. Remember that?"

Stella nodded. "I haven't forgotten that, no." She paused. "Loreen, give him a chance. That's all I'm asking. He won't arrive at the house until after you and Gabe have gone to work, and he won't be there when you get home at night either. So have coffee with him or something like that. Take a walk around the park. I don't know. He won't force either you or Gabe to speak with him, and he won't go over my head either. I respect that. He's showing *me* respect—something he never did during our marriage. And I'm not forcing his hand to do that either.

"The way he is now, the way he speaks to me, the way he acts. He's not the same, Lo. And the fact he was in intense counseling for five years? That's a long time. An impressive amount of time. And the fact he's still in therapy? That's a really great thing. People do change, Lo. I believe that, though I didn't at first, even though your Uncle Marcus does. He said so to Kat, and she was so pissed off at Marcus, but I believe him. I do. And now you're telling me your dad worked to get his license as a therapist while in prison? You have to admit. That's pretty amazing."

Loreen pushed her chair back, stood, then turned to gaze out the window, her back to her mom, silent. "So not only do you want me to condone your having Robert spend time with my helpless baby brother, you're asking me to get to know him, because you're telling me he's a changed man."

Stella stood and walked closer to her daughter, held her by the shoulders and turned her around to face her. "That's what I'm asking."

Loreen scanned her mother's face, as if memorizing each and every facet, then placed her hands over her mother's hands and squeezed. "Okay."

Stella encircled her daughter in her arms and hugged her tightly. "Thank you, Loreen."

"But someone's gonna have to convince Gabe to do the same. You know that, don't you? He's really angry about this whole Dad ingratiating himself into our lives again thing. He thinks it's totally messed up. And what about Aunt Kat? Did you tell her all this?"

Stella walked to the door, grasped the handle, and stood still, her back facing Loreen. "No, I haven't told Kat yet. She hasn't asked me, so I know Charlie must not have told her. Maybe I won't have to convince Gabe or Kat about any of this." She turned around. "Maybe you could tell them I'm not as off the wall as they think I am."

Loreen gazed at the ground, shaking her head back and forth several times, then looked up at her mom. "Okay. I'll do it. For you, Mom. Because you're asking."

Stella stared at her daughter. "Thank you, Lo. That means a lot to me."

Chapter Sixteen

Stella's cell phone chimed early the next morning.

"Stella Crockett?"

"This is she."

"This is Nurse Maureen Ohara. Dr. Hamilton would like to speak with you before you visit your husband this morning."

Stella's heart beat ramped up. "Is something wrong? Has something happened to David?"

"Not at all. Dr. Hamilton wanted me to get in touch with you, though, and give you that message."

Stella's heart rhythm slowed down a bit, and she loosened her grip on her cell phone. "I'll be there in a few minutes. Is the doctor in the ICU or…?"

"He's in the conference room. You know where that is?"

"Yes, I'm familiar. Thank you for telling me."

Stella glanced in Charlie's bedroom. Robert was sitting in a chair next to the bed, pencil in hand, pointing out something to Charlie, speaking in a low voice. Charlie nodded several times, then wrote something down on a sheet of paper. Robert glanced toward the doorway and gave Stella a little wave. Charlie said "hi", then went back to doing his homework.

After a quick shower, Stella jumped in her car, trying to keep her foot from stomping on the gas pedal, so she could arrive at the hospital in record time. She knew that was silly. David was still alive, but whatever it was Dr. Hamilton had to say, he obviously didn't want Nurse Ohara to deliver the message to Stella.

When she arrived in the ICU, she recognized Nurse Ohara, who pointed down the hall, and Stella waved and raced to the conference room.

The door was open, and Dr. Hamilton stood and gestured for her to take a seat while he closed the door, then sat across from her at a round table that could probably seat twenty to thirty individuals. They greeted each other, and Stella folded her hands on the table and waited.

"This morning at six a.m. David woke up."

Stella leaned forward in her chair and stared at him, heart fluttering in anticipation of his next words.

He cleared his throat. "I asked Nurse Ohara to phone you before you arrived this morning. You and I should discuss his behavior and how to deal with that."

"His behavior? Is he acting strange or something?"

He leaned back in his chair, elbows on the armrests and steepled his fingers. "Nurse Ohara checked on your husband and noticed his eyes flickering. She waited for several minutes, and he turned his head toward her and asked where he was. She immediately asked him several questions. He knows his name, that he's in the hospital, that he lives in Monarch Bay. What he doesn't remember is the actual accident or anything that happened afterward. Our protocol is not to overwhelm the patient by asking too many questions after waking up. Many patients are confused and agitated and scared, and we may exacerbate their situation by pressuring them in any way. We don't know what they'll end up remembering, because some of them instantly recall people and places and things. Others take longer to regain their recollections."

He tapped his pen on the table. "Some make a full recovery and are completely unaffected by the coma. Others will have disabilities caused by the damage to their brain. Some don't regain their memory at all. We talked about that after David arrived here at the hospital, but I wanted to prepare you again for the possibilities."

"Doctor, do you think it really helps that I've been talking to David while he's been in the coma? Every day I tell him about what's happening at home, about his favorite sports team, about each member of his family, what they're doing. I did everything you told me to do."

"I believe with some patients, it indeed makes a difference. Then again, for others, the brain damage inhibits them from taking any information in whatsoever. It's a good sign David knows who he is and where he is. My point is, let's take this slow. He'll probably sleep a lot, then wake up for short periods of time, and we don't want to overwhelm him with too much information or force him to try to remember anything."

Stella could hardly contain her nervousness and excitement. David was awake! That was a good thing. And she hadn't even had a chance to go to church and pray. At this point, she promised to go and at least give thanks that he was alive and talking. "What about the reverse, doctor? If he asks questions, should I answer them truthfully?"

Dr. Hamilton nodded. "It is my advice that, yes, you should. We don't want to tell him too much. That may make him more agitated. And then he may get angry. You never know what the patient's reactions will be. So, I'd answer his questions, but don't volunteer too much and no need to elaborate to any great extent."

Stella nodded. "Thank you." She stood. "May I go see him? I mean, right now… or?"

Dr. Hamilton pushed his seat back. "Yes, please do. And if you could, please notify the nurses how he's doing afterward, so they can apprise me when I read his chart."

Stella thanked him again and rushed down the corridor to his room, heart in her throat, anxious to see her husband awake and talking, hoping he'd remember his family who'd always meant the most to him—her and Charlie and everyone else who made up his world. She abruptly halted at the entrance to his room and took a deep breath, glanced around the corner and saw his eyes open, staring at the ceiling. She let out the breath she'd been holding and entered the room.

She wanted to do everything right, not push him, not stress him out, stay calm and happy and try not to pry information out of him, nor endeavor to jar his memory. She had to exude a peacefulness that she didn't really feel, but she could fake it—for him. She'd do anything for him. And he was alive. That was what she wished for, prayed for.

She slowly approached the side of his bed. "Hello, David," she whispered.

He slowly turned his head in her direction. "Hello."

His voice sounded rough, lower than normal. Probably because he hadn't spoken in days. She'd lost track of time, every day blending into the next with the sameness of it all. But now everything would be different. She wouldn't be sitting by his bedside reading to him, hoping he heard her voice and remember all her words of love and the memories she described of their life together.

"I've been waiting for you to wake up. Do you feel okay? Are you in any pain?"

His brows furrowed. "Are you a nurse? You're not dressed like the other nurses?"

Stella's chest felt as if a boulder had been laid on top of her, so she remembered to take a deep breath, calm herself. All in good time. The doctor said his memory might return slowly in bits and pieces. She had to be patient and understanding.

She smiled. "No. I'm not a nurse. You don't recognize me?"

He stared at her, studying her face. His eyes wandered from the top of her head to her shoulders and back up. "Should I?"

"I've been here every day, reading to you. You had been reading a book by Jodi Picoult called *Nineteen Minutes*. I was almost finished with it. She's one of your favorite authors, and I didn't even know it until I found her book at your bedside."

He squinted, lips drawn in a straight line. "Why would you be in my house? In my bedroom?"

Was she supposed to tell him the truth? Suddenly she couldn't recall what the doctor said would be best. She had to say something. Tell him why she would have known who his favorite author was. She'd sort of talked herself into a corner with only one way out. "David, I'm your wife. We've been married for five years. We share the same bedroom." She reached out to cover his hand with hers.

He drew his hand away slowly, staring her in the eyes. "I've never seen you before. And you're not Patti. Where is she? I want to see her."

Oh, my God, a good six years of his memory—lost. Then again, that didn't necessarily mean it was a permanent memory loss. That could change. It was early days. In fact, he'd only been awake a few hours. She shouldn't expect much. She drew closer. "Yes, Patti was your wife, David. But she passed away. Of breast cancer. That's when we met."

"That's a lie," he growled. "Nurse! Nurse!" he shouted. "Get this woman out of my room. I want to see my wife. Where's Patti?" He thrashed around in his bed, the IV pole swaying back and forth.

Stella reached out to steady the pole. If it fell, it might rip the needle out of his arm.

Nurse Ohara and Dr. Hamilton rushed into the room.

"Diazepam twenty milligrams stat," the doctor called out.

David's face turned deep red. He was hyperventilating, screaming at the nurses and Dr. Hamilton. "She's not my wife. She's lying. What is she doing at my house, rummaging through my bedroom? She's a thief.

She took my book. What else did she take? Call the police. Patti can look through the house and see if this woman stole anything else. Get her away from me. I hate liars. Help! Hel… " His words slurred to a stop, and his eyes slowly closed.

Dr. Hamilton turned to Stella and gestured toward the door.

Stella's heart beat rapidly in her chest so hard, it felt as if she'd run a mile in less than a minute. She exited the room and sidestepped to the corner, out of David's view, bent over, hands on her knees, and breathed in and out slowly.

She saw men's shoes several feet away and straightened up. "I'm sorry. I don't know what I did wrong. I wasn't pressuring him. I—"

"Stella," Dr. Hamilton said, grasping her forearm. "It's okay. We'll just have to approach David a bit slower. He's just not ready. He's only been awake for a few hours."

Stella nodded. "I know. He didn't know who I was, doctor. He thinks he's still married to his dead wife. That was more than five years ago."

Dr. Hamilton's expression remained calm. "Totally common, Stella. Don't be too alarmed. Yes, there's a possibility he won't remember you, but I would say, with time and with a little help jogging his memory with pictures and stories… he could come around. His memory of the distant past right is now at the forefront. The present is just not available at the moment. That could be permanent. Or not. I'm sorry I can't be more specific but—"

"I understand, Dr. Hamilton. You explained that all to me. Obviously I went a bit too fast for him. That's all on me. And I apologize for upsetting him."

He nodded. "No need to apologize, Stella. You're doing the best you can, and you've never been in this situation. Every patient with a TBI is different. Every single one. We'll just take it day by day."

He reached in his pocket and extracted his cell phone, glanced at the screen, then looked up at her. "I'm sorry. I have to scrub for surgery. I think it would be best if you don't try again today. Take the day off. Get away from here. Do something different. Relax. Try again tomorrow. That's my advice."

"Of course," she said, as he rushed toward the elevator bank.

Stella didn't know what to think, how to feel. Disappointment clouded her thinking, and she took a moment to decide what she should do. Her legs felt like two blocks of concrete, her heart as heavy as lead. She walked like a zombie to the elevators, and the doors were already open. Staring at all the buttons, she automatically pressed the one for the lobby. She'd go home. What else could she do?

After the doors opened, she slogged through mental quicksand to the parking lot and walked like a zombie to her car. She felt so weak, it was as if she hadn't eaten in days. She'd go home and make herself a decent meal, sit down with her feet up, try to relax. As if that were possible. She slumped into the driver's seat, exhausted.

She drove home, staring out the window, trees wafting in the breeze, tiny birds flitting from limb to limb in the park. When she stopped at the light, she watched as hundreds of butterflies flew from one branch to the next, orange and black wings fluttering softly until they landed. Monarchs. The reason this town had been named after them. Monarch Bay.

She loved living here. Loved having the twins still living here as well, especially now. Loreen had moved back home to save money, and Gabe would be graduating from San Luis Obispo soon and was still living near the university. But now that she needed him at the bakery, he'd instantly arrived and settled himself in Charlie's bedroom in one of the single beds. Kat and Marcus and Peter lived several blocks from her and David's house.

Family meant everything to Stella, so she was happy with the living arrangements in such a beautiful small town on the coast of California, the weather mild, the beach inviting. Much better than the constant rain and cloudiness of Oregon, where she and Robert and the twins had lived. But an arrow had lodged itself in her throat all the way through to her heart. It hurt.

She felt stupid for feeling this way. Betrayed. Lonely. Forgotten. Abandoned. Her husband didn't know who she was. So now who was she? Would the feelings he had for her ever return? She shook her head, trying to think her way through the morass of negative thoughts and emotions.

Everything would be all right. David would remember her. She had to believe that. Otherwise, what did she have and who was she?

When she arrived home, she tried her best to be quiet so as not to disturb Charlie and Robert. Their voices trailed into the kitchen, where Stella stood in front of the refrigerator. She couldn't make a decision to save her life.

"Stella?"

She turned around. "Robert."

"Are you okay?"

Stella nodded. "I'm okay. How're you and Charlie doing?"

Robert smiled. "A lot more than just okay."

"What do you mean by that?"

"You know, Stella, he was telling me about his teacher and classmates and friends and such. He's adorable. I experienced something I'd never felt before with my own kids. That specialness. Helping him with his homework… I was doing something to make him feel good, even when I had to correct him on some math work. He still smiled at me. I wasn't scaring him by trying to control him or sternly telling him what to do. And the constant anger I used to feel for the kids interrupting the life I had with you… it's no longer there, of course. In fact, I don't remember the last time I was angry about anything, Stella. Instead of seeing Charlie as an intruder in my life, interacting with him is something I look forward to. It's very freeing." He caught her gaze. "Am I making any sense?"

Stella nodded, tears gathering in her eyes. "Yes, you're making perfect sense. I still look forward to seeing the twins and Charlie. And the twins are adults now. But they'll always be my babies, no matter what their age."

"You're a good mother, Stella. I admire you. All these years you've had to be both mother and father to Gabe and Loreen. They've turned out to be fine individuals. That's all on you, Stella. I had absolutely nothing to do with it. Especially when we lived in Oregon, all I did was provide a place to live and food on the table while they were growing up."

Stella shrugged. "Well, there is that. We didn't lack for food and water."

"Doesn't say much about me, that's for sure. But I'm going to try to remedy that… maybe one day I can."

Stella stared into his eyes. "Loreen agreed to talk to you."

"What?" he said, a bit loud. He lowered his voice. "Sorry, but that comes as a complete surprise." He smiled. "A good one though. Wow! Did she say when? Does she know much about me now?"

"She looked you up on the internet. She's the one who told me about your license as a family therapist. Why didn't you tell me that?"

He puffed out a breath. "I was serious about learning more about why I acted the way I did when we were together, Stella. And all that psychology information I found absolutely fascinating. So when they opened it up as a possibility to study in prison and get an advanced degree, I jumped all over it, applied, got accepted into the program, studied hard, and got my degree in less time than I would have on the outside. Nobody to stop me from studying all day, every day. No job to go to. I had all the time in the world. All of that… seeing a therapist, studying for my degree… it changed me. I'm a different man." He held his hand out like a stop sign. "Not trying to convince you of anything, Stella. Don't get me wrong. The only way you'll know I've really changed is if you give me a chance to prove that to you."

Stella tilted her head. "You're doing that right now, Robert."

"Little by little, Stell. Little by little."

Chapter Seventeen

Several days later Stella took Charlie to the doctor, who replaced the orthopedic boot with one less restrictive, allowing him to begin walking on his own, albeit slowly and carefully.

Stella texted Robert that she wouldn't need him to help out with Charlie and brought her son to school, discussed his situation with his teacher, and told Charlie she'd pick him up later. She stopped by the hospital to check on David, hoping their visit would be a more positive one. However, his day was filled with various x-rays, along with an MRI, so Stella took the opportunity to sit in the park and relax.

She found an unoccupied bench, sat down, and tried to meditate, breathing in to the count of three, breathing out from her belly to the count of three, until her pulse slowed. Anxiety and stress had become her constant companions, which affected her sleep as well as her appetite. She was always tired and never hungry. Her body was telling her to slow down and eat healthy, and she promised herself she'd try her best, starting today.

In the recesses of her mind someone called her name, but the voice was incorporated into a dream until she opened her eyes.

"Robert! Oh, my God, you scared me to death."

"I'm sorry. I called your name several times, then realized you must be asleep. I was about to leave." He sat on the bench, then stood immediately. "May I?"

"Of course."

He sat back down and looked up at the sky. "It's an absolutely gorgeous day. How's Charlie? So the doctor released him to go back to school?"

"He put a different orthopedic shoe-like contraption on Charlie's foot and he's able to hobble around. He wanted to go to school so bad, and, with the doctor's permission, that's exactly what happened. I just dropped him off."

"Good for him. He's a little trooper, that one."

"And I want to thank you again for looking after him. Though I have to admit, I didn't end up spending that much time with David. I probably could have stayed home with him myself."

Robert smiled. "I'm glad you didn't, though. I really enjoyed spending time with your son, getting to know a young person who's only five years old." He shrugged. "A new experience for me, Stella."

"Yes, I guess it was, Robert."

"Care to take a short walk?"

Stella stood. "Sure. I need the exercise. David's having a bunch of tests run today, along with x-rays and an MRI, so I left and came over here to relax."

"Oh, geez. I'm sorry. Don't feel like you have to walk around with me. You were sleeping for a reason, Stella. You're obviously tired. I'll leave you be. Just thought I'd ask—"

"No. I'm serious. I need to move, you know. Every day I sit in that god-awful chair in David's room. It's so uncomfortable. But it's not like I can do jumping jacks inside the ICU."

He laughed. "Then let's walk a bit."

They sauntered around the edge of the park, then took a side path to look at the pond and ducks and children playing on the grass.

They were silent until they reached a line of ducks. The mama duck waddled in front with ten ducklings following her, their little rear ends wiggling side to side. Stella stared off into the distance at the dark green hills surrounding Monarch Bay.

Stella's gaze led her to a cluster of clouds, and she smiled, then pointed. "Look at that one. It looks exactly like a duck. There's a head and two spindly legs and a bit of tail feathers sticking out the back. Can you see it?"

Robert followed the direction she pointed. "Yeah, I do." He chuckled. "That's so funny. Right after we just saw, what, eleven ducks all in a row a few seconds ago?" He chuckled.

She turned to him. "I haven't heard you laugh like that in… ages. Years actually."

"I never found anything funny during my marriage. I was an unhappy man. All I ever looked for were the bad things in life, and once I walked down that road, man, I was able to turn anything and everything into a negative experience. It was all I'd known most of my life. It was almost as if it was the only way I felt comfortable. I know it doesn't make much sense to you. It took me years to understand it myself."

Stella thought about what he said for a few moments. "It does make sense to me." She paused. "You know what I said about the doctor asking me to leave the other day?" She shrugged. "I messed up, Robert. I told David I'd been reading to him from one of his favorite books I found on his bedside table. That set him off. He got so angry. He asked me why I was in his house, in his bedroom, looking through his things." She halted and turned to Robert, lips trembling. "He doesn't know who I am, Robert. He wanted to know where his wife, Patti, was." She covered her face with her hands, sobbing. "I'm a stranger to my husband."

Robert took her in his arms and hugged her lightly. "It'll be okay, Stella. I've done some research on the internet, and there's a good chance his memory will return. This could be temporary. He might suddenly recall everything all at once or, with time and seeing you and talking with you, the recollection of you and him together may gradually enter his head, and he'll know who you are after awhile." He stepped back and gently pulled her hands away from her face, looked in her eyes. "You have to have hope, Stella. And think positive. Take it one day at a time. I mean, he's alive, right? That's a huge thing to happen, given the serious traumatic brain injury he suffered."

She nodded, swiping at her cheeks with her fingertips.

Robert reached into his pocket and placed a tissue in her hand.

"Thank you." She dabbed under her nose and eyes. "Since when did you become so empathetic?"

He smiled.

She shook her head. "Never mind. That was a rude thing to say."

"I deserved it. I take no offense, believe me."

Stella took in a big breath, let it out slowly. "You're totally right about David. I know that. The doctor said as much from the beginning. But to experience it, to see the complete… I don't know… hatred in his eyes for me. It just shook me to the core."

"I understand. I do." He paused, watching her. "You're shaking. Have you had anything to eat today?"

She shrugged. "I don't know. Not that I recall."

He touched her elbow. "Let's go get some lunch. I'm starving. You've got to be hungry. Plus you need to keep up your strength. I know that sounds like a cliché, but it's true. My therapist explained to me about nutrition, because I had a tendency to neglect eating. I'd eat a granola bar and a coke and call it a day. Not a good thing."

"Okay. Let's go somewhere quiet, where no one will see me and ask a bunch of questions about David's condition."

"I'm not that familiar with the places in Monarch Bay. Up to you, Stell."

She didn't flinch at him using a more endearing name for her. It almost felt right somehow, given the way he was treating her, with such kindness and understanding. It felt good. Made her feel calm inside, after what had happened at the hospital. "The Blue Cat again. It's pretty good food, and most people don't take lunch at this time."

He checked his watch. "You're right. Should we walk there? It's a nice day."

Robert stuck out his elbow, and Stella hesitated for a second then curled her fingers around his arm. They sauntered around one long side of the park without speaking. Birds in the trees tweeted a greeting. A woodpecker pecked out a rhythmic tune, the sun glistened on the dark green grass spread across the park, and children shouted from afar. Stella almost felt happy for a second, then checked herself.

She had no right. David was lying in a hospital bed with a traumatic brain injury… and now believed he was still married to Patti. Holy crap! And here she was, meandering across the park, holding onto her ex-husband's arm, headed to the Blue Cat for lunch.

She suddenly halted mid-stride, and Robert almost tripped alongside her. She shook her head as she backed away from him. "What am I doing?"

"Stella, what's wrong? What happened?"

She shoved out both hands toward Robert.. "I can't do this. David's in the hospital. My husband's fighting to get his life back, and I'm walking around this beautiful park with you, on the way to have lunch together, as if everything is hunky-dory." She paused, stared him in the face. "Loreen warned me. She said you'd try to talk me into believing you. That you'd changed. That you're a different man."

Robert took several steps away from her, mouth agape. "I'm not trying to do anything, Stella. I'm just being me." He placed both his hands on his chest. "I have changed. I know I have. I don't expect you to believe my words, but I'd think my actions would speak for themselves. I'm trying to show you, I'm not the same man you were married to. But if you don't give me a chance, how will you ever know?"

She closed her eyes, shaking her head from side to side slowly, as if in a trance. "No. No. I can't be taken in by you again. It's like when we first met." She opened her eyes. "You were a nice guy then, and look what happened."

"I know that, Stella. Don't you think I anticipated how you would react to my telling you about what happened to me in prison? Why should you believe me? I could be lying through my teeth." He paused, took several steps toward her. "But I never expected you to just take my word for it. I want to prove to you I'm a changed man. Because it's true, dammit. I'm not the same person I was. And I told you all about what I learned through therapy. I've been working on putting my life back together for five, going on six, years. I swear on my… on my kids' lives, I'm the real thing. I swear to God, Stella. Please, please give me a chance. Please."

Stella hesitated. Should she do this? Was she going down a road that she shouldn't? She was a married woman. What if someone told David they'd seen her strolling through the park on the arm of her ex-husband? "I'm sorry, Robert. I shouldn't be doing this. People will talk. And it could get back to David, even the two kids. And they'd be right to question me about it. I'm sitting here thinking… what the hell am I thinking?"

"Why did you decide to trust me with the care of Charlie, if I'm such a psycho? That doesn't make sense."

Tears threatened, and she let them flow down her cheeks. She was so confused. She didn't understand why she'd asked Robert to care for Charlie or acquiesced to his offer of having lunch together. Her mind whirled. Was she pissed off at David for thinking he was still married to Patti? Yes, there was a part of her that took affront to David saying that and kicking her out of his room, shouting at her. But that was an ignorant way to feel, and she knew deep down, it was all the TBI. He wasn't the David she knew and loved speaking that way to her. And he could still recover his memories of them together.

He would remember. She knew he would. She believed he would, if she had anything to say about it. Which she did. Because she planned to visit him the next day and the day after that and the day after that and do everything in her power to make him like her, enjoy her company, and eventually realize he was her husband. And what about asking Robert to take care of Charlie? He'd volunteered, and she'd taken him up on his offer. That was on her.

"I'm sorry, Robert. You're right. I'm the one who asked you to take care of my son. And, no, I don't think you're a psycho." She held her head between her hands, tears rolling down her cheeks. "I don't know what's happening to me. I feel like I'm going crazy or something."

He reached out a hand, and she grasped it. "It's okay. Let's call it a day, Stell. You go back to the hospital or go home and take a nice long bath, pamper yourself. Tomorrow's a new day. I can even pick Charlie up from school, if that will make things easier for you today. Whatever you want, I'd like to help you out. Lord knows, it's hard doing all this alone."

She dropped her hands to her sides and stared at him. "Okay. Okay. I'm going to go home now. You go to lunch. I'll get something to eat when I get to the house. But I'll pick up Charlie today myself. I don't want to disrupt his routine. He may be feeling weird today wearing that orthopedic shoe thing. Kids can be mean, maybe make fun of him. I should be there when school gets out."

"Sounds good, Stella. You take care of yourself."

She nodded, not knowing what she was even doing, standing in this park, talking with her ex, as if everything in her life was flowing along hippity-skippity, when in reality her life was in shreds. David didn't believe they were husband and wife. She was a total stranger to him. Her heart was breaking in two so hard, her chest hurt.

She turned and ran the few blocks to the hospital parking lot. When she arrived at her car, she wondered where she was headed then, recalled, she was starving. Maybe she was feeling and thinking oddly because she needed to eat something. She had to get her head on straight before she picked Charlie up from school.

Charlie, David's son. And David didn't even know that. Holy shit, as Kat would say. Her life was unraveling, and she better get her act together, before she lost her husband and Charlie lost his dad.

Chapter Eighteen

Stella's exhaustion got the best of her that day, and the moment her head hit the pillow that night, she slid into slumber for nine hours and awoke feeling refreshed, ready to meet the day… or rather, ready to meet David and try again.

During the night sometime she'd received a text from Kat, which she could hardly believe was real. Kat said even though she didn't agree with Stella allowing Robert to take care of Charlie after he sprained his ankle, she wasn't going to fight with Stella about something that was really none of her business.

She said Charlie was Stella's child, not Kat's, and Kat would have to acknowledge that Stella was able to make her own decisions and promised not to butt her nose into Stella's private family issues. She ended by saying she loved Stella and always would, and she respected her and would try her best not to make waves. She acknowledged Stella was going through a hard time right now and didn't want to make things worse by arguing with her.

The relief Stella felt after reading Kat's text was literally palpable. Her stomach unclenched, and it felt as if a significant weight lifted from her chest. She wouldn't have to argue endlessly with her sister, and that was a gigantic problem Stella wouldn't have to deal with.

She headed to the hospital, fearful of what, or rather, who she'd meet there. Would David be her husband today, or was she still a stranger to him? She told herself to take her time, don't push him, just have a quiet visit, talk about the weather, Monarch Bay, anything but the fact they were married and he was madly in love with her.

She pasted a smile on her face, nodded at Nurse Ohara, and walked into David's room. "Good morning." She set her purse with the book *Nineteen Minutes* on the chair and stood to the side of his bed. "How're you feeling today?"

David turned his head toward her, the scowl obvious on his face. "What the hell are you doing here? I thought I told you to get out of my room yesterday," he yelled. "I don't want you here, bitch. You're a liar and a thief. You lied about being my wife. You stole the book that was in my house." He fumbled around the side of his bed. "Where the hell is that call button, goddammit. I'm reporting you to the nurse." He pressed the button over and over like a crazy person, jamming his finger on the button so hard Stella thought it would break apart in his hand. "Nurse!" he shouted. "Goddam useless shits. Nurse!"

Stella ran out of the room, smack into Dr. Hamilton. The file in his hand fell to the floor, and he backed several feet away, eyes wide.

"What's going on in there?" he said.

Stella caught his eye and pointed toward David's room. "I didn't say anything." She felt herself dragging breaths from deep in her chest, causing her to hyperventilate within seconds.

Dr. Hamilton grasped her shoulders and turned his head to the side and called out, "Get a chair over here." He looked at Stella's face. "Take a deep breath. Try to calm yourself."

She felt his hands press down on her, forcing her to sit in a chair that appeared behind her. He knelt on the floor in front of her, grabbing both her hands in his. "Take one deep breath. Now. Nice and slow. Count with me. Breathing in. Hold, one, two, three. Breathing out, hold one, two, three." He repeated the pattern three times.

Stella's breathing slowed considerably, and she stared at Dr. Hamilton's face as it shimmered into vision. "I'm sorry. I didn't do anything. I—"

"It's all right, Stella. Stay calm." He patted her shoulder. "Remember what I told you. It's going to take time. Don't give up on him. Just keep on coming. One of these days, we're all hoping his memory will return… bit by bit or however it goes. Believe that. I've seen it happen many times."

"And you've seen it happen that they don't ever remember too. Am I right?"

Dr. Hamilton sighed. "Of course. But if you don't continue trying, Stella, you'll never know, will you? I'm not giving up on him. The nurses aren't either." He stood. "And neither will you."

She nodded, feeling as if a ton of bricks lay on her chest. She placed a hand on her throat. "I feel sick."

Nurse Ohara put a small cup in her hand. "Drink this. Apple juice. Have you eaten today?"

"I don't remember. I don't think so."

"I'll bring you to the cafeteria myself then," Nurse Ohara said. "It's my lunch break."

"No," Stella said, placing her hand on the nurse's forearm. "I can go myself. I'm guessing you have little down time around here. I don't want to be a bother. I'm going to drive home and eat and take the day off."

"Are you sure?" Nurse Ohara said, eyeing Stella with a look that said she doubted Stella was telling the truth.

"I'm positive." Stella stood, looked down at herself. "See. I'm not wobbly. I'm okay." She tipped the cup to her lips and drank the apple juice. "I'll be fine." She picked up her purse from the floor where someone had placed it and shifted it onto her shoulder, then glanced from the doctor to the nurse. "Thank you. Thank you for helping me out today. I'll be here tomorrow to visit again."

Dr. Hamilton and Nurse Ohara backed away, and Stella rushed to the elevator bank.

Tomorrow was another day. Another opportunity to try again with her husband. She had to have faith… hope… whatever she needed to get through this rough spot. If it actually was a spot and not the permanent road of his future. Speaking of faith, she'd pick up a sandwich, park in the lot behind St. Salvador's Church off Main Street, eat her lunch then go inside. And pray.

It had been years since she'd eaten a cucumber and cream cheese on wheat bread sandwich from Linda's Lunchery. She enjoyed every bite and washed it down with a cola for an added caffeine pick-me-up. After setting the alarm on her phone, she endeavored to meditate for five minutes, then exited her car and walked around to the front of the church.

Designated an historical monument, St. Salvador's was like nothing she'd ever seen during her childhood days she'd gone to church with her foster parents. The particular church she and Kat and Fiona and Nason had attended on Sundays was rather bland—cream-colored walls, a few small paintings of the Stations of the Cross, a small altar with no fancy adornments, uncomfortable hard-as-concrete seats, and the kneelers were unpadded and hurt Fiona and Nason's knees, as well as Stella's and Kat's.

But St. Salvador's? Just the intricately carved doors to the church were awesome, towering what looked like twelve-feet high by five-feet wide with foot-long, brass handles. Inside Stella found a foyer with black-and-white swirls throughout the marble floors leading to the church proper, where rows and rows of oak wood seats ran up both sides of the church. At the far end stood a black marble altar garnished with a hand-sewn cloth, which draped over the sides to the floor. Beautiful stained glass windows decorated the walls, with figures of the Twelve Stations of the Cross spaced evenly along the sides. Stella glanced up at the ceiling, which looked similar to photos she'd seen of the Sistine Chapel. Her mouth fell open, so mesmerized was she by her experience in this church.

Who wouldn't feel close to God here? Her footsteps echoed off the walls, like the clip-clop of a horse, and she began tip-toeing toward the front pew. There she knelt as close to the inner sanctum as she could without reaching the altar. Bowing her head, she let her thoughts wander as she tried to remember what it was like to pray when she was young.

"God," she whispered. "If you're still talking to me since I've ignored you for years…" She glanced up at the cross hanging on the wall behind the altar with a young Jesus, arms spread wide, holes in the middle of his hands dripping blood. "Jesus, you probably don't want anything to do with me, but I'm here anyway." She folded her hands and leaned forward against the pew. "I don't know when I lost my faith in you. I think it happened during my marriage to Robert. I couldn't believe you'd allow him to beat me and rape me over and over for ten years and not intervene in my behalf. I remember all the times I called out your name. I'd say, 'God, help me', over and over."

Tears sprinkled her cheeks as the memories rained down upon her. "I needed someone to help me back then. Where were you? Where? All I can guess is that you wanted me to become a stronger woman by forcing me to act on my own. Maybe it was your grace that guided me to the discovery of my sister Kat because of the man I hired to find her. Then somehow you placed that kind trucker, Tom Mizzaranni, right in front of me with the help of that waitress, Maisie, at the truck stop cafe. If that was you, thank you from the bottom of my heart, because it brought me here, to Monarch Bay, where I met David."

She sniffed and grabbed a tissue from her pocket and swiped beneath her nose. "That's why I'm here really, God. I mean, the rest of that stuff already happened, and if you had a hand in it, believe me, I owe you, big time. But now I need a favor. For me and my family, but it's also for David. He's a good man. He deserves better than to have lost his memory of all he has here. I'm a good wife to him, God, and my kids love him. Our son, Charlie, adores him. And now that's all been taken away."

She closed her eyes as tightly as she could, shaking her head back and forth. "Please help him. Please do something, anything, so he at least remembers us, his family. I don't care if he doesn't remember our wedding day or Charlie's birth or any of that. I just want him to know who we are. We can start our life together fresh and new. The memories aren't as important as the fact he doesn't know me, God. I'm a stranger to him, and he's still in love with Patti… and she's dead! I'm here, right here, right now, and I love him more than I've ever loved any man." She stared at the statue of Jesus on the cross again, willing her thoughts to penetrate through whatever it was that flowed from her to God—that spiritual connection she used to feel years ago as a young girl. "Please, please help David remember." She stood. "Thank you."

She slid out of the pew and turned to her right, gazing at the six Stations of the Cross along the right wall. A shaft of light hit her in the face, and she covered her eyes with her hand, like a visor. She shifted her gaze from side to side, trying to figure out where the light was coming from. She couldn't figure it out, because there were no beams of light emanating from any of the six stained glass windows of the Stations of the Cross on the right side of the church. It was as if the beam of light came out of nowhere, yet it was hurting her eyes to look directly at it.

Then it was gone. Poof! She stood in the center of the aisle, searching for a place the light could have come from. There wasn't anywhere but the stained glass windows on the right side of the church, where the beam had shone through. She turned to the left side of the church. The sun's beams filtered directly toward her, hitting her in the face. This didn't make sense. Where had that sunbeam come from on the right side of the church if the sun was shining through the stained glass windows on the left side?

She twisted around and looked at Jesus on the cross again. "Was that you?" she said in as quiet a voice as she could, since she was in a church and yelling seemed inappropriate. She walked backward several steps, then turned around and walked out of the church, bewildered yet awed. What had just happened?

When she reached her car she suddenly felt nauseous and bent over, wrapping her arms around her stomach. She opened her mouth to vomit, and just as quickly as the feeling came on, it disappeared. She straightened up, took several deep breaths, got into her car and drove away.

Chapter Nineteen

That afternoon Stella took a nap on the couch, while Charlie played in his bedroom. Her rather odd, unusual, and inexplicable experience in St. Salvador's had kicked her butt. She slept for two hours and woke up, ravenous and thirsty. After a croissant she'd picked up at the bakery earlier and a cup of fresh coffee, she slowly began feeling more like herself.

After talking to Kat on the phone about her second visit with David since he awakened from the coma, they realized visitors from the family were not yet a good idea. There was no getting around the fact the kids, as well as Kat and Marcus and Peter, would have to explain their relationship to David, which would circle around to his being married to Stella… and the doctor didn't want David any more upset and disturbed than he already was.

Any patient waking from a coma, suffering from a TBI, would be agitated and nervous, not knowing their place in the world, not remembering experiences they were being told they had in the past. Dr. Hamilton and Nurse Ohara explained it was a highly stressful time for TBI patients. Stella promised to keep Kat and Marcus apprised of the situation. Kat didn't bring up the subject of Robert, which meant the world to Stella. It would have been too much to handle right now.

The following day Stella woke up feeling funky—stomach upset, dizzy. She spoke with the nurse at her general practitioner's office and apprised her of the situation with David. It was a small town; they were already aware of what had happened. The nurse thought Stella's symptoms were concurrent with anyone going through what she was experiencing. However she suggested Stella come in that afternoon to see Dr. Holmer. There had been a cancellation at two o'clock, and Stella took it, hoping Robert would be able to pick up Charlie from school.

After much thought and deliberation, Stella decided not to visit David that day. It would just add to her feeling nauseous and stressed out before her appointment, but she wanted to try again the following day, hoping something, anything would be different. Also, perhaps she'd give God a chance to think about what she'd explained in church. Or was she being a total idiot for thinking that way?

She texted Robert and asked if he'd pick up Charlie. He jumped at the chance. Stella couldn't believe how happy he was to spend time with her son. The difference between the Robert in Oregon and today's Robert was striking.

After a thorough examination, as well as Stella explaining all she'd been going through with David's memory loss, the doctor asked her about her eating and sleeping habits since David's accident. Then he took blood and urine samples and sent her home with a prescription for a mild stress reliever.

When she walked through the front door, she heard Robert's voice and Charlie laughing out loud. She smiled and wondered what they were doing, so she tip-toed down the hall to Charlie's bedroom and peeked around the corner.

Robert knelt in the middle of the floor with an obviously handmade paper hat on his head with horns or something sticking out the sides. A blanket draped across his middle and a strip of black material hung around his neck, meeting at the back of his neck in a knot. She could only guess he was meant to be a horse or a bull, but wasn't entirely sure until… Robert let out what was supposed to be a horse's whinny.

Stella backed away from the door, hand covering her mouth, trying to stifle a laugh. She peeked around the doorway again. Charlie stood facing Robert with a broom in his hand, the handle wrapped in silver duct tape. "On guard, Maximus. I am the king. Back away," he said loudly.

Stella didn't know what they were pretending. It almost looked as if they were jousting, but Charlie should have been riding a horse, not standing on the floor in front of the horse with a jousting stick, if that's what it was supposed to be.

She couldn't hold it in any longer and laughed out loud.

Both of them jerked their heads in her direction.

Charlie smiled. "Hi, Mom! It's the Renaissance times."

Robert stood and slipped the paper helmet off his head. "Hi, Stell. Just playing horse and jouster… or something along those lines."

"Shouldn't Charlie be on his own horse or at least be on top of your back with that jousting stick if, that is, you're supposed to be a horse?"

Robert slipped the blanket off his waist and tried to pull the collar off his neck at the same time. "That would be what one would surmise. But don't ask me. I'm just following orders here."

"I'm the jousting guy, and there's another guy on Robert's back. You just can't see him is all," Charlie explained.

Stella covered her lips with her fingertips. "Who's winning… or whatever it's called?"

"I'm the king, so I have to win," Charlie said.

"Ohhhkayyy." Stella strung out the word, then smiled at the two of them.

"Guess it's time for me to go then," Robert said, gesturing toward the doorway.

Stella took a few steps back. "Thank you for bringing him home. And for playing along with him." She glanced at Charlie. "Say goodbye to Robert."

Charlie waved, then flopped onto his bed, poking the broom handle toward the ceiling.

Stella followed Robert to the front door. "Thanks so much for picking him up, Robert. Truly, I really appreciate it."

He opened the front door, stepped outside, and turned toward her. "He's a great kid, Stella. Then again, so were Loreen and Gabe."

She smiled. "Thank you. As a matter of fact, they'll be here for dinner soon." Within seconds, a car pulled into the driveway. "Speaking of which."

She walked past Robert to their car, leaving him standing alone on the doorstep. She had to warn the kids, Robert was here. Gabe and Loreen could make up their own minds as to whether they wanted to stay or leave.

Loreen rolled her window down. "Wassup, Mom?"

Gabe leaned toward his sister and looked over at Stella. "Who was that?"

Stella glanced back at the doorway. Robert must have gone inside. "Your father."

Loreen's eyes widened. Gabe leaned back in his seat and gazed out his side window.

"It's Dad?" Loreen whispered. "Is he staying for dinner?"

"I didn't ask him to," Stella answered. "Do you want him to?"

Loreen chewed at her bottom lip. "I guess that would be all right with me." She turned to Gabe. "What about you, bro?"

Gabe shrugged, still looking out his window. "According to you, Loreen, he's a…" he gestured quotation marks with his hands, "changed man."

Loreen huffed out a breath. "I didn't say that. How would I know anyways? I haven't spoken to him. It's Mom who's convinced he's changed his ways. I just wanna see if she's right or not."

Gabe shrugged again. "Fine by me. Whatever."

Stella leaned her head inside the car. "Neither of you has to do anything, and I'm not even asking you to. But he's your father. He always will be. I just think if you give him a chance, you just might change your mind."

"Have you?" Gabe said.

"So far, I'm impressed," Stella said. "But I'm not forcing the issue. It's still all so new. I really don't expect either of you to feel different just because I do."

Gabe shoved the car door open. "Let's just do this thing. Get it over with."

Stella came around to his side of the car and stood before him. "Please don't do this, if it's going to make for a hostile atmosphere."

He looked her straight in the eyes. "I said whatever, Mom. I'll paste a smile on my face and shake his hand. Then we'll see what happens after that."

Stella nodded, walked to the front door with Loreen and Gabe following her.

Robert left the front door ajar, and when Stella pushed it open he stood in the foyer, looking like someone had given him a death sentence.

"Hey, Pops," Gabe called out with a smirk on his face.

Robert shoved out his hand. "Gabe? Nice to see you after all this time. How're you doing?"

"I feel about as good as you look right now," Gabe said. "I've heard from Loreen that my Mom thinks we should give you a chance. You know… to prove you're not the bastard you always were when we were living in Oregon. You remember, don'tcha, Dad?"

Robert glanced at the floor, then up at Gabe. "I deserve everything you call me and say to me. I was an asshole, a bastard, whatever names you can think of. That was me. But I'm not that man any longer, son. And I'd like you to give me the opportunity to prove that to you. If you'll let me."

Gabe glanced at Loreen.

Loreen walked toward her father and stood a foot in front of him. "You look the same… Dad."

"But I'm not," Robert whispered. "I swear to you, I'm not."

Loreen nodded. "I guess we'll see."

"What's for dinner?" Gabe said.

Stella let out the breath she'd been holding since they'd entered the house. "I just have to pop a homemade lasagna in the oven a neighbor dropped off the other day. I had put it in the freezer, so while it's baking, maybe you three can sit in the front room and chat for awhile. I have to make a salad and garlic bread."

Robert and Loreen and Gabe filed into the front room, while Stella went to the kitchen to get dinner ready. She hoped all would go well. She wasn't happy the kids hadn't had a father for the last five years. They were better off without Robert the way he'd been for most of their lives, but if he really had changed, which she thought he had, she'd be happy they would have both parents instead of just one.

Stella heard the hum of conversation while she was putting the salad together and spreading garlic mixture on the French bread. She was taking it slowly, wanting them to have "alone time" together. Suddenly she heard laughter as well, and she smiled. This was good. Really, really good. It made her feel validated in her observations of Robert's behavior.

He appeared to be a pretty nice guy, thoughtful and caring and attentive. And the way he acted with Charlie, playing the horse, surprised her to no end. He'd never played around with Loreen and Gabe. They weren't accustomed to, nor had they ever seen, this softer side of Robert.

When it was time for dinner, Stella called everyone to the table. Gabe walked into the dining room with a smile on his face, and Loreen appeared content. Robert was the last to be seated, and he glanced at Stella and winked at her with a smile. She guessed the three of them had gotten along quite well, and her insides relaxed. She even felt hungry for the first time in days.

During dinner they talked of nothing serious—the upcoming Monarch Bay Festival, the beach, the bakery, town matters like expanding the park, Gabe's studies at the university, Loreen's accounting endeavors, plans for taking a vacation.

"Maybe one day during the summer we could all go camping?" Robert said, looking from Loreen to Gabe to Charlie. "You, too, Charlie."

Gabe took a bite of lasagna and nodded. "That might be fun."

Loreen smiled. "Yeah, maybe."

Charlie jiggled around in his seat. "I've never been camping. Dad's never taken me. He's always busy at the bakery."

Stella frowned at Charlie. "Is that really how you feel, baby? That he doesn't spend enough time with you? You've never said anything like that before."

Charlie shrugged. "He says he has to work in order to put food on the table and clothes on our backs. But he never talks about vacations. Robert said maybe one of these days we can play baseball and go to the park after school."

Stella glanced at Robert, who lifted his eyebrows.

"Only if your mom is okay with that, Charlie," Robert added.

"Well, as soon as Daddy gets out of the hospital we'll have to do something about that. I think your Daddy works too much. Maybe we should hire another baker to help him out. Then you and he could play baseball and go to the park too."

Charlie shrugged. "Okay."

Stella spent a few minutes pushing her salad around on her plate, contemplating if that would ever happen with David and Charlie. What if David never remembered having a young son or a wife or any family at all? Granted, Stella was happy he'd recovered from the coma, but that was only the start. His life was more than waking up. He had a life at the bakery, a loving wife, a devoted son, and other family members who loved him and needed him. What if that never happened? What would he do? Patti wouldn't be there to love him either. She was dead. Stella was the one who was alive.

When they finished dinner, Robert stood and asked to help out with the dishes, and Stella demurred, saying she'd take care of it. It soothed her to perform something mindless, like filling the dishwasher with dirty dishes instead of ruminating over the huge changes in her life and David's future place in her life as well.

Robert thanked her for dinner, hugged Loreen and Gabe goodbye, and took his leave. But not before he and Charlie high-fived and Robert promised to see him again sometime, if it was okay with Stella. Robert didn't mention the park or playing baseball, and Stella realized he was trying to be sensitive about the subject concerning David's work ethic and spending time with his son. She realized again the difference between this Robert and the Robert of her past and smiled. It was not only refreshing, it brought to the forefront how she remembered him when they first met. Her heart clenched, recalling how madly in love she'd been with Robert back in the day.

She caught sight of herself in the window above the sink, grinning. She shook her head, telling herself these memories had nothing to do with her life today.

Or maybe they did.

Chapter Twenty

The next day, Stella woke to her cell phone pinging at nine in the morning. She grabbed it after the fifth ring, finding it hard to wake up. Maybe it was the Valium she'd taken the night before that Dr. Holmer prescribed. She pressed the button to answer it, heart beating rapidly. Was it something about David? Had he fallen back into a coma? Was that even possible? She realized she'd never asked that question and felt like an idiot. It had never crossed her mind.

"Hello, Mrs. Crockett. This is Carolann, Dr. Holmer's nurse. Do you have a moment to speak with the doctor?"

Stella waited only seconds before Dr. Holmer came onto the line, greeting her kindly, as always, since she'd known him for years, and he'd delivered Charlie five years ago as well.

"I have good news for you. Your blood work came back perfect. No anemia, which is something I told you I was looking for. But another thing I didn't ask you about was the type of contraception you and David have been using, but I guess I got my answer to that."

Stella frowned. "We're not using anything right now, doctor. You're the only physician I've seen in Monarch Bay, so you know I'm not on the pill or have an IUD or anything. So how did you find out we aren't using anything?" Her mind still felt foggy after having been jogged out of a deep sleep, confused as to what he was even talking about.

"All makes sense, Stella, because you're about six weeks pregnant and you can expect this little one in about thirty-two weeks, so approximately eight months from now."

Stella's stomach flipped over, and bile crept up the back of her throat. Her cell phone slipped from her fingers onto the floor with a clunk as she ran to the bathroom. Lucky the lid was up as she bent over and vomited. Spit and bile flew out of her mouth, and she knelt closer until the wave passed, then she slumped onto the bathroom rug.

Suddenly remembering Dr. Holmer's gentle voice telling her she was going to have a baby, she grabbed a wash cloth, wet it, and wiped off her face then rushed to find her phone.

"Dr. Holmer? Dr. Holmer?"

"Still here, Stella. Are you okay? Sounds to me like you have a bit of morning sickness."

She swallowed. "Sorry about that. I never had morning sickness when I was pregnant with the twins. Maybe it's just the surprise of it all."

"Good surprise or bad?"

She paused. "I don't know how to answer that, doctor."

"No need to say a thing, my dear. I know what's going on with your husband right now. You think about all this and get back to me. If you and David are looking forward to having another child, then congratulations, and you'll need to set up future appointments. If this isn't something you want, contact my office, and we can chat about alternatives."

Stella nodded, then realized he couldn't see her, so she thanked him and ended the call, plopped back onto the pillows, and stared at the ceiling. "What should I do?"

She contemplated what this might mean for her… and David's… future together, if they would ever have a future together. Her cell phone rang. Kat.

"How are you, Stella? And David? I haven't wanted to bug you about it. I've kept up with the latest news, because I talk to Loreen every day. She told me about David's memory loss… about him thinking he's still being married to Patti and all that. What the hell happens now?"

"I have no idea, Kat. Dr. Hamilton says this is typical post-TBI behavior and to just roll with it. Of course, I'll continue visiting him. I'm going today, see how he reacts. Oh, my God, the last time I was there, Kat, he yelled at me to get out of the room." She began to cry, which turned into hiccups of sobs, nose running, tears clouding her eyes. "He called me a liar and a thief and a bitch. I don't even recognize him anymore, Kat. And all of it reminded me…"

She shook her head, grabbed a tissue from the side table, and swiped at her cheeks.

"Reminded you of what, Stella?" Kat whispered.

Stella remained silent. She couldn't say the words. "Nothing. Nothing. I'm just upset is all. The poor man has been in a terrible accident and is suffering from a traumatic brain injury. What is wrong with me? I should be way more understanding than I sound. It's just that it brought back—"

"Of course you're upset, Stell. And you've never been in a situation like this before. Cut yourself some slack, girl. Your feelings are hurt. Whether they should be or not doesn't matter. They are. David's always been a lovely and tender and caring guy. How he is right now must be such a shock. And I know what you were gonna say. The way David's acting reminds you of Robert. Shit, that must be awful to deal with. A man you… well, a man you *used to hate*."

"Not you, too, Kat. Please don't start."

"Not gonna start. I don't wish you anything but happiness in your life, Stella. And you're happy with David. I mean, you were. And you will be again. He'll get through this. The doctor told you this is typical of TBI patients, and there's no reason yet to think David won't be one of them. Hopefully, he'll recall everything about his life prior to the accident, so please don't give up on him, Stell."

Stella sighed. "I haven't given up hope, Kat. Just because Robert appeared on the scene does not mean I've reverted to old behavior. You never knew Robert. And the Robert who came back into our lives isn't the same man he was when we were married."

"You don't know that for sure, Stella. That's all I'm saying. People like him can be like chameleons. They change with the temperature around them. Act like the people around them want them to act. Then when they've got you convinced of the, quote unquote, new person they've become, then their true self appears. And sometimes by that time, it's already too late. He'll suck you in, then spit you out, just like he did after you were married. Before you were married you told me he was the nicest man on the planet, then boom… you marry him, and he morphs into a fucking dick. I don't wanna see that happen to you again."

"I'm not the same woman I was with him either, Kat. Remember that. I'm not going to be sucked in, as you call it, a second time. I'm not that stupid or naive. You can even ask the kids. Loreen and Gabe and Charlie and I had Robert over for dinner. They had a good time together. I'm letting them digest what went on between the three of them, so I haven't asked about the particulars. I don't want to be pushy or seem nosey. I'll let them come to me and give me an update, if there is one.

"But while I was in the kitchen fixing dinner I could hear them talking, and they even shared a few laughs. During dinner, it was really pleasant. Charlie adores him. So cut me a break, will you? People can change." Silence answered Stella's speech, and she blew out a puff of air. "Are you not speaking to me now?"

"Of course I'm speaking to you. I love you is all. I don't want to see you or the kids get hurt. Again."

"Neither do I. You know that without having to say it, all right?"

"Stella, I get it. I'll back off, because I know you know how I feel about Robert. But you're right. I haven't been around him like, ever. So I'm gonna save my opinion for later. Just take my words of caution as me worrying about my sister. I love you. I love your kids. And you're the one who told me all about Robert and how it was when you were married. It was frightening. You know that. But, yeah, people can change. Marcus keeps telling me that too. As angry as he was… and me too… about Robert arriving in Monarch Bay after his short stint in prison, Marcus has known some bad guys who, after they got out of jail, well, he said he couldn't believe they'd changed so drastically from when they went in. So, I get it, okay? Just be careful."

"I love you, Kat. And tell Marcus thank you for being so understanding. And that's all I'm asking of you as well. Just cut me a little slack here and hold onto your opinion until you meet Robert, see what he's like yourself. I promise to listen to you, no matter what side you're on. I know you're only showing how much you care, and I certainly am the last person who would blame you for everything you're thinking right now. Hell, I'm the one who told you how terrible life was with Robert, so I can't blame you for your feelings. I get it." She yawned. "Thank you for calling, Kat. I have to start my day. Get to the hospital. Try again."

"Good luck with that, Sis. Keep me up to date. One of these days, hopefully soon, Marcus and I can visit David too. When he's ready."

They said their goodbyes, and Stella showered, ate a light breakfast, and drove down Main Street, hoping to stop by Patti's Pastries to pick up a latte, say hello to Lo and Sunny before going to the hospital. She'd just pulled into the only spot available down the street when a man and woman walked past her car and entered a small restaurant that had recently opened, Break an Egg.

Stella did a double-take when she noticed the way the man gestured while talking. He looked like Robert. OMG, it was Robert! And the woman, who Stella didn't recognize, with long, blonde hair, perfect make-up, walking like a runway model in a flowing summer dress that whipped round her perfect body from the breeze, grasped Robert's forearm and smiled at him in such a way, it made Stella recall how very much in love she'd been after dating Robert for a short time back in the day. He'd been solicitous, generous, kind, helpful. His every action had endeared Stella to him like a magnet. She guessed some things never changed.

Wait until he springs the proposal on you, bitch. Stella shut her eyes and covered her mouth with her palm. What was she thinking? More importantly, why was she thinking these things? Was she jealous? She was married to a wonderful man. Robert was her past. David was her future. Though *which* David would be her future was the question.

If David remained the way he was today, Stella couldn't imagine them staying together. If he hated her that much, and his temper never calmed down so they could talk to one another, how could she stay with him? And, yes, David reminded her of Robert when Stella was married to him. She'd already admitted that to herself and Kat. But she also knew it was early days, way too soon to make any foolish decisions about her and David's future together.

Robert and his what… girlfriend?… entered the restaurant, and Stella waited until she knew she wouldn't be seen, opened the car door, and rushed down the street to the bakery. She spoke with Sunny for a few minutes while he made her a latte. Loreen was on a break and had gone for a short walk, so Stella left, hoping she wouldn't run into Robert and his date, also hoping David was a little kinder to her when she visited him.

And what about the baby growing inside her? She couldn't share what should have been great news for David. In his mind, they weren't even married, and he didn't know who she was. But giving the baby up, either for adoption or having an abortion? Neither represented a path Stella was prepared to walk. She and David both wanted this to happen. And now that she was pregnant, Stella couldn't imagine not going through with it. She'd love the baby, and she could raise it herself, if that's how it turned out.

Life as a single mom wasn't so terrible. That's how it had been with Loreen and Gabe. Robert had brought home a healthy paycheck and forced her not to work outside the home, so raising the two kids had been her responsibility and hers alone. She knew how to do that and do it well. And she'd have Loreen and Gabe to help out. They'd stepped up to the plate immediately after David's accident, and they'd do it again, if Stella suddenly became a single mommy to a newborn. The twins would take over the tasks necessary to keep the bakery open. She just knew they would.

She suddenly realized she'd driven on autopilot to the hospital. It had become part of her daily routine, though she hadn't spent much time with David since he'd awakened from the coma. Maybe today would be different.

When she entered his room, he was reading a book. He didn't look up when she said hello, and she took that as a disappointing omen to how the rest of the visit would transpire. Maybe she could take a different tack. Not talk at all. Pull up a chair and read one of the magazines on the table at the foot of his bed.

She reached for one with pictures of yummy pastries covering the front page and sat at David's bedside, crossed her legs, and thumbed through a few pages until she came to an article she found appealing.

David coughed, and she glanced up at him. "Do I have to ask you again what the hell you're doing here? I told you I don't appreciate you coming to my room. If Patti were to see you here, she'd be very angry. I don't need some groupie hanging around, making me look like I'm two-timing my wife."

Stella had no clue what she was supposed to say. She combed her memory, searching for Dr. Hamilton's suggestions. Don't make him angry, don't try to jar his memory, talk about something innocuous that wouldn't make him mad. She pointed to the article in the magazine. "This is all about how to bake the perfect croissant. Do you like chocolate croissants, because I sure do? I was thinking of bringing you one the next time I'm here. Sunny, the baker at Patti's Pastries, is known all over Monarch Bay as the premier chocolate croissant baker." She looked him in the eyes, holding her breath for his response.

"I think I like chocolate croissants. Patti always made them… to perfection, I might add. Have you ever tasted one of them?"

Stella nodded. "I know Patti. We're friends. And yes, she taught Sunny all he knows about making chocolate croissants."

He frowned. "You know my wife? I thought you said—"

Stella grinned. "Of course I know your wife, silly. She and I are close friends."

"But you told me that you're my wife."

Stella shook her head. What should she say? He was talking to her, which was a miracle in itself, for the first time since he'd awakened from the coma. She didn't want to ruin this opportunity, this possibility to make inroads with him, create a connection. "You must have misunderstood. Sometimes that happens after a traumatic brain injury. I'm sure Dr. Hamilton mentioned that."

David nodded slowly. It looked as if he was thinking, perhaps trying to put the pieces together to make sense of his new world. "Have you seen her lately? The doctor said she's out of town, so I haven't seen her, nor has she called. Do you know if something's wrong? If you're her good friend, she must know I'm waiting to hear from her."

"She told me last night she wasn't feeling too well. She went to the doctor right before your accident, and they sent her out of town for more tests. But the results aren't in yet, and that makes her extremely nervous. As soon as she finds out anything, I'm sure she'll call and return to Monarch Bay."

"What tests? What's wrong with her? How was she feeling before she went out of town? Where did she go?"

Stella reached out, touched David's forearm. "She had a mammogram and they saw something suspicious. She went to Los Angeles to have more tests done. I think a biopsy, but I'm not sure. She and I have only spoken for a few minutes since she's been gone. I'm sorry, David. I don't know more than that."

"Thank you for telling me. I've been asking the doctor every day, but he says he doesn't have that type of information and wouldn't be allowed to give it to me even if he did, due to the HIPPA laws or something like that."

Stella realized she'd just made herself the fount of information for everything Patti. She'd have to play her cards just right. Get him to trust her and see where things went from there. At least he was talking to her and not calling her names, yelling at her, asking her to leave the room.

But it was a dangerous game she was playing. Even though everything she told him was the truth, it was all from the past. Patti had those tests done in L.A., but she'd died from what the biopsy had revealed. The chemo hadn't worked. Radiation had turned out to be worthless. She'd been given a few months to live, and then it had been over, quite quickly, soon after Stella met David and Patti, when she had worked at their booth at the annual Monarch Bay Festival.

So she wasn't really lying. Just playing around with the "timing" of the truth. Hopefully before too long David's memory would return, and he'd realize all these things had happened in his past, and his future was now with Stella and not Patti. She could only hope.

At this positive juncture, Stella stood. "Well, I've got to go, David. It's been nice talking to you." She looked him in the eyes. He was staring at her, but he didn't look happy. He seemed confused. But that was better than being angry. She waved to him and walked out of the room, letting out a breath she didn't realize she'd been holding. Maybe she'd done a bad thing. But she looked at this as a road full of possibilities. She could work this, so that she came out as his friend. Better than him hating her as he had before today.

Exhaustion grabbed her like a thief in the night. Since David's accident, her world had been topsy-turvy. Robert entering the picture had turned her life upside down and sideways. And David's memory loss had jerked her around to the point, she didn't know which way was up. She suddenly felt as if she couldn't go another step without collapsing.

She pressed the elevator button for the cafeteria, where she ordered a latte with a double shot of espresso and took a seat at the window, where she could look outside and contemplate anything but what her life was at the moment: a real "shit show", as Kat would say.

"A shit-show, all right," Stella mumbled, then took a sip of hot coffee, tasting the fluffy foam, breathing in the strong scent of Columbian espresso, wondering in the back of her mind if she really was jealous of the woman accompanying Robert to the restaurant.

She closed her eyes and took another sip, warming her hands wrapped around the paper cup.

"Stella?"

She jerked her head up and opened her eyes. Robert.

"We have to stop meeting this way," he said with a grin.

Didn't she know it.

Chapter Twenty-One

Robert took a seat across from Stella. "How's David doing?"

Stella let out a deep breath. "I haven't told the doctor yet, but I did something I hope won't backfire in my face."

He frowned. "Tell me about it. If you feel comfortable doing so."

"Sure." She sipped her latte, then turned it round and round on the table. "You know how I told you he doesn't remember me, and he thinks he's still married to Patti? So we were talking about chocolate croissants, of all subjects, right? I told David Patti and I are close friends."

"Why would you do something like that?"

She tapped the table with her fingertip. "Here's what I'm thinking. David's stuck in the past. He has no memory of the present or me. If he never gets his memory back, he and I will no longer be a couple. In his mind, I'm no one. It'll be over between us.

"So I told him about Patti's breast cancer, as if it's happening right now. I'm hoping by sharing with him information about Patti, it will get to the point where I can explain the chemo and radiation aren't working and then tell him she passed away in the night or something like that.

"David hasn't even gotten out of bed yet. The physical therapist is doing passive PT on him while he's lying in bed, so his muscles won't atrophy. But my point is, he won't be able to go to a funeral for Patti anyway, and I can tell him she just wanted to be cremated, and I can even bring him her ashes. We have them at our house. Then I'll have integrated myself into his life, and I'm hoping he'll fall in love with me again, and we could get married and have our lives back." She raised her index finger. "And if his memory does return, then he'll know what I've told him is the truth, Patti died, and he's married to me now."

Robert shook his head. "So if his memory doesn't return, Stella, everyone in the entire town of Monarch Bay is going to go along with this charade once David's back on his feet while working with the townspeople at the bakery every day? No one's going to mention that Patti died years ago and that you and he have been together for five years?"

He reached out and covered Stella's hand with his. "This may not work, Stell. If his memory doesn't return, it'll backfire. And when David finds out you lied to him and it was all a ruse, he'll hate you for it. Then what'll you do? You'll be left with a second divorce and three kids. And will he want anything to do with Charlie after he finds out he's the child you and he planned to have? Who knows? But if not, Charlie will forever be traumatized by a dad who ignores his existence. Your plan may work, but only if David's memory returns and he realizes that yes, you're his wife, and Patti passed away."

Stella chewed at her bottom lip, continuing to twist her coffee cup round and round, staring at the foam as if it might pop out an answer to this dilemma. Suddenly she felt a tear on her cheek.

Robert reached out and wiped it off gently with his finger. "I'm sorry I made you cry. That wasn't my intention. But I don't want to see you get any more hurt than you already are. It's bad enough David's memory is stuck in the past, but you have to believe, or at least hope, one day he'll remember you, and all the feelings and love he felt for you will return. I'm telling you, your plan has the opportunity to ruin any future life you and David might theoretically have if his memory doesn't return. But if you were to just let things flow naturally and give him time for his memory to resurface, you and he might have a chance."

Stella nodded, then looked Robert in the eyes. "Thank you for your advice. I agree with you." She let out a huge sigh. "Oh, my God, Robert. What am I going to do now? I've really messed up this time."

"You could ask the doctor his advice. What comes to my mind is…" He tapped his chin with his finger. "If David mentions Patti again, you could say, in a kind way, you don't know what he's talking about. Have the doctor explain that sometimes a patient's memory tricks them into believing things that didn't happen, but that when his memory does return, he'll know the truth. David will have to chalk it up to his brain processing a lot of misinformation that, in reality, isn't true. It's a function of a brain that's suffering from a TBI."

He shrugged. "Sounds plausible to me, Stell. I've read quite a bit about TBIs since this happened, believe it or not. What I've told you is something I read. Take it or leave it. I just thought it might help you, since you've gotten yourself into a corner that's going to be a little tricky to get out of."

Stella turned her hand palm-side up and interlaced her fingers with Robert's. "Thank you for telling me this. I made a mistake. I didn't have time to think about all the ramifications of my plan. I was caught off-guard and just said those things to David totally on the fly, no preparation whatsoever. And now look where it's gotten me. I'll have to speak with Dr. Hamilton and tell him what I did and how he would like me to fix it."

Robert lightly squeezed Stella's hand. "I'm sure he'll understand. You were caught off-guard, as you said, and you just blurted out whatever came to mind first, without thinking it through. Believe me, patients with TBIs really do live in their own world until their memories resurface, if that happens. Hopefully, David's memories will return, and you and he will be able to rekindle your relationship and live your well-deserved happily ever after."

Stella stared into Robert's eyes. "You've really changed, Robert. If you'd been like this during our marriage, we'd…"

"Still be married," he finished for her. "I think about that every single day. I have so many regrets. I'm working with my therapist on not hating myself over what I did and how I acted when we were married, how I treated you and the kids." His eyes glazed over. "I was a horrible husband and a terrible father."

Stella's eyes teared up again. "Yes, you were. But, Robert, you now have the opportunity to live a much happier life, one in which you'll feel good about yourself and people will enjoy being around you. Your happily ever after is in the works as we speak." She smiled. "I saw you with a gorgeous blonde on your arm the other day. Perhaps she'll be the next Mrs. Walker."

Robert smirked. "We just met, Stell. You probably saw us when we were getting breakfast the other day?" Stella nodded. "That was not a date. We met in the real estate office where she works and talked for a bit. She's my realtor. Then we saw each other on the street the next day and continued our discussion over coffee."

Stella grabbed a napkin and dabbed under her eyes, then took a sip of coffee. "Why would you need a realtor, Robert?"

He smiled. "That's something I wanted to talk to you about. Not only do I love Monarch Bay itself—it's a quaint little town, and the people are friendly, and the beach is gorgeous. I'd like to set up my practice here. I have my license as a family therapist, and, if I bought a house, I could have a tax write-off, since I could set up my practice at home. I don't want to live in an Airbnb forever. But more importantly, I want to get to know my kids, Stella. And I need to settle down somewhere. So why not here, so I'll be near them, you know?"

"I understand. Have you spoken with the kids about your plan? And, not to be nosey, but where on earth are you getting the money for the down payment on a house in Monarch Bay?"

"You're not being nosey at all. Do you remember me ever telling you about my grandfather? He was really my only living relative during the time we were married. It's not like he and I had a close relationship, but we kept in touch through the occasional letter here and there. He died while I was in prison, and I was the only person named in his will. He had real estate and land around the New York area. He left me everything—two houses, an apartment building, land." He laughed. "I'm fairly wealthy, if you can believe it."

Stella chuckled. "Who woulda thunk, right? Well, congratulations for that happening to you. Not that your grandfather passed away, of course. So what about talking with the kids about your plans to make Monarch Bay your home?"

"Oh, right. Yes. Both of them have been texting me. We go back and forth. I've stopped by the bakery almost every day and have a short chat with each of them. I don't expect them to love me as their father overnight. That's way too much to hope for. But I do want to show them I'm not the same father they grew up knowing."

"I'm happy about all of this, Robert. Neither of them has told me a thing. Then again, I haven't been all that available for them to talk to me either. All three of us kind of go our separate ways. They go to work at the bakery, and I fly off to the hospital. Oh, and I talked to Kat last night. She can pick up Charlie from school every day and bring him over to her house, so Peter and Charlie can play together, and I can still spend my day with David. You won't have to put Charlie on your to-do list any longer, but I really want to thank you for helping me out when he sprained his ankle. Your assistance was invaluable, Robert. I mean it."

His dark eyebrows drew together. "Wow. Wasn't expecting this. Though, of course, I knew your sister took care of Charlie after school. But I've grown fond of your son, Stell. He's a great kid. I'd like to continue a relationship with him. After all, he is Loreen and Gabe's brother… and my ex-wife's son. I could still pick him up after school. At least sometimes?"

Stella had not expected this reaction, although it made sense. Charlie was a great kid, fun to be around, funny, smart, well-behaved. She glanced out the window at the blue sky, cirrus clouds, bright green trees in the hospital courtyard. She faced him. "Why don't I talk to Charlie? He'll be six soon, and he's old enough to tell me how he feels about your idea. I've never asked him, though I can see through your interactions, he likes you. But he may feel different since he loves his cousin Peter and is accustomed to hanging out with him at Kat's place after school."

He nodded. "Of course. No problem. Whatever you and he decide. I just wanted to say what was on my mind and in my heart. If I hadn't said something to you, you'd never have known."

"You're right. And I'm happy you and he get along so well. Oh, and I'm beyond elated that you and the two kids are communicating with each other so often. I want them to have a father in their lives. I mean, this type of father, the father you've become, now that you're out of prison and had been seeing a therapist, and obviously you're still in therapy, working on yourself. I think that's one of the most honorable things a person can do—take the time and effort to improve their mental and emotional states through therapy. Noticing that something's wrong is a huge step. And trying to correct it? Well, that's something so many, many individuals just don't take the time to do. They either think therapy is a bunch of hocus-pocus or they feel they aren't so bad and the people around them can just accept them as they are, even though no one is happy, not the person with the problems nor the other people in their lives. Congratulations for making the effort, Robert. I'm proud of you. Really, I am."

Robert smiled and didn't break their gaze for what seemed like at least a minute. Stella grew a bit uncomfortable and cast her eyes down into her coffee cup.

He pushed back his chair and stood. "Can I ask you something?" She nodded. "Would you like to get dinner sometime this week? Just to get out, forget about your troubles, have a glass of wine or something? Just talk about the weather and politics or whatever with me. It's been so long since I've treated myself to dinner in a real restaurant. And you're having a tough time of it these days. We can treat ourselves to a night that's problem-free. What do you say?"

Stella got up from her chair. "I think I'd like that, Robert. It's not like we don't have a connection. We have two children together, and you've been taking care of my son. The dinner will be my treat. I'd like to show my appreciation for you coming to my aid with Charlie."

"No need, Stell. I'd do it all again in a heartbeat. Let's not worry about who pays the bill. Unless I'm totally out in left field, I'm probably wealthier than you are right now. I actually have money to throw around. Let me do that. It'll be fun for me."

"Okay then. I'm free every night. Now that I don't have a husband to come home to."

Robert caught her eye. "That could change in a second. Don't plan on being single forever. David will come around, if you have anything to do with it, right?" He smiled.

Chapter Twenty-Two

Stella woke up the next morning feeling nauseous again. She wasn't pressuring herself to make a decision about the baby growing inside her, but if she was honest, she'd already decided to keep the child. It was absolutely ludicrous to even entertain the thought of an abortion or adoption. Women's rights meant a lot to her, and it was her right to keep her baby. Period.

As far as being a single mother, she'd "been there, done that". She had no help raising Loreen and Gabe, and though she'd have to figure out some sort of babysitting schedule so she could be at the bakery and still be an at-home mom, she refused to stress herself out about it right now. For all she knew, David would be awake and totally recovered, and they'd share the responsibility for their baby, just as they'd done after Stella gave birth to Charlie.

Stella wasn't looking forward to talking to Dr. Hamilton about what she'd told David, nor was she excited about visiting David, since she couldn't predict what kind of mood he'd be in. She had to talk to Kat and the kids and tell them she was pregnant. Maybe over dinner this evening? Or maybe she should do it separately.

She showered and ate some toast and a soft-boiled egg, which did away with the morning sickness quite quickly. Loreen had left her a note saying she was going to the bakery earlier than usual to get some accounting issues resolved. Stella dropped off Charlie at school a little early, then headed over to Kat's place to make her announcement.

Stella hadn't spent as much time at the hospital with David because of his outbursts and kicking her out of his room, but maybe that would change, if his memory returned or if he was amenable to having her hang out with him, now that he knew she was Patti's friend. She could only hope he wouldn't ask her any more questions about Patti's breast cancer, though that wasn't likely. Oh, she wished she had never opened up that

Pandora's box. But it had allowed her to talk to David for the first time without him becoming angry. She could only hope that was a permanent change of behavior.

When she arrived at her sister's place, Kat opened the door, looking fantastic, as always, with her bleached-white, cropped hair and perfect make-up and wild clothes. Kat had a beauty that surpassed the typical "attractive woman" image. She was striking in her carriage and forthrightness of speech. She said what she meant and meant what she said, often sprinkled liberally with swear words and laughter as a side dish.

"I missed you, girl," Kat shouted, bringing Stella in for a hug, then pulling her inside and slamming the door. "Peter's in his room doing math homework. Let's sit down and have a cuppa."

Stella laughed out loud. "You're a veritable pick-me-up, aren't you?"

"You betcha." She gestured outside. "Let's sit on the deck with Remy. He's getting old and enjoys lying in the sun. Probably good for his aging bones. He has hip dysplasia. Typical of labs in general, poor guy."

Stella walked out onto the deck and knelt down next to Remy. He'd saved her when Robert shot David and turned the gun on Stella five years ago. Remy had attacked Robert and kept Stella from being shot too. She owed this dog her life. Remy turned his head and looked at her, gave her hand a nice long licking, then fell back asleep.

Was this what she had to look forward to with Uje? She was only a couple of years old, so Stella didn't want to even think about it. She had enough on her plate without adding to her "anticipatory anxiety," which was something she'd been fighting for years. The future was unknown, and she had to tell herself that, like a daily mantra, in order to ward off the depression that often lurked right at the edge of her mind, especially since Robert had shot David. She still had PTSD from that night. It was a daily workout, trying to deal with the constant anxiety that had become her companion.

"Here ya go, Sis. Decaf latte' tall, lotsa foam." She set a large ceramic cup on the picnic table.

Stella took a seat across from her sister, picked up the cup, and breathed in one of her favorite scents. "I'd love to buy one of those machines you have for making these, except I'd probably end up drinking one or two in the morning then a couple at the bakery, then one after dinner at night. No one needs that much coffee.”

Kat took a sip from her mug. “That’s why they invented decaf, silly.”

“But the calories in all that half-and-half. I mean, that’s what I love about those drinks. They’re so creamy and delicious. And I tend to drink them instead of eating breakfast… and sometimes substitute them for lunch too. Easier and quicker, so I get more work done.”

“You don’t need to lose any weight, Stella. You look a little peeked right now. But with all the stress you’re under, I guess I shouldn’t be surprised.”

Stella stirred her spoon round and round in her latte’. “It’s more than that. Which is why I came over this morning. I have news.”

Kat sat up straight, looked Stella in the eyes. “About David? Has he got his memory back? Can Marcus and I visit him? What about Peter and Charlie? Are they ever going to be allowed inside the hospital? Even for just a few minutes? It would do David good to see his son and—”

Stella put her hand up like a stop sign. “Hold up. Hold up.”

Kat tapped her lips with her fingertips. “Sorry. I get all hyped up sometimes, and I think I drank too much coffee this morning too.”

Stella smiled. “Not to worry. I’ll answer all your questions, but this is news that has to do with… well, both David and me, of course, but then again, who knows—”

Kat placed her cup on the table. “Will you spit it out? What the hell is this news you’re taking so long to tell me. Open your mouth, girl, will ya? The anticipation is killing me. Gawd!”

“I’m pregnant. Due in eight months.”

Kat slammed her hand down on the picnic table. “No fucking way! Are you serious?”

Stella nodded. “We’ve been trying for months. I was waiting to figure out what I wanted to do before making the announcement, and you’re the first to know. And Marcus, of course.”

“He’s on another long haul. Won’t be back for weeks. But wow! Really? This is… you don’t seem too excited, Stella? What’s up with that?”

“Kat, come on! David doesn’t even know who I am. He doesn’t even know who Charlie is, for God’s sake. Even though I told him that story, which…”

"Which what? You look like the cat that swallowed a mouse, or whatever the expression is. What the hell are you keeping from me? I'm your sister. Out with it, girlfriend. Shit."

"Okay, okay. I talked to Robert—"

"What the fuck? You're still talking to him? About what? Why? I mean, I know he was taking care of Charlie when he sprained his ankle, but Marcus is gone and I'm back in the game now. No more excuses for your son to hang around that asshole any longer."

Stella stirred and stirred the foam in her latte until there was none left. "I can truly say now, he's a changed man."

"Fuckin' A. Are you still stuck on that jag? Jesus, Mary, and Joseph."

Stella glanced up at her sister. "Will you cut it, Kat? I'm a big girl. I know what I'm doing."

"Apparently not. It's bad enough you let him be around Charlie. Now you should cut him out of your life entirely, since you don't need him anymore. What are you hanging around him for anyway, Stella? You don't need him in your life."

"It's like I said, Kat. You don't know what he's like now. He's consistently kind and understanding, and Charlie loves him."

Kat literally sneered at Stella. "Please... do not tell me you're in love with Robert, Stella. That you're gonna divorce David cause he doesn't know who you are, and you'll leave him all alone in the hospital, fighting to get his memory back, all for that piece of shit who beat you and—"

"Stop it!" Stella shouted then stood abruptly, knocking over her latte. Coffee splattered all over her skirt and blouse, dripped off the edge of the picnic table. Remy rushed over as fast as his tired legs could carry him and began licking up the sugary coffee on the deck. "Shit, shit, shit! I'm sorry. I'll get some paper towels." She rushed into the kitchen, Kat fast on her heels.

"Please, don't, Stell," Kat whispered behind her.

Stella turned to face her sister. "I know you're mad, but stop treating me like I'm an idiot. I know what I'm doing. People change, Kat. Can't you get that into your head? We've already been over this a million times. Are you that forgetful? I don't think so."

Kat grasped Stella's hands and held them tightly. "I'm sorry. You know how I am. I have a short fuse sometimes. It's not my place to judge.

Marcus lectured me about this already, and I get it, okay? But it's been hard for me to accept the fact, you're allowing this man back in your life after everything that happened. I just can't wrap my head around it."

Stella stared into her sister's eyes. "Once an abuser, always an abuser?"

Kat nodded. "Pretty much. Yes."

"What about change? What about forgiveness? What about everything Fiona and Nason taught us growing up after mom and dad died?"

Kat continued to nod her head, up and down, up and down. "I know. I know. I'm sorry. You were always the kinder person. More understanding and forgiving and—" she waved her hand back and forth, "—willing to see the good in everybody. I'm not like that. What's that expression? Fool me once, shame on you. Fool me twice, shame on me? I'm more fool me once, you're dead meat, man. I'm not gonna let it happen again, bro."

Stella reached out, and Kat encircled her in a hug. They stood together, rocking back and forth for several minutes, both crying.

"I love that you care about me and my family, Kat. You're the perfect sister. Always have my back. Always ready to come to my rescue whenever I need it." Stella pulled away. "You're the best. But this time, I want you to trust me. Robert doesn't mean any harm to me or my family. In fact, I saw him with a woman the other day. He says she's just his realtor, but I think he may be dating her. She looked happy, holding onto his arm and all that. He's going to buy a house here in Monarch Bay, so he can get to know the kids better. And he loves Charlie. And vice versa. He's Loreen and Gabe's father, Kat. I can't deny them the opportunity to get to know him as he is now. And they're adult enough to make up their own minds. I'm sure Loreen must have told you she and Gabe and Charlie and I had dinner together. It went far beyond my expectations. It was actually fun.

"Oh, and the other day, I accidentally walked into the house and saw Robert playing with Charlie. It was like seeing a man I've never met before. He was dressed up as a horse, and Charlie was playing a jouster. It was hysterical. And he and I are going out to dinner soon. If he's going to be back in our lives, he and I have to establish a relationship of sorts. We'll be seeing each other quite often, I would imagine."

"Okay. I get it, Stell. I'll keep an open mind. I promise. Marcus will be proud of me. He says I can be as stubborn as a fucking bull in heat."

Stella burst out laughing. "Nice analogy, Kat. Marcus is hysterical."

"He keeps me laughing. I'll give ya that."

Stella held up her index finger. "One more thing." Kat lifted her eyebrows. "Robert volunteered to pick up Charlie from school several days a week, and I'm going to say yes. Charlie loves spending time with Robert and vice versa. I have to ask Charlie first what he wants to do, but I'm pretty sure of his answer. Maybe you'll let Peter come over more often, and that'll give you a break, too, get you out of the house for awhile and do something different. Have some fun for a change. Especially when Marcus comes home after his long hauls. Then you and he can take the afternoons to go on a ride on his Harley or something, you know? Just think about it."

Kat tilted her head. "I never would have expected this from you, Stell. You're really giving this guy a second chance."

"Not a second chance with me, personally. But he's family, Kat. And to me family is everything. It's what gets me up in the morning and keeps me feeling fulfilled in my life. That's why this hurts so much that you and I are so at odds about his Robert thing. I don't want to fight with you or even disagree with you, Kat. But you've gotta let me live my life the way I see fit, based on my knowledge about Robert and what he's like now. Trust me. I know you think I trust too much, but I think you don't trust anyone ever. Can't you just accept, we're two different people? I'm not right, and you're not wrong. I'm just being me, and you're being you. And that's totally cool. I accept our differences. Can't you?"

Kat sighed and plopped down at the kitchen table. "Marcus says the same thing. That I'm too rigid in my principles. That I have to acknowledge and respect that people feel different about… well, almost everything. It's what makes the world go round." She paused, smiled. "And round and round and round and—"

Stella burst out laughing. "Okay. I get it. And I'm with Marcus. Let's have a truce about this Robert thing."

"I'll talk to Marcus about allowing Peter to go over your house and play with Charlie while Robert's kid-sitting."

"Thank you for that. And if he's not comfortable with that, I'm totally cool with it. I respect, he's going to have an opinion, and so be it." She took a seat next to Kat. "Are we cool? Please say we're okay."

Kat leaned over and hugged her sister. "We're cool. I love you."

"And I love you." Stella stood. "Now I've got to get to the hospital, explain to Dr. Hamilton my extraordinary screw-up telling David Patti's alive and has cancer."

Kat's mouth dropped open. "You did what?"

She knocked on her skull with her knuckles. "Crap. I didn't have a chance to tell you."

"Tell me what, exactly?"

Stella explained her interaction with David, as Kat's eyes grew wider and wider while Stella told the story. "I don't know what I was thinking, Kat. Like I could convince him of all of this… as if he and I would be living in a bubble, and everyone in Monarch Bay would suddenly think Patti had died recently. Oh, and also that everyone in Monarch Bay would forget David and I have been married for the last five years and have a son. God, I'm an idiot, Kat."

Kat stood and hugged her sister. "You were desperate. I get it. And caught in the middle of a really unusual situation, wanting your husband to talk to you and not kick you out of his room every time you come to visit. I get that." She pushed Stella toward the front door. "Now, go to the hospital and talk to the doctor. I'm sure he can tell you what to do going forward. I'd say give David our love, but he doesn't know who we are… yet. But good luck with the doctor and all that."

She gave Stella another hug. "And with that new little kid you're cookin' up there."

Stella and Kat hugged again at the front door, and Stella drove off, waving to her sister through the side window. Both Robert and Kat had been so understanding after hearing Stella's impossible tale of deception with David.

She wasn't so sure what Dr. Hamilton's reaction would be.

Chapter Twenty-Three

Dr. Hamilton was exiting David's room as Stella reached the nurses' station.

"Have a few minutes?" he said.

Stella nodded, followed him into the conference room, and took a seat.

Dr. Hamilton shut the door and sat across from her, cleared his throat. "I heard from David he wants to be kept apprised of his wife's breast cancer and chemo and radiation. He's afraid she may die. He says you told him you were Patti's friend." He leaned back in his chair. "What's going on, Stella?"

"I was thinking how he may not ever get his memory back. So I was trying to figure out a way to ingratiate myself into his life. I was hoping he and I could be friends and that our relationship would blossom after Patti supposedly—" She made air quotes. "—died. That he'd fall in love with me after she passed away, as he did in the past."

Stella leaned her elbows on the table and covered her face with her hands, took a breath then dropped her hands onto the table. "And what I told him was all true. It's just that it already happened five years ago. But what I forgot about was the fact that once David got out into the community of Monarch Bay, everyone would know Patti died years ago and that David and I are married and have a five-year-old son. So David would know I lied to him and…" She looked him in the eyes "… I've made a total mess of things. I'm so sorry, Dr. Hamilton. I'm an idiot. God help me, I don't know what I was thinking. My ex-husband used to tell me if I had a brain, I'd play with it. Maybe he was right."

Dr. Hamilton tapped his pen several times on the table. "It's okay, Stella. I understand your motives. You were desperate and you love and miss your husband." He sat up straight. "Don't be so hard on yourself. You're not stupid, as your ex-husband may have told you. That's absurd. But you are in an unenviable situation."

He leaned his elbows on the table and leveled his gaze at her. "I think I told you, TBI patients often recall memories that aren't even true. We'll just chalk this one up to that, okay? I already explained to David about this part of his condition… that sometimes his memories aren't really memories at all. I convinced him you never told him that. That it's really all in his mind, his imagination, if you will. I explained that what he's saying you told him simply never happened. He just thinks it did."

Stella blew out a loud breath, so relieved, she wanted to hug Dr. Hamilton. "Thank you, doctor. Thank you so much. I appreciate your help. And I'm sorry. So sorry I messed up."

"You're dealing with a lot. The nursing staff and I recognize that. You're not the first person in this hospital with a relative or friend who's suffering from a TBI. David's angry, Stella. He was okay when I left him but Nurse Ohara said he began ranting and raving when she went into his room to take him down to physical therapy. They had to sedate him, and he's sleeping comfortably now."

Stella stared at the tabletop for several seconds then looked up at the doctor. "He's just so… he's not the man I married, Dr. Hamilton. I mean, he's completely unrecognizable. A different person. I can't even express how difficult it is to be around someone I don't even know. He's a total stranger to me, just as I am to him, I guess."

She covered her lips with her fingertips, holding in a sob. "I feel horrible saying these things, but David was always the most kind and gentle man, Dr. Hamilton. And to see him now hurts so much and at the same time he makes me so angry because he's so mean and just… cruel. The way he talks to me? Sometimes I just want to run away and hide. Other times I'd like to slap him across the face, he's so disrespectful."

Dr. Hamilton nodded. "I understand. And it is horrible to watch a loved one acting so out of character. But I can't stress how important it is to remember that personality changes after a head injury are some of the hardest TBI symptoms to deal with, for both the patient and their loved ones. A brain injury can make patients suddenly angry and aggressive, or even cause them to feel nothing at all. And the most common post-TBI personality disorders are borderline personality disorders, avoidance of the reality of their situation, acting paranoid, obsessive-compulsive behavior and narcissistic behavior as well.

"All these cases have one thing in common: damage to areas of the prefrontal cortex, in particular the orbitofrontal cortex. Although they may be extreme examples, the idea that damage to these parts of the brain results in severe personality changes is now well-established. And aggression is one of the most common consequences of traumatic brain injury."

Stella grimaced. "It's all so depressing. I love him. I mean, I used to love him. But the David he is now? I don't know him and as terrible as it is to admit this, I don't love the David he is now." She stood, her legs wobbling. "So should I see him today?"

"I wouldn't advise it. Let's take it a day at a time. You never know what tomorrow will bring."

Stella nodded. "I understand. I'll try again tomorrow."

"You might want to check with Nurse Ohara before you go into his room tomorrow. I think that's best."

"I agree. And I promise to do that," she said, then walked unsteadily out of the room and took the elevator to the first floor. She'd go home and have some time to herself, think about when she should announce her pregnancy to Gabe and Loreen, maybe sit in the backyard for a bit.

Just as she passed Patti's Pastries, she saw Gabe and Loreen talking outside the bakery. She pulled up in front and walked toward them.

"Hey, Mom!" Gabe and Loreen said together.

They were twins, after all, and this type of behavior happened often, even now, when they were much older.

"Do you two have a moment?"

"Sure," Lo said, glancing at her brother. "My office?" She turned, and Gabe and Stella followed Loreen. "Sunny's watching the front, so don't worry. We have some time before the next rush."

They took seats in Loreen's office and shut the door.

"Everything the same with David?" Gabe said.

"Dr. Hamilton thinks I should find out how David's feeling every day, before I visit him. He doesn't want him to be constantly upset after I leave because that could possibly postpone his recovery and cause a delay in him regaining his memory too. We don't want to risk that happening."

"Dad said he asked you if he could sometimes pick up Charlie from school and take care of him," Loreen said.

"Robert did ask me that, and I've thought about it, and I think it's a good idea. Charlie wants to spend time with Robert too. I want our family back. I mean, I want you two to have a father and a mother. And your father is Robert. And Charlie loves Robert. I haven't asked you two how you feel. I've been so busy, and you both are keeping us afloat here, and I want to thank you for that. It means everything to me. And it would mean everything to David, too, if he remembered. Or I should say, when he remembers. He'll be grateful."

"No problem," they said in unison, then both smiled at her.

"And to answer your question," Loreen said, looking at Gabe then back at her mother, "Gabe and I are happy about how much Dad's changed. We're still a bit guarded, naturally, but it seems like he's turned his life around. That's awesome."

"He wants to buy a house here in Monarch Bay and open up his own practice," Stella said.

"He didn't tell either of us," Gabe countered, glancing at Loreen. "He's going to buy a house here? Does he expect us to live with him or something?"

Stella shook her head. "Not that he told me. He just wants to establish a relationship with you two. Something he never had before, though he knows that's all on him. He was the bad guy. He just wants a chance to prove to you both, he loves you, and the past is the past, and that's not who he is any longer."

They both nodded.

Loreen stood. "So that's it?"

Gabe lifted his butt off the chair, saw his mom's face, and sat back down. "Something tells me that's not exactly why you stopped by, Mom."

"No, it's not." Stella paused. "There's something important I have to tell you."

They both raised their eyebrows.

"I'm going to have a baby."

Their mouths dropped open at the same time.

"No way!" Gabe said.

"It's David's?" Loreen asked.

Stella made a face. "For God's sake, Loreen, who else's baby would it be?"

Loreen shook her head like a dog after having a bath. "Of course. I don't know why I even said that. I'm sorry. David must be—"

"David doesn't know yet. And I have absolutely no idea when the doctor will allow me to tell him. David's not ready. He hasn't even talked to either of you or Charlie or Kat or Marcus or Peter. He barely can stand being in the same room with *me*."

"That's right," Gabe said.

"Well, congratulations anyway, Mom," Loreen said.

Stella smiled. "Thank you. I'm happy. David and I wanted another child." She shrugged. "Our wish came true."

"Does Dad know?" Gabe said.

"No. I haven't told him yet either. Naturally, I wanted to tell you two before I say anything to Robert. Robert and I are still getting to know each other."

"Do you see yourself with Robert in the future?" Loreen said in a soft voice.

Stella looked at her daughter as if she'd grown a second head. "Why are you asking me that, Lo?"

Loreen shrugged. "I don't know, Mom. What if David never recalls the fact you're his wife? I'm not trying to be an asshole. I don't know what I would do in your place anyways."

"Me neither," Gabe added. "I like David a lot. But what're you gonna do, if what Lo just said happens, and you're always a stranger to him?"

"I guess I'll cross that bridge if I have to, guys," Stella said as she stood. "Right now, I'm going to go home and take a nap. I'm exhausted."

"We have this place covered, Mom," Loreen added. "Don't worry 'bout a thang."

Stella hugged them both. "You're both amazing."

"We expect a raise, ya know," Gabe said with a laugh.

"As soon as my accountant says it's in the budget," Stella answered.

Loreen smiled. "Get outta here, little brother."

"I'm not your little brother… little sister."

"Ask Mom, Gabriel. I think I was born first. Ha ha."

They all laughed… together… and Stella's heart lurched. If only life could be as sweet as this moment.

Cherish the good times, Stella reminded herself. And gird your loins for battle, as it says somewhere in the Bible… or was that from the movie *Gladiator*? Didn't matter. Stella had to ready herself, in case the way she wanted their future to go didn't turn out as she expected.

Chapter Twenty-Four

Stella woke the next morning, nauseous once again, wondering why she never felt this way when she was pregnant with the twins. She thought it would have been harder on her body to carry two babies, not just one. Then again, she was older now. Gabe and Loreen were twenty-four. Plus, she'd been working her tail off at Patti's Pastries for almost six years, often ending each day in a state of exhaustion.

But she wasn't working now. Loreen and Gabe said they were handling the bakery, and everything was humming right along. She had to start taking better care of herself, since the stress she was under was greater than she'd ever experienced… second only to her life with Robert back in Oregon, of course.

But what was happening now ran a close second. Her husband didn't know he was her husband and maybe never would remember. She was almost forty-three years old, and, after trying to have another child for several years, knowing the likelihood was slim, here she was— expecting another baby at her age, without a husband to help her through it. Stella had thrown out her birth control pills, and she and David had told themselves they'd see what happened. If nothing happened, they'd be okay with it. They already had Charlie and, though the twins were Stella's children, David loved them as if they were his own. Now the newest addition to their family would have one parenting parent, Stella. And a parent who wouldn't understand who this baby was in relation to him! Holy crap! What a bizarre situation.

Maybe today she'd walk to the hospital. It wasn't the same as being on her feet all day at the bakery. Yes, working there was exercise, but it was more standing and moving around than anything "cardio". And it certainly wasn't relaxing. She loved the customer interaction, though. It was fun having all their "regulars" come in each day, sharing a laugh or a short story.

She didn't picture herself staying home every day, just because she was pregnant, either. Loreen explained the bakery was running in the black. Perhaps Stella could come in for a few hours a day, so the twins could take a break, instead of Lo and Gabe practically living at the bakery every day.

But she'd worry about all that later. Her focus had to be on her husband's recovery. If he recovered. Because if he made a total recovery, he'd want to go back to the bakery. He loved it there. It was his second home—a dream he and his wife, Patti, had fulfilled together, one that Stella and David continued after Patti's death. But to be honest, Stella was tired. Tired of the same thing every day, and she was ready for a change. And this baby could "be" that change.

She'd have to check with Loreen to see if she could swing it without having her there all day. It was hard to plan a future when the future was so up in the air, especially if David never returned to Patti's Pastries. She couldn't expect the twins to continue working there indefinitely either. Maybe Loreen would stay, since she'd gotten her degree in accounting. But Gabe's plans never included working in a bakery. They could hire someone to take over his duties, though.

She had to stop. It was all too much to think about and planning really wasn't possible. She'd take one day at a time, as Dr. Hamilton had suggested, and learn to live in the here and now… for now. She dropped Charlie off at school and headed to the hospital to see David. When she arrived at the ICU, she realized her stomach was in knots. She didn't know what state David would be in. Would he even welcome her arrival?

She waved to the nurses standing behind the counter, saw Nurse Ohara and stopped to talk to her for a second. She told Stella they hadn't needed to give him any tranquilizers, and he appeared calm. Stella thanked her, took a deep breath, and walked into his room.

She smiled when she saw him. His hair looked freshly washed, and even though no one had given him a shave, the dark stubble on the sides of his face and over his upper lip and chin gave him that sexy look she'd always been fond of. David was a handsome man, even more good looking when he smiled. A smile that always gave her goosebumps.

"Good morning, honey," she said, not realizing until after she'd said the words, naturally they were inappropriate and he wouldn't understand. But she'd gotten caught up in the past for a few seconds and said what came to mind.

The look on his face spoke volumes, and she took in a quick breath, not knowing how to get herself out of this predicament.

"I don't think my wife would appreciate you calling me 'honey'. What are you doing here? It's Bella, right? Well, I'd enjoy a day without you coming in and telling me stories that aren't true. You've been lying to me about being friends with my wife. In fact, I think you've been stalking me for years. At least that's the feeling I get from what you told me.

"Patti's not sick. I'm going to get her number today and call her. I don't think she knows I've been in an accident. You would have told her, if you really were friends. She'd never ignore me, so you must have told her she didn't need to return, and that I was fine. Stop messing with my life!"

Stella sucked in her lips, holding in any comments that instantly came to mind. She'd have to tread carefully. But what could she say? She'd never be able to see him again, if he continued to think she meant nothing to him, that she was not his wife, that he didn't have a child who needed him desperately, a family that missed him, and a child on the way. The look on his face spoke volumes. His hatred and irritation was killing her.

Allowing him to believe Patti was alive just wasn't right. She truly believed that. If he thought Patti would return the moment he phoned her, what would happen when she never answered his calls and never phoned him back? Someone… maybe Stella… had to take responsibility and explain Patti was never coming back. For how much longer could they allow him to believe the unbelievable? At some point, probably very soon, he'd know something was up, and there were no more excuses anyone could fabricate to remedy the situation.

Stella was the only person who cared enough about David to tell him what he needed to know. It was cruel to lead him on like this, allowing him to believe such a huge lie, that his dead wife would answer his call eventually and come rushing to his bedside. Maybe… and she'd read this somewhere on the internet, written by a neurosurgeon… jarring his mind with the truth could possibly jar his memory as well. And as painful as that might be and as angry as that would make him, he'd then have no choice but to face reality. They were allowing him to believe a dream that was impossible to come true. They couldn't continue the illusion - that his wife, Patti, was alive. That charade was coming quickly to its inevitable end.

What was the worst that could happen? He was angry at Stella for lying about being Patti's friend, and he didn't want her to visit him. But that wouldn't help him face the truth, would it? He would continue to wait for Patti, and eventually he'd be angry at Patti when she never showed up. What difference did it make who he was angry at? He was angry with Stella anyway and abusive in the way he responded to her.

Maybe it was the fact she was pregnant, combined with raging hormones. Maybe it was the fact he reminded her of the "old" Robert the way he yelled at her and made her feel like crap. Something exploded inside her chest and stomach, her entire body, and words spewed out like vomit, which was actually what she felt like doing, since she'd eaten nothing this morning, and her stomach gurgled and churned.

"She's not coming home, David!" Stella shouted. "She died over five years ago," she screamed, then placed both hands over her chest. "I'm your wife, David. I am. I am. Not her. She's gone. And, yes, she and I were friends. She was a wonderful person. Everyone loved her. She was sweet and caring and beautiful and kind."

His eyes looked as if they'd bulge out of the sockets, and Stella inched closer to him and looked him in the eyes. "I, Stella Crockett, I'm your wife, David. We've been married for five years, and we have a son together. His name is Charlie, and he adores you. Both of us adore you. So stop treating me like I mean nothing to you, because whether you remember me or not, I'm here to tell you, you're madly in love with me." She backed away from his bedside, tears flowing down her cheeks, throat sore from yelling.

A hand grasped her by the elbow and pulled her out of the room. Stella turned and faced Nurse Ohara.

"Stella, honey, come with me." Nurse Ohara gently led Stella into the ICU waiting room and helped her sit on the couch, then grabbed a tissue and folded it into Stella's palm. "You have to calm down. Please. Shouting at him won't do anything but raise his blood pressure, and that's not good for him. I know you're upset, and I understand. I've seen this happen so many times, and it's heartbreaking but, honey, you have to get hold of yourself… for David's sake."

Stella nodded over and over, until she felt like one of those bobbleheads on the dashboard of a car, which made her laugh and laugh. Then she couldn't stop crying, and she ended up sobbing, arms crossed over her abdomen, rocking back and forth, hurting so much, she thought she'd be sick right there on the shiny floor of the waiting room. She took a deep breath, shut her eyes, and leaned back. "I'm sorry. I'll leave. I'm so sorry. I'm sorry."

The nurse patted Stella on the shoulder and sat beside her. "It's okay. But I think you should go home, lie down, and rest. This is all very upsetting to you and the family. I totally understand. But you have to take care of yourself, before you have an even worse breakdown than you did today. I'm guessing your general practitioner could call in a prescription for you, for Valium or something, to help out for the short term."

Stella shook her head and looked Nurse Ohara in the eyes. "I can't. I'm pregnant with David's child."

The look on Nurse Ohara's face was unreadable. "Seriously?" Then a smile broke out on her lips. "Why, that's the best news I've heard all day, and, believe me, we don't get much of that around here. Congratulations. I'm assuming David doesn't know?"

"No, he does not. And I'm not going to tell him. It's probably best he doesn't know. I mean nothing to him, so neither will this baby. He'll just think I'm making up some story anyway."

The nurse grasped Stella's forearm. "Have faith, Stella. I've seen worse cases than David's, where the patient suddenly regained their memory. He just might be one of them. And when or if he does, this news will delight him. It truly will." She stood and helped Stella off the couch. "Go home, Stella. Take a lie down."

"I will. And I'm sorry. Please tell Dr. Hamilton I'm sorry."

"It happens fairly often, mind you. And being pregnant, your hormones are jumping all over the place. He'll understand. I understand. Now go home, sweetie."

Stella nodded and headed for the elevator. The doors opened, and Robert smiled at her.

She shook her head. "We really have to stop meeting like this."

He took her by the hand and guided her inside the elevator. "It's obvious you're upset. Let's go somewhere out of this hospital and have a cup of tea or coffee or a soft drink."

"That would be nice."

"You can tell me what's going on with you. Although I'm sure even I could enumerate several things myself. It's a topsy turvy world you're living in right now."

She nodded. "Tell me about it."

"No, you're going to tell me."

She laughed, and when they reached the lobby he guided her outside to a car she'd never seen before. "What the heck is this?"

"It's my mid-life crisis gift to myself. A brand new Dodge Challenger SRT Hellcat convertible. Eight-hundred horsepower."

Stella laid her hand on her chest. "My Lord, Robert. This must have cost you a fortune."

"Which I have." He laughed and opened the passenger door. "Seventy-five grand cash, out the door. Let's go for a little spin before we get something to drink."

Chapter Twenty-Five

Robert headed to the Pacific Coast Highway, known as the PCH to those in California, and headed south. He pressed a button, and the top cover ever so slowly lowered into a compartment behind the back seat. Stella's hair whipped round her face, as the wind blew through the inside of the car. Robert tapped a small drawer beneath a conglomeration of dials and knobs and took out a scrunchy and handed it to her.

She smiled and wrapped her hair into a ponytail, enjoying the feeling of freedom that came with the speed and comfort of the car.

He glanced at her, and their eyes met, and they burst out laughing.

"Pretty cool, huh?" Robert said, placing his hand over hers.

Stella turned her hand palm-side up and interlaced her fingers with his. "I've never ridden in a car this expensive or this fast. Aren't you afraid of getting a ticket?"

He squeezed her hand. "You worry too much. Let's just drive for a bit. I know a great place on the beach to grab a sandwich and watch the waves. You up for it?"

She nodded, leaned her head back on the headrest, and breathed in the salty scent of the ocean. The peacefulness of this moment magnified the contrast between right now and what awaited her back in Monarch Bay. She wanted just a few minutes… a few minutes… of not thinking and not doing anything.

David was a sound driver, never tailgating or going too much over the speed limit. Stella put on her sunglasses and took a few seconds to watch him. He was still such a handsome man. Accompanied by the complete change in his behavior, she'd grown fond of just being with him, talking to him, sharing herself with him, as she'd never done while they were together.

There was an ease he exuded that had never existed between them. And she enjoyed it. A connection slithered between them and grabbed her unaware and unwanted, inching its way into her heart. At this realization, her breath caught in her throat. Tears slid down her cheeks. Was she falling in love with Robert—again?

She felt his fingers tighten around hers, and she glanced at him.

"Are your eyes watering from the wind, or are you crying, Stella?"

She shook her head over and over and just let the tears come, exhausted from worrying about everything—about David, Charlie's relationship with his father, Loreen and Gabriel running the bakery without her, her future as a single mother with a newborn. And now, aware of her feelings for Robert, which seemed so terribly inappropriate at the moment, her exhaustion escalated. What the hell was she thinking? Actually, these weren't thoughts. They were feelings, overwhelming and unexpected in their arrival.

Robert took the next exit and pulled into a small parking lot next to a restaurant overlooking the beach, shut off the engine, and turned to face her. "Tell me what's wrong. Besides the fact you've been spending almost every day trying to get your husband to remember you, along with being on the receiving end of his anger because you're trying to pass yourself off as his first wife. You've got to be ready to fall asleep on your feet. And now you're crying when I was trying to get you away from all that, so you could feel refreshed and enjoy this beautiful day."

Stella held in the next stream of tears, waiting for her to give in to them. "Let's take a walk on the beach. No shoes, no scrunchy, no jacket. I want to feel the ocean breeze in my face and hair and just be."

"Your wish is my command, m'lady." He walked around the front of the car and opened her door, reached for her hand, and guided her out of the car. He kept hold of her hand as they walked to the boardwalk, then hopped onto the warm sand.

Stella pulled away from Robert and ran to the edge of the ocean. She focused on the bubbles and foam left on the sand after the water receded, faced the ocean, and walked toward the incoming waves. The water nipped at her knees, and the edges of her dress soaked up the salty waves like a sponge.

Robert laughed. "You're loving this, aren't you?"

Stella turned toward him, her back to the ocean, feeling the constant lap of the waves against her legs.

He wrapped his arms around her waist and gazed down at her upturned face. Their eyes met, and something Stella couldn't describe lurched inside her gut, up through her chest into her heart.

He slowly lowered his head, and their lips met in a whisper of a touch, so soft and so light, she didn't know if she imagined it or just wished it was happening. Then she felt his tongue sweep gently across her bottom lip, and she opened her mouth and kissed him as she never remembered kissing him before. It was unlike any kiss she'd experienced when they were together back in the day. It was tender, unforced, quiet, yet the pounding of the waves brought with it a feeling of triumph and excitement and a bit of fear. Fear she wanted this too much. Fear she was enjoying it too much. Fear she was falling back in love with the man she'd hated so much she wished him dead hundreds of times. And now he was making her feel the most alive she'd felt in months.

It suddenly felt as if she could no longer catch her breath, and she pulled back, leaning against his arms around her waist. "Oh, my God, Robert." She lay her head on his chest. "What are we doing?"

"This is all on me, Stell. I never stopped loving you. I've always loved you. But I was a terrible husband and a terrible person when we were married. I had to reach hell and climb my way up the longest ladder ever, in order to understand why I behaved that way, to realize I could change, if I wanted to. And I desperately wanted to.

"You know what? It was pure chance I was on the freeway when I saw the exit for Monarch Bay. I wanted to take the turn-off, knowing you still lived here, but at the same time I knew I shouldn't intrude on your new life with David. So I forced myself not to put on my blinker. Then all of a sudden… I don't know what you'd call it, kismet, an accident, fate. Hell, whatever it was, I swerved into the right lane and took the exit anyway. And it brought me directly to you, which is what I wanted all along.

"I worked so hard on myself, Stella, and, yes, I hated the person I'd become. But when I felt the shift and the changes I made over those five years, I slowly felt worthy of love. Maybe not yours but someone's love. And when I saw you again, I wanted that love to come from you. So I told myself to just be my new self, don't try too hard to convince you of anything, just be me—the man I never was for you or for the kids." He stepped away from her, arms spread out like wings at his sides. "So here I am, Stella. And if you want to try again, I'm willing… and wanting."

Stella's heart felt as if it were cracking in two—one half loving the David he'd been and the other half loving the Robert he was now. Robert's face blurred in front of her teary eyes, and she whipped around and ran. Ran as fast as she could through the edges of the waves, her dress soaked all the way to her waist, chest heaving with the struggle to get as far away from Robert… or maybe as far away from where they'd kissed… as she could.

Running, running, gasping for each breath until she threw herself onto the sand several feet from the foam and the seaweed and the waves, tears endless. It hurt to breathe, and her heart hurt so bad she didn't know what to think or how to feel.

Robert knelt beside her, encircled her in his arms, and pulled her up until she stood leaning into his body as he held her tightly, not letting her fall, holding her weight against him carefully, allowing her to catch her breath, waiting for her sobs to subside.

He said nothing as she slowly moved to his side, his arm around her shoulders, helping her walk back to the car.

When they reached the passenger side, Stella leaned her back against the door and glanced up at his face. "I don't know what to do, Robert. Help me decide what to do."

His gaze held hers. "That can't be a decision I make for you, Stell. I'm here if you want me, but we both know David's memories could return at any time. And then where would we be? I love you, Stella. I always will. But you're married. I want a relationship with my kids, and I plan to live and practice in Monarch Bay. So you have to decide whether we'll be exes with a connection because of our kids, but we have nothing to do with each other… or we can be more than that, because you leave David. I can't imagine what you're going through. And I won't even try to say what I'd do if I were in your place, because I don't know." He opened the car door and helped her inside.

They drove in silence back to Monarch Bay, pulled up in front of her house. He kept the engine running.

Stella grabbed the door handle and stared at her house, the front yard, the trees and flowers and mail box then, turned to Robert. "I need some time, Robert. I love you. I do. But I love the David I loved before the accident."

Robert nodded. "I'm not going anywhere, Stella, but I won't force this. I promise you. I won't do that to you. You're in a terribly difficult situation, and it's your decision, not mine."

She leaned over and kissed him gently on the lips, pushed the door open and ran into the house.

Chapter Twenty-Six

Stella texted her daughter and asked if she could pick up her little brother and have him hang out with her at the office because she wasn't feeling well, wanted a little lie-down for a few hours before everyone came home for dinner. Stella was so upset with herself for what she'd told Robert and how she'd acted with him, the guilt was eating her up inside.

What the hell type of signals was she sending her ex-husband by sharing details about David's behavior and how she felt about Robert to his face? She could have kept everything to herself and worked it out on her own, given time and a "let's see how things go" attitude.

But she felt so utterly and hopelessly alone and lonely and sorry for herself to boot. This was supposed to be an exciting time. She was pregnant with the child she and David had dreamed of. A literal miracle at her age. And who could she tell who would be as elated as she? Yes, Kat thought it was really cool Stella was pregnant, when Kat could never have a child of her own. Hence, when Loreen found out she was carrying her boyfriend Harley's baby at the age of seventeen, she and Harley had decided to allow Kat and Marcus to adopt baby Peter. Loreen had been a solid part of Peter's life since the beginning, babysitting and visiting and attending every pre-school event and birthday party. But Kat, being the one-of-a-kind sister she was, was truly happy Stella was pregnant for the third time.

Other than her sister, who was there to tell about this pregnancy? Her kids were happy for her, but the one person who could really share the miracle of it all would have been David. And now, he could not have cared less, because Stella was nothing and no one to him. And that hurt Stella so bad she could almost taste the foulness of her hatred for him. A strong word—hatred. But Stella was so pissed off about his memory loss that, even though it was intellectually an unrealistic way to think, she couldn't help the negative feelings growing inside for David, to the point she admitted to Robert, she still loved him.

She wanted to jump up and down with joy over the upcoming birth of her child but had no one to jump up and down with. She and David were supposed to be celebrating. Instead, Stella only felt let down and rejected by David. Though she knew she was being selfish. For goodness sake, she wasn't the one who'd been in a horrific accident, but her desire to share this event overwhelmed her. She wanted to shout it to the rooftops. Instead she'd morphed into a resentful witch, kissing another man while married to David.

Maybe she should see a therapist about these feelings and thoughts. She didn't know what the hell she was supposed to do. Should she wait and wait and wait—for what could be years—for David's memory to return? Or should she grab the one man who understood what she was going through, being a therapist himself, as well as still in love with her, and share the news of her pregnancy with Robert now, before telling David.

No. She knew that wouldn't be right. To tell her ex-husband she was pregnant with David's child before David knew? Wait! Perhaps this news would jar David's memory. He was stronger now. He'd been in physical therapy as well as occupational therapy for awhile. Nurse Ohara said he was walking and feeding himself, becoming more independent each day.

The one and only hitch was his memory. That had not changed. He'd made no advancements in that area. He was stuck in a pre-Stella world. She wondered how much longer they would keep him in the hospital and how long would he live at the rehab center afterward. Would they expect him to go home upon his release from rehab? But where would he go? His home was with Stella. They couldn't afford for him to get his own place while paying the mortgage on their house. And if David would soon be independent enough to get around on his own, would it hurt to be honest with him about her pregnancy? Once people in Monarch Bay found out, it would be the talk of the town anyway, and David would soon find out the truth.

Stella shook her head, trying to rid herself of the constant meanderings concerning her and David's future, since it didn't look promising they'd ever have one together as man and wife. He wouldn't want her to nurse him back to health. She was a stranger to him. He would be uncomfortable having Stella as his nursemaid.

"What the hell am I going to do?" she whispered to no one.

She felt the walls slowly close in on her, and she glanced around, claustrophobic, sick to her stomach. She had to get out of this house. Aloneness was getting her nowhere. She just kept going round and round in her head about what to do about David, when or if to tell him about their baby, whether to ignore her new-found love for Robert and honor her marriage vows to her husband, to move on with David and hope he'd eventually recall she was his wife and that he loved her… or leave David for Robert.

It all came down to how long she decided to wait for David's memory to return. And if it never returned, she asked herself, would she stay with him just because… or should she divorce him after… a few months or a few years? Was she willing to wait months or years? And for exactly how many months or years before she decided to leave him, if he never remembered who she was? Would she expect Robert to wait for her? Did she want Robert to wait for her? If she extricated Robert from the mix, would she desert David and set out on her own as a single mother? Would she desert Robert and set out on her own as a single mother, when she knew damn well Robert wanted her?

Did she want to spend months or years or decades married to a man who didn't love her? Would it be fair to her children? Fair to her? Fair to David? He could eventually find someone else. He wasn't in love with Stella anyway, right? Didn't her new baby deserve a loving and caring father? And if that father couldn't be David, could it be Robert?

Stella sat on the seat in front of the mirror of her vanity dresser, staring into her own eyes, as if she were looking into a friend's. What would she tell this fictional friend? What would she advise this woman to do?

Stella leaned her elbows on the top of the dresser and cradled her head in her hands. She couldn't stop thinking and deliberating and wondering and obsessing about David and the baby and Robert and on and on. She felt as if she were going crazy. She glanced up at her face, saw a woman confused and sad and lonely and also a bit wild. She stood, pushed the seat away with the backs of her knees, grabbed the marble paperweight and threw it at her reflection, glass shattering into hundreds of pieces, flying every which way—onto the floor, on the top of the vanity. Several shards missed her face, others nipped into her arms and chest.

Her gaze moved downward. Tiny pieces of her beloved mirror surrounded her feet. She'd saved for months to buy that mirror at the local antique store down the street from Patti's Pastries. And now, it all lay in shards all over the floor. Just as her heart had shattered into pieces since David's accident.

Slowly she tip-toed through the chaos she'd created and rushed down the hallway, grabbed her purse and slammed the front door after herself, ran down the street, not knowing where she was headed, not caring who saw her, not understanding how her behavior would help her come to any decision whatsoever.

She ran as fast as she could down side streets she didn't recognize, houses she never knew existed until she no longer had breath inside her lungs to go further, bent over, heaving in air like a drowning person, hoping no one saw her and called the paramedics. Minutes passed before she lifted her head and looked at her surroundings and saw no one.

Stella continued walking slowly, trying to catch her breath, until she came to Main Street. She crossed over to the side opposite the bakery, and the cool ocean breeze lowered her temperature until her face no longer blazed hot along her cheeks. She rested a hand on the wall of the building and stared ahead of her, only to catch sight of Robert and that same blonde woman he told her was his realtor, entering the same restaurant, Break an Egg, both laughing as the door swung shut behind them.

Had he been lying to her? Was this all a ruse to ingratiate himself into her life and her children's, only to revert to his old behavior?

Oh, my God. She couldn't take it any longer. She walked as fast as she could four blocks to the hospital and took the elevator straight to the ICU and ran past the nurse's station to David's room.

She stood at the threshold, staring at the man who'd been her world for five years, Charlie's father and the father of her unborn child, thinking how no one else was going to tell him the news.

It had to be her.

Chapter Twenty-Seven

Stella tentatively approached David's bedside. He had a book in front of him, concentrating, eyebrows furrowed, lips moving silently. The book she recognized as one she read to Charlie at bedtime and realized David had a long road ahead of him. He graduated college and read adult novels every night before falling asleep. But maybe the progression from kindergarten to college-level reading advanced quicker than normal, because the information once stored in his brain was capable of returning by exercising the part dedicated to processing that type of information. She didn't know.

If that was true, perhaps the information she shared with David about being his wife had made inroads. Maybe he was able to talk about his past with Stella, now that she'd forced the truth to the forefront. She'd know momentarily, and her legs and hands shook as she waited for him to acknowledge her.

After several moments, Stella placed her hand on the side rail of his bed. "David?"

His head jerked up, and he dropped the book onto the bed tray. "What do you want?"

Stella let out an audible sigh. "David, do you think we could start again? We aren't enemies. Can we talk like civil human beings? I don't want to shout at you like I did, and I'm sorry about that. I was angry. And I don't like it when you yell at me either." She laid her hand over her heart. "We were once so close and now you can't stand the sight of me. That hurts my feelings. I know Dr. Hamilton explained to you what it's like to recover from a traumatic brain injury. Your memory may or may not come back. He also told me introducing tidbits of your past life may jog your memory, and slowly you may recall your past. That's what I want to happen for you."

She reached out and covered his hand with hers. "I want to help you remember. I have some great things I'd love to talk to you about. They're exciting. I'm hoping you'll allow me to share them with you. I think you'll enjoy them. I know I can't force you to recall experiences from your past. It doesn't work that way. But a nudge in that direction might eventually do the trick. Would you like to try?"

David looked down at their hands, pulled his from under Stella's fingers, then looked her in the eyes. "I don't like what you said about Patti. I don't believe she's dead and that I'm married to you. I don't even know you. I don't recognize you. I'm not in love with you. I don't feel comfortable talking to you, especially about my wife."

Stella kept her breathing slow and steady. "But you must know that Dr. Hamilton and the staff and I aren't all conspiring against you, trying to feed you false stories about your past. You actually think we all got together and made up lies in order to screw around with your brain? David, you've got to know that's not what's happening here. We know… all of us know… your memory has been compromised by the TBI. You know it too. But the only way to go on with your life… from here… is to recapture your past—your *real* past—just before you had the accident. We aren't lying to you, David. Don't you understand that?"

"Okay, okay," he said, raising his voice to almost a shout. "Everybody's told me all this stuff. But none of it makes sense to me. I can't force myself to love you… Stel-… Stella, right?"

She nodded. "Yes, Stella. I know you can't force anything, David. But we're all hoping sometime down the road, something will change and you'll remember me and Charlie and Loreen and Gabriel and Kat and Marcus and Peter. We're your family, and we love you. We're here to help you remember. Perhaps if you allow us to visit you and talk about your past in a friendly way… maybe all of that will act as a trigger. And slowly your recollections of all the time you spent with me and our family will rise to the surface, and you'll be like, 'I remember, Stella.' That's what I'm hoping will happen, David.

"Won't you please just try? Give me a chance. Give yourself that chance. It's an opportunity I swear you won't regret." Tears slid down her cheeks, and she let them glide past her chin and drop to the bedside. She was so damn tired, exhausted. She wanted to lie in bed for a week and wipe out all memory of David's accident and everything that had followed.

David lay back on the pillow and stared at the ceiling. "Dr. Hamilton said I should take it slowly. That jarring my memory could backfire and do the opposite and hinder me from ever recalling my past."

"Or it may *not* backfire, David. That's the thing. It's a gamble. Everything I want to share with you may worm its way into the crevices of your brain, and you may remember some of it, maybe not all of it, but that doesn't mean you've forgotten everything. Little by little, bits and pieces of your past might resurface. But you have to start somewhere. You can't just sit here in this bed until your memory returns. It looks to me like you're reading, and I was told you're getting occupational therapy and maybe soon you'll walk out of here on your own and continue therapy at the hospital until you regain most of your physical abilities.

"But we should also work on strengthening your mental and emotional abilities. That's what I'm here for. I want to help you." She paused, held his gaze. "I love you, David. Let me help you. Believe what I'm telling you. Somewhere inside you, I'm hoping and praying, you know I love you. And I know I'm asking you to do something that seems completely impossible and frightening, and you just do not want to do it. But let's start this journey together. Believe in yourself, David. I do. I really believe that with my help, you'll be able to regain at least some of your memory. I really believe that. I believe in you. Have some faith in yourself." She choked up, voice wobbling. "Try… try to have some faith in me."

"I guess so."

She smiled.

He practically sneered. "You said we're married. When did this happen? After my wife Patti supposedly died of breast cancer?"

Stella nodded. "We could show you the obituary, David. Or better yet, I have pictures that were taken at the memorial service you had for Patti. I worked with you to organize the memorial service. There's a book everyone signed, like an album of things people said about Patti after she passed. It's a beautiful tribute to her, David. It's all proof that what I'm saying… what we're all saying… is true. I have pictures of our wedding too. My two kids, Loreen and Gabriel, are in the pictures. They've been wanting to come visit you since your accident. And so do my sister, Kat, and her husband, Marcus, and their son, Peter. You and Marcus are best friends. Oh, and here's…" she scrambled in her purse for her wallet, "here's a picture of our son Charlie." She handed it to him.

David slowly reached out his hand and took the photo from her. He glanced at it, then up at Stella, then back at the picture. "He's a cute little kid. How old is he?"

"He's five. In kindergarten. He misses you so much, David."

David let out a long, deep breath. "Anything else up your sleeve?"

She cringed at the way he had asked the question but tried not to let it get to her. He was treating her as if she were making up an unbelievable story, that she was still lying, trying to convince him of things he knew were false. It hurt, she wouldn't deny it. And she had to accept that, for right now, that's what he was feeling, and it wasn't unusual. But she was doing the right thing. He wasn't yelling at her, and maybe, just maybe, he'd accept this new reality. She'd bring their photo albums and let him look at them, alone. That might work. And he appeared open to giving it a try.

"For now, I think this is enough, David. And I'm thinking, why don't I bring a photo album. I'll drop it off at the nurses' station, and you can look at it whenever you like. Take your time. All the pictures are marked with dates and names. I think it's a great idea."

He handed her the photo of Charlie and turned his head toward the window. "Sure. Whatever you want."

She placed her hand on his forearm. "Isn't that what you want too, David? To remember? That's all I'm trying to help you with. We all want you to get your memory back. You do, too, right?"

He refused to look her way, shook off her hand, and waved toward the doorway. "Just go, will you?"

She took a step back, tears threatening once again. "Sure. No problem. I'll see you later."

He didn't answer, and she walked out the door, feeling she'd made an advancement in the right direction. He wasn't happy about it, but he could learn from this type of activity. And she'd do her damndest to help him come over to the bright side, the right side. She was his future, and so was Charlie. And so was their child. He had to remember. He just had to.

Chapter Twenty-Eight

Charlie stayed at Kat's place for dinner that night. Stella was so tired she went straight to bed after visiting David. Her plan was to bring photo albums to the hospital the next day, and, if she felt the timing was right, tell him she was pregnant with their child.

Ambivalence swirled though her entire body. What would she do when he looked at her, aghast, after she explained they both wished and dreamed of this day? That it was a miracle of God she'd become pregnant at her age. That this was supposed to mark a turning point in their marriage where Stella and David would make some crucial decisions about whether she would be a stay-at-home mom and he'd cut back on his hours, if Sunny was interested in taking over the baking and Loreen decided to stay as their accountant. And that, if any of those options fell through, it would impact both Stella's and David's future.

About a year ago they'd decided they didn't want to schedule their lives around the bakery but rather schedule the bakery around their lives. They worked hard and long to make Patti's Pastries an exemplary legacy in honor of David's wife, Patti. Both of them wanted that for Patti, and they were proud of what they accomplished in five years' time. But it did consume their lives, and they wouldn't be this young and this fit forever. They never took vacations with the family, nor alone together. They seldom went out on dates. The bakery literally ruled their comings and goings, and the only place they came and went was the back door to Patti's Pastries.

But now… if Stella and David weren't going to be a couple, and if Stella became the only one who could work at the bakery, Stella would opt out completely and sell it. She wanted to spend time with her new child, and that meant being a stay-at-home mom. Gabe had no intention of working at the bakery after having spent four years at the university, and though Loreen was doing what she'd been trained to do, Stella knew her daughter had aspirations of working at a large accounting firm in a big city, perhaps getting her master's degree, so one day she could make partner at an accounting firm.

So either David and Stella conspired together to reach the dreams they once talked about, or Stella would let it all go and sell the bakery to the highest bidder, if David agreed. What else could she do, if he wasn't a working partner? She guessed he could keep his share of the ownership and hire people to run Patti's Pastries, but that had never been in their plans.

However, if Stella and David were no longer partners—in their marriage, that is—then David's plans for the bakery could be anything he wished, because Stella would want out. She wouldn't work with him if he didn't believe she was his "wife".

She lay on top of her bed, arms spread out, as if she were making angel's wings, and breathed in and out deeply, trying her hardest to relax. Though, ever since David's accident, she couldn't remember the last time she wasn't stressed out. And she couldn't have a glass of wine to take off the edge of constant nervousness that invaded her belly every single day. She had to think of the baby. He or she now ruled Stella's life, but in a good way, as inconvenient as his or her sudden appearance was, given the fact the baby's father had no clue he even *was* the father.

"Oh, God," Stella shouted, turning onto her stomach, burying her face in the duvet covering their bed. "What am I going to do?" She grabbed a pillow and stuffed her face in the middle of the cushy down fluff and screamed as loud as she could with all the frustration and indecision spinning round and round inside her head down to her belly, making her shiver and shake.

The doorbell rang, and she popped her head up out of the pillow, listening. If it was someone selling something, she wasn't interested, no matter what the savings. And no one would be coming over in the middle of the afternoon to visit anyway. She waited to see if they left of their own accord, then the doorbell rang once again.

"Crap," she muttered. Shoving herself off the bed, she made her way to the front door, not even squinting in the peep hole, her mind fuzzy with ideas and speculations about her future. She opened the door. Robert stood on the porch steps, looking bereft and sad. She frowned and shook her head. "What are you—"

"Can we talk?"

Stella jerked her head back, surprised at not only the serious tone in his voice, but the look of total helplessness in his face. She pushed the door wide open and backed up, gesturing him inside.

"Thank you," he mumbled, staring at the ground as he walked past her into the front room, then stood beside the couch.

"Have a seat," Stella said. "Can I get you something to drink?"

He shook his head. "I think we should talk."

"Okay." Stella sat on the edge of the chair across from him and folded her hands in her lap.

Robert gazed downward for several seconds, hands dangling between his knees. "I wasn't being totally upfront the other day."

Stella sighed. "And here I'd just begun to believe you, unlike when we were married. It was so refreshing. And now I'm finding out you haven't changed at all?" She laughed lightly. "What a fool I am."

"No, it's not like that. I don't take back a word I said. I still love you, Stella. I told you I always have, and I always will. That's all true."

"Then what part was a lie?"

"I didn't say I lied. I said I wasn't being completely upfront." He cleared his throat. "Remember when I told you about that blonde woman who's working as my realtor? Who, by the way, found the most perfect house off Main Street that I decided to buy."

Stella leaned back in the cushions, arms folded over her chest, giving him an exasperated look. "Get to the point, Robert."

"Okay. She and I had gone out to lunch several times to discuss exactly what I was looking for and what my future plans were. I told her about Loreen and Gabe, and she knows about you being my ex-wife and all that." He stared at his hands. "We had dinner together last night. She said she had good news and wanted to talk about it. I agreed, of course. The conversation sped off to a more personal note, and I guess I didn't realize how many drinks we had over the course of the meal.

"She and I connected right from the beginning when I met her. She's divorced and had mistreated her husband, just as I mistreated you. She's been in therapy for about seven years and considers herself a changed woman. Kind, empathetic, understanding. We talked for hours. She admitted having feelings for me, and I won't deny she's attractive in many ways."

Stella rolled her eyes. "So you two slept together." She shrugged. "You can't possibly think I'd think you were being disloyal to me,

Robert, or that you were two-timing me with another woman. We aren't anything, you and I. We aren't together in any way, shape, or form. I'm married. You're not my husband. If anyone would be cheating, it would be me. All you and I have done is kiss. And only once. My supposed 'virginity' is still intact. You can see whomever you want, sleep with whomever you want. It's none of my business."

Robert stood, walked toward Stella, and knelt on the floor in front of her, grasping her hands in his. "That's not where I was going with this story, Stell."

Stella tried to pull her hands out of his, and he wouldn't let go.

They stared into each other's eyes for almost a minute until tears rolled down her face. He kissed her cheeks and chin and touched his forehead to hers.

"My point is, when this very attractive woman was telling me all of this about her life, and we realized how much in common we had, and she explained I'm the first man she's met since her divorce and that she's falling in love with me… I felt a connection with her, yes. But not love, Stella. I mean, I like her. She's a nice lady." He pulled back and looked into Stella's eyes. "But I don't love her. I never could. There's something between you and me that's more than a connection. It's more of a forever bond we share.

"I put you through hell while we were together. I know that. And after I went to prison and started therapy, all I ever wanted was to get back to you, whole and fixed and complete and… and worthy of your love, if you'd give it back to me. I don't feel anything for this woman. Yeah, I like her, but she and I could only be friends, nothing more than that. But she's not interested in being just friends. She wanted me to come to her house last night, spend the night, see how it went, see if we were compatible sexually before we went any further. The thought of that repulsed me. The thought of going to bed with anyone but you made me feel sick to my stomach. It would have been a total betrayal of what I hold most dear and what I want to happen between us."

"But, Robert, there may never be anything between us. You can't put your life on hold for me. David may get his memory back tomorrow. And once he finds out I'm carrying…" She stopped, jumped up, walked around to the other side of the couch and stood, hands on the head rest, leaning toward Robert. "I'm carrying his baby, Robert. And David doesn't even know yet. I wasn't going to say anything to you until I told him first. That was the right thing to do. I owed him that. And now I've opened up my big fat mouth and told you before I've had a chance to tell my husband."

Robert stood slowly, slid his hands into his pockets, and blew out a puff of air. "Wow. Well, congratulations, Stella. That's exciting, right? You wanted this?"

Stella nodded. "David and I were trying, but it's been about a year and nothing." She shrugged. "I found out I'm due in a little over seven months now."

Robert rounded the couch and grasped Stella by the shoulders, slowly turned her to face him. "If he doesn't want you… or this child, Stella… I do. I'll take you any way I can have you. I'd love his child as if it were my own, if that's how you want it. I know I have no rights to you. You're no longer my wife, and you're married to a man you love deeply. I'd come in as second best, I'm sure, in comparison, but I'd take that over not ever having you."

She scoured his face with her eyes, looking for something, anything to indicate he was lying to her, not telling her the whole truth, trying to get his way, exaggerating his feelings, trying to sway her in his direction. All she saw was pure, unadulterated adoration and love. Like when they first met, and he begged her to marry him, telling her he'd never met anyone quite like her, that he'd give anything in the world to have her as his wife.

"I don't know what to say," she whispered. "I don't even know whether I should believe you or not. Your words are reminiscent of when you and I were madly in love back in the day and you asked me to marry you. I believed you then, Robert. Why should I believe you now?"

He came as close to her as he could without smashing up against her, his hands sliding from her shoulders to her forearms. "There's no reason you should believe me, other than the fact I know who I am now, Stella, and if you choose to be with me, I'll prove it to you every day of my life. That I'm a new man. I love you and I don't expect anything from you. I don't want to control you. I want you to be just you, in control of your own life, as I am of mine, but not in control of you. I want a union, with both of us working as a team, along with the kids and Charlie and, if you want, with your new child. If you'll have me. And if you won't, I'll walk away. I'm staying in Monarch Bay because of the twins, but I won't push myself on you or them. And if none of you want me here any longer, I'll just leave."

"Or stay and be with your realtor friend," Stella said into his face.

"No, that's not how it is. She said I had to choose, and I said that was an easy answer for me. I want you. And only you. I told her I don't want a relationship with her. I want one with you. She was furious with me. She stormed out of the restaurant and said she never wanted to see me again, and she'd give the listing to someone else in her office to handle. I paid for dinner with a smile on my face. She made a fool of herself. I never led her on, and I never would have. I liked her, as I said. Just not in the way she wanted."

He leaned a bit closer, lips almost touching hers. "I want you, Stella. Forever. If you'll have me."

She opened her mouth to speak, not knowing what she could say or should say.

He placed his finger lightly on her lips. "Shhhh. You don't have to answer that. I just want you to know." He came a little bit closer.

Stella felt an overwhelming pull like a magnet, drawing her closer to him in her soul and her mind… and then her body collapsed into his, and she parted her lips and allowed his tongue inside, pressing her body against his, hard and tight, molding herself against his shape, feeling they were one person, but a couple at the same time.

Her mind lost all thought of what she should do about David, what she wanted to happen with David, what her plans were if David's memory never returned or if it did return. All mental meanderings and worries flew out of her head like balloons into the sky, and she melted into Robert like a candle to a flame.

Hours later Stella found herself beside him in her bed, naked, awakened by the sound of Loreen and Gabe talking to each other in the kitchen.

She opened her eyes to find Robert staring at her.

He kissed her gently on the lips. "What should we do?"

Chapter Twenty-Nine

At first Stella didn't understand where he was going with that line of questioning. Did he mean, what should they do now that they'd slept together and Stella was married to another man? Was he asking about her future plans and how they involved him and her? It was a loaded question, and she sure wasn't up to answering it at the moment, since her two kids were now home.

Robert leaned over her and whispered in her ear. "I can hide here and leave after they're gone or…"

"What about your car? They've probably already seen it anyway," Stella whispered back.

He smirked. "I don't know that they have any idea what type of car I drive. Do you know how many silver Camry's there are in any given city?"

Stella nodded then glanced at the bedside clock. "They'll both leave in a few minutes. Let's just stay in bed. They won't come in here to wake me up. They know I need my sleep. Don't worry."

He smiled as he snuggled his body closer to hers. "I can think of something to do while we're waiting."

A part of Stella wanted to make love again, but the just-woken-up Stella, the one who was thinking straight and had her wits about her, kissed his cheek chastely, then pulled away. "I can't, Robert. I haven't had a moment to think about what happened last night."

"And all through the night too," he said quietly.

Her face heated up, along with other body parts, with the memory of their lovemaking—different than she'd ever experienced with him during their marriage. Back then he'd been a selfish lover, never interested in satisfying her. It had been "slam, bam, thank you, ma'am" all those years, unexpected, abusive attacks in the middle of the night.

But last night he'd taken his time, and they'd made slow, languorous love off and on between napping and catching their breath. That had definitely been a Robert with whom she was not familiar. Miraculous. And she'd enjoyed herself, enjoyed being with him. They talked of things having nothing to do with David or the fact she was married, nor did they touch on the subject of Robert's time in prison.

They spoke of music they both enjoyed and films, and she told him all about her sister, Kat, and her husband, Marcus, about the bakery and her work there. He spoke of his plans to open a practice as a family therapist, that he was looking for another therapist to pair up with, so they could have an office outside of the home, and if that didn't work out, he'd convert one of the bedrooms of his soon-to-be house into a therapy room.

For Stella, it was like getting to know the real Robert for the first time, the Robert she'd never met during their marriage, the man hidden under all the hatred for his past and need to control everyone around him and his cruel machinations to be the one who ruled the roost at home. The Robert of last night, the man she'd become reacquainted with since David's accident, was enjoyable to talk with and to be around.

Stella had no clue what all this meant in terms of her future. The front door slammed, the murmurings between the twins waned, followed by the rumbling of an engine disappearing down the street. As she popped out of bed Robert grabbed her wrist, and she turned toward him.

"We should talk," he said.

Stella slowly sat on the bed, then nodded. "You're right. We do have to discuss all this…" She wafted her hand between the two of them. "…that's happening between us. I know. But I need some time, Robert. You've got to understand that. Last night came out of the blue. I don't even know how I feel about it." Her face flushed at the memory. "You're the lover I always wanted you to be when we were married. And now…" She shrugged. "We're no longer married."

"Take all the time you need, Stell." He cleared his throat. "But are you planning on… I don't know… just waiting for David to wake up to the truth that he's your husband and the father of your future baby or…?"

Stella bent her head back and stared at the ceiling, hoping a lightning bolt would suddenly burst through the house, and God's voice would tell her exactly what she had to do, though she knew that was never going to happen. She couldn't beg God for another favor anyway. She'd already pleaded with him to grant David's memory to return and couldn't ask another favor, especially since she hadn't had anything to do with Him in years. What was she thinking? That she was so special to Him, He'd grant all her wishes like some Wizard of Oz?

"Robert, on the one hand you say you'll give me all the time I need, and you'll essentially back off. Then with your next breath, you ask me what my plans are." She could feel tears, imminent behind her eyes. "I refuse to start my day crying over this. My hormones are raging, and I've been emotional over everything since David's accident. I need a freaking moment, Robert. Or, actually, more like days or weeks to think about this. Please."

Robert took her hand and turned it palm-side up and kissed the tips of each of her fingers—one of the most sensuous moves he'd made since last night. She marveled at the change in him, feeling as if she were living a dream. Was this really the Robert who'd beaten her to the point of bruising her, shattering her cheek bone, causing her nose to bleed? The difference between the two Roberts boggled her mind. Night and day. Black and white. Asshole versus knight in shining armor.

After kissing her fingers, he folded her hand closed and leveled his gaze to her eyes. "I'm sorry it seems like I'm pushing you. And I'll admit, I'm giving you mixed signals. Take all the time you need. My saying, 'Hey, Stella, what have you decided?' is disrespectful, and I apologize. But you know what? I'm getting mixed signals from you, too, Stella, which makes it hard for me *not* to go down the road leading to our getting back together. Do you agree with me? Am I totally off the wall here?"

She shook her head while fondling a piece of his hair that had fallen over his eyebrow. She finger-combed it back into place, then kissed his forehead. "I'm sorry, Robert. I realize, I, too, am giving you mixed signals. I'm so confused. I don't know what to do. I love you. I told you the other day." She swiped at her wet eyes. "But you have to understand, I'm mixed up. My emotions… my insides… feel like they're in a blender, twirling round and round, and where they'll stop—" She shrugged. "I— don't know."

She paused, held onto his hand with both of hers. "I want to… no, I need… to go to the hospital and talk to David. I planned on telling him about my pregnancy yesterday, but the timing was off. I got him to a good place.

"He was listening to me, and maybe, just maybe, buying into the fact that what I was saying just might be the truth. So I didn't want to overload him with even more surprising information and tell him about the baby. I'll see how it goes today."

She stood, walked a few steps to the en-suite bathroom, then turned toward him. "When you think about it, Robert… put yourself in my shoes. What would you do?"

He stood in all his glorious nakedness and crossed the room, stopping in front of her, noses practically touching. "If I'm being honest, Stella, I don't know what I'd do either. All I know is, my heart belongs to you, and I love you, as I've always loved you, but this time around it'll be different. I'm different. We together would be different. I can make you happy, Stella. I swear to God, I can. And I will."

She lay her head on his chest, listening to his heart beat slowly and steadily beneath her ear. "I've only felt safe with one man in my entire life, and that's David." She lifted her head, and their eyes met. "You can't blame me for wanting that again… with him. But since I don't know if I'll have that again with David, I don't know if I want to gamble with the entire rest of my life, hoping he'll change… that he and I will return to how we were and we'll get our happily ever after.

"Do I grab onto what's right in front me, right now, hoping you and I will make it work this time? Or do I gamble with the rest of my life, stay with David, hoping to regain what he and I once had?"

She pinched her lips together, hard. "I've never been a gambler. I don't like to bet. And these are very high stakes, Robert. Do I pick door number one with David behind it and wait to see what happens? Or do I pick door number two, where you're waiting for me right here, right now, and I won't have to wait a single moment to, hopefully, be happy again?"

Tears coursed down her cheeks. "I have no idea. I'm hoping beyond hope, something will come to me, like a dream in the night, unexpected yet not unwanted in its arrival. Just as I realized I have to have faith there's a God who's watching over me, I have to have faith something's going to happen that will help me resolve this dilemma, and I'll be able to make a choice that makes sense that's best for me and my family."

Robert gently wiped the tears from her face and smiled. "I'll wait for you. No more pressure. I promise you that. In fact, it might be less confusing for you if I stay away for awhile. It'll kill me, but I can do it… for you. What do you say? A plan?"

Stella closed her eyes for a few seconds, then opened them. He was still standing there. This was all real. It wasn't a dream. What was happening with David was a nightmare. And Stella didn't know which direction to point her heart. "It's a plan," she murmured, her heart threatening to burst out of her chest. She hurt inside, her life in emotional upheaval.

"I forgot," Robert suddenly said. He fumbled in the pocket of his jacket hanging over the back of the chair, pulled out a sheet of paper. "I suggested Charlie draw a picture of his daddy. He did, and then he asked me to take it to David. I told him I wasn't allowed to see him, just as Charlie isn't, because David has to get better before he has visitors, but that I'd give it to you." He handed the picture to Stella.

She held the paper out in front of her. "It's David," she whispered.

"It is," Robert said, smiling. "Charlie asked me if I thought his daddy would like to put it up on the wall in his bedroom at the hospital, and I said, of course, he would." He chuckled. "I think it's a pretty good rendition, don't you?"

Stella rubbed her eyes, trying to stave off a wave of tears. "It really does look like David. Charlie captured his dark brown hair, the eyes and nose… perfectly." She glanced at Robert. "He misses David so much, it hurts me inside. I can't imagine what it's doing to the poor kid to go this long without seeing his father."

She laid the picture on the vanity table and turned to Robert. "Thank you for encouraging him to draw this. It'll mean a lot to…" She paused, shook her head. "Actually I don't know that it'll mean a damn thing to David, since he doesn't have any feelings for his son right now. He might not ever have any, which would be devastating for Charlie."

Robert encircled her in his arms and rubbed her back as she cried. "You'll work it out, no matter what happens, Stella. Maybe showing David this picture will jar his memory. You just never know. That's the most difficult part of memory loss from a TBI—not knowing when or if the person will recollect the past or just parts of it. I think forgetting people is the worst. The rest isn't all that important really, but to forget your wife and kids and family? It may be harder on all of you than it is on David."

He leaned back. "He might know, intellectually, he has a family, but emotionally, he hasn't a clue. It's the feelings, not the mere knowledge, that's the most important part. You can't expect him to fake his way through this. In fact, what's going to happen when they release him? Where's he going to live? Here?"

Stella pulled away and rummaged through her closet for something to wear. "I don't know. I don't even want to think about it. And I know it's coming soon too." She turned around, holding a hanger with a pretty pink and yellow summer dress. "For both David and me, it would be like living with a stranger. He looks like David, but he doesn't act like him. There lies the rub. Are we expected to occupy the same bed as before? Pretend we're lovers? Fake it till we make it?" She stared at the dress she'd selected. "I just can't picture that."

"I understand. It's an untenable situation for both of you. How does he feel about that?"

"We haven't spoken about it. I need to talk to the doctor first. I don't know what they're planning or when. If David's walking and talking and can take care of himself, and if he needs to go to physical therapy at the rehab center, then they release him, where do they think he's going to live?" She threw the dress on the vanity stool. "Shit." She ran her fingers through her hair. "What the hell am I going to do, Robert? I can't think straight." She looked him in the eyes. "Especially when you're standing here in David's and my bedroom after I spent the night making love with you. I'm cheating on my husband. I'm a horrible person."

Robert walked toward her, and Stella put out her hands to stop him. "Don't, Robert. Please."

He halted several inches from her. "I should go."

She nodded.

He grabbed his things and walked slowly out of the bedroom.

The front door closed quietly, and Stella dropped to the floor, covered her face with her hands, and sobbed, completely overwhelmed and out of control, her confusion and lack of direction taking over. "God, what am I supposed to do? Please, just tell me what to do?"

Chapter Thirty

Stella decided to take a short break before heading to the hospital to visit David. Maybe seeing proof of the family who loved him in the photo books and the fact he was Charlie's father might make a difference in his behavior. She enjoyed surprises such as surprise birthday parties and other such good news. But hoping David's memory would resurface sounded, even to her, a bit over-the-top and ridiculously hopeful and unrealistic. It could be days, weeks, months, years… or never. And there was that rub again. It might never happen.

Stella grabbed Uje's leash from the coat rack in the foyer and called out her name. The poor pup hadn't been walked in forever. Stella's routine had gone completely off the rails. When Uje greeted Stella after work, Stella was accustomed to taking Uje on a walk to the beach and back, then fed her dinner. These days, Uje was lucky she got breakfast and dinner at all, since Stella's mind was somewhere else. And taking Uje for a walk wasn't in the forefront of Stella's thoughts. The drama in Stella's life had taken over completely. That had to change. Beginning with a brisk walk along the beach right now, today, with her pup.

Uje jumped and hopped around like a dancing bear cub when Stella tried to clip the leash onto her collar. Uje stormed toward the front door, dragging Stella along with her as she kicked off her shoes. Going barefoot was a luxury most people could never afford, but along the coast in California, it was typical to see people without shoes.

Stella and Uje half-walked, half-ran to the boardwalk, then crossed the sand. Even at this time of day, the breeze blew comfortably warm against her cheeks and through her hair. Leaning down to unclip Uje's leash, Stella dropped the leather lead and her hoodie onto a small hillock of sand and rushed to the water's edge. As she dipped her toes into the ocean, a sudden rush of letting go and just "being" overcame her. She stood, arms spread wide, head tilted back, letting the sun caress her face as she breathed in through her nose, out through her mouth, letting go of every thought and worry that had held her tightly every day since David's accident.

With her eyes tightly shut, she could hear Uje beside her, running into the water, then running out, back and forth, shaking off the ocean and sand each time she returned. Then she'd begin again, over and over, barking and yapping in joy and to capture Stella's attention as well. Stella ran down the beach, Uje following her, to where the ocean foam met the sandy edge and continued running until she was out of breath. Then she turned around and ran back, exhausted and spent. She dropped to the sand next to her hoodie and leash, and Uje licked her face. Stella couldn't help but laugh, something new and refreshing these days.

Feeling more awake and alive than she had in weeks, Stella waited until her breath evened out, then rinsed Uje off under the spigot at the side of the bathrooms. Satisfied she'd taken a time-out, she walked home, feeling ready to meet up with David. At least that part of her day felt good. She wasn't at all sure how the rest of it would pan out.

She ate a piece of toast, hoping to stave off the morning nausea, not sure if it was caused by the baby or stress. What she was sure of was, stress was not good for a growing fetus. She had to do her best to stay calm and take care of herself, or she might have a miscarriage. She wasn't twenty years old. Having a baby in her early forties carried higher risks, but Stella was healthy, not overweight, exercised regularly, meditated. But she had to be careful, if she wanted to carry this child to term without complications.

She promised herself she'd slow down. It felt as if she was living on a bullet train, going from one stop (home) to the next (the hospital) and back again. Loreen and Gabriel had stepped up to the plate and taken care of everything at the bakery, for which she was eternally grateful. Financially, Patti's Pastries was running in the black. Business was booming, in comparison to the month before David's accident.

The kids were obviously doing a fabulous job running the bakery on their own, with Sunny taking on all the baking. Sunny had spoken to Loreen about a close friend who yearned to be a baker and would practically work for free in order to gain the experience necessary to get into a program in San Francisco. Loreen asked Stella her opinion, and Stella gave her daughter the green light. It seemed a win-win situation and so far was working out, which was a huge burden lifted off Stella's shoulders.

Kat consistently picked up Charlie after school a couple of times a week and also dropped off groceries. She had a key to Stella's house but never took advantage of that, except to do Stella the favor of bringing home cooked casseroles and the necessities for dinners.

Stella was blessed beyond measure with a family who cared for her and David. They all were going beyond anything Stella would have dreamed to make her life easier, especially now that she needed to rest and eat well for the child growing inside her.

Stella found an old album containing pictures of her and David's wedding, including Loreen and Gabriel and Marcus and Kat. The album started from the beginning of their life together at their wedding, then segued to Stella pregnant with Charlie, then to the hospital at Charlie's birth and afterward when they arrived home. There they were, photos of Loreen and Gabriel and Kat and Marcus and Peter at various family get-togethers.

Dr. Hamilton told her photos were an excellent way to slowly introduce David's past into his present before actually introducing all the individuals in person, which could be an overwhelming experience and possibly backfire, causing him too much stress and information overload. At the very least, Stella hoped David would believe she wasn't lying to him about the life they shared. He'd see for himself, he was married and had a family whom he loved and who loved him dearly.

Stella arrived, carrying a satchel with two photo albums and a smile on her face, hoping and anticipating David's positive reaction. He wouldn't be able to deny the truth staring at him in the faces of his family, and maybe, just maybe, this would be a turning point.

When she entered his room, David was leaning on a walker in front of the window overlooking a garden with a view of trees and flowering plants. The area was a peaceful and beautiful place to focus attention and to walk through with benches and fountains interspersed throughout.

"David?" Stella whispered, not wanting to startle him.

His head jerked around, and the expression on his face wasn't what she hoped for, lips angled downward, eyebrows dipped in a scowl.

Stella forced a smile anyway. "I brought the photo albums I told you about. Would you like to take a few minutes to look through them with me?"

He sighed audibly and turned his walker in her direction, shuffling toward her. "You know, Sheila, I—"

"It's Stella. My name is Stella, David."

"Sheila, Stella," he waved his arm, as if swiping away a mosquito or a gnat. "Whatever, okay? I'm tired. My head hurts from trying to remember what everyone is telling me I've forgotten. It's fucking exhausting, all right?"

She nodded. "I can't imagine how difficult this must be for you. I'm sorry if it feels as if I'm pestering you, because that's not my intention." She paused, calculating every word, so as not to upset him further. "Everyone is so eager to see you, talk to you, know you're okay. They want to visit you, too, David. But Dr. Hamilton thinks it would be too much. And I agree with him. That's why we thought giving you a little distance by introducing your family to you slowly in pictures, rather than in person, might be a better way to guide you back to your present life."

"I can't remember any of my goddam life, Sheila. Shit, I mean Sharon." He shook his head like he was trying to get water out of his ears. "Whatever," he shouted. He closed his eyes and took a deep breath. "I'm trying. Let me get back into bed, and you can show me the damn pictures."

Stella could feel her blood pressure rising, pounding inside her head, heart racing. She, too, took a deep, cleansing breath and stepped back, giving him room to get into bed.

After he situated himself, she brought the table over in front of his chest and placed one of the albums on top, then opened it to the first page.

He scanned the photos, his face expressionless.

She pointed slowly from photo to photo. "This is me, and, obviously, that's you. We got married on the beach, down the street, right off the Monarch Bay boardwalk, where they hold the annual Monarch Bay Faire. This is my sister, Kat, and her husband, Marcus. That's Gabe and Loreen, the twins from my first marriage."

She turned the page. "And this is me, pregnant with our son, Charlie. I was huge by then, nine months pregnant, just waiting for him to come out."

On to the next page. "And here's Charlie. He weighed seven pounds, nine ounces, and, man, he was a hard one to push out." She chuckled. "Here he is in the bassinet, about ready to go home. He was already sucking his thumb. Still does occasionally, if he's stressed. But he's almost six years old. First grade's right around the corner."

She pulled out the drawing Robert had given her. "And this is a picture Charlie drew the other day. It's you, David. See? He wanted you to have it. Your dark hair, mustache, goatee." She eased herself into the chair next to his bed, allowing him to turn the pages and look through the album on his own. She didn't want to overwhelm him, so she backed off and remained silent.

He studied the pages she'd shown him, slowly going backward to the beginning. Then he closed the album and turned his eyes to meet hers.

"I'm sorry. Nothing rings a bell." He paused and sighed. "Honestly, I'm tired of trying to remember. I don't know these people, and no pictures or meet and greet is going to change that. They're all strangers. Do you have any pictures of me and Patti? I'd like to look at those." He paused. "Maybe if you just dropped them off at the nurse's station, that would be fine with me." He bowed his head. "To be honest, Sheila, I can't do this anymore. It's too much." He looked to the side of her, not meeting her eyes. "I'd prefer if you just… just didn't come by any more. Please." He slid into a lying position and turned his back to her, pulling the covers up to his shoulders.

Stella sat quietly, utterly deflated, like a burst balloon, then stood slowly reached out as gently as she could and grasped the album. Holding it close to her chest, she picked up her satchel and walked out of the room. When she reached the elevator bank, someone called her name.

"Stella, wait!"

She turned around. "Dr. Hamilton."

His eyebrows drew together.

"It didn't seem like it went well. David wouldn't even talk to me just now, when I stopped by to check on him."

As hard as she tried to keep her emotions in check, tears escaped down her cheeks. She quickly swiped them away and shook her head. "He doesn't recall any of us. Not me, my two kids, our son, Charlie, my sister, Kat, her husband, Marcus, who was David's best friend. None of the pictures rang a bell. In fact, he said it's all too stressful for him, and he'd prefer if I stopped visiting him."

She shrugged. "I've done everything you asked, doctor. And I never even got a chance to tell him I'm having his baby." She sucked in her lips to stop them from trembling, feeling too open and raw. "I… I'm going home, Dr. Hamilton. I have to take care of myself. Stress isn't good for the baby, and, my doctor told me, at my age, I have to be careful. This is all so disappointing—"

He placed a hand on her arm. "I understand. You're in a difficult situation. An impossible one at this point. I agree with your doctor. You need to take care of yourself and your baby. Take some time away from here. Would you mind leaving the photo albums, though? I think that eventually, if we leave David alone, he might look through them when we're not around. I believe he's curious. He wants to get his memory back. He just might end up looking though them when he feels up to it and there's no pressure. You know what I mean?"

She nodded, swiping again at her tears. "Here." She handed the satchel to him. "There are two albums inside with pictures of his entire family. And thank you for your help." She pressed the button for the elevator. "Call me at any time, night or day, if anything changes."

"I'll do that. And, by the way, we're moving him to a rehab facility in San Luis Obispo soon. Not too far away, but definitely not around the corner."

She glanced at the floor. "That's only about a thirty-minute drive." She shrugged. "Doesn't seem like I'll be taking it that often anyway."

The elevator arrived with a ping. "Thank you for everything, Dr. Hamilton. I appreciate all you and your staff have done for David."

He nodded. "Of course, when the time comes I'll keep in close touch with the staff at the rehab facility and pass on anything important. You can also call them, and when you visit, introduce yourself. They'll have all your information anyway."

"Thank you." She took the few steps into the elevator.

"So you won't be visiting him here again?"

Stella closed her eyes for a few seconds. "Right now, I never want to come back, doctor. But I will anyway. Just in case, you know? Maybe I'll catch him on a good day? I'm just not feeling well right now. But, yes, I'll be back."

He nodded, and she gave him a little wave.

What a nightmare today had been, not at all what she had hoped for or, frankly, expected. She'd allowed her mind to go to a place she should never have dreamed, picturing David's eyes lifting to hers with a smile on his face, shouting, "Stella, I remember. I remember everything, babe." Kissing her and holding her close while she cried with joy that her husband had come back to her and he remembered everyone… and they lived happily ever after.

"What an idiot I am," she mumbled.

She wanted to talk to someone, and that someone was Robert. But that wasn't fair. She'd be giving him mixed signals and false hope. Stella had no idea what to do. After reaching the car, she slid into the driver's seat, laid her head on the steering wheel and sobbed.

Until a pain completely unfamiliar to her gripped her abdomen, taking her breath away. "Oh, my God, no." She leaned her head back on the headrest, cringing as each cramp squeezed her insides over and over. She tried to breathe through the pain, taking deep inhales and long, slow exhales. Too early for Braxton Hicks. She hadn't a clue what this was, nor its significance or what it meant for the future of her pregnancy.

Struggling to snatch her cell phone out of her purse, her breath catching with every stab of pain, she pressed the number for her doctor's office and explained to the nurse what was happening. The office was located next to the west wing of the hospital, and when she told her where she was parked, the nurse replied someone would be out in a moment.

Stella breathed through each cramp, and within what seemed like seconds, one of the male nurses from the doctor's office knocked on the window, startling her. He opened the car door and helped her sit in the wheelchair he'd brought to take her around the corner.

As she gripped the armrests of the wheelchair, she couldn't stop crying. "What's happening to me? Am I losing my baby?"

He patted her shoulder, telling her to keep calm, and wheeled her as fast as he could to the entrance to the building, through the sliding glass doors, down the hall to her ob/gyn's office, past the waiting area to a private room, where he helped her onto the table, covering her with a light blanket.

Dr. Ormond entered the room immediately, his nurse following him, pushing the ultrasound machine to the side of the table.

"Hello, Stella. Breathe deeply. I'm going to have a look at your uterus, see how this baby's doing. I know it sounds impossible, but don't catastrophize this incident. It may be nothing."

Automatically, Stella's upper teeth bit down on her lower lip, and she felt blood drool into her mouth. "Please. Please don't let anything happen to my baby," she whispered.

The nurse laid a hand on Stella's arm, lightly caressing with her fingers. "Breathe, Stella. Slow, deep breaths."

The cramping wasn't as bad as when she was sitting in her car. She was able to take deeper breaths. Her abdominal muscles loosened and relaxed. The cool gel under the ultrasound wand soothed her abdomen with every pass.

A second nurse entered and took her blood pressure, listened to her heart. They hooked her up to another machine, lines and squiggles beeping and bopping up and down on the screen.

It seemed like hours had passed, when the doctor stepped back, and the nurse gently wiped the gel off with a soft cloth, unhooked her from the machine, unwrapped the blood pressure cuff, then stood to the side.

Dr. Ormond leaned over Stella. "Everything looks fine. Baby looks good. Your blood pressure's gone down from when you first came in." He helped Stella sit upright. "Stomach cramps during early pregnancy are relatively common and usually not a cause for alarm. These cramps are typically part of the normal physical changes in the body that occur in preparation for the baby. But I'm glad you came in. If this happens again, call the office right away." He smiled. "You're fine, Stella. Now I suggest you go home, relax, take care of yourself, eat, and drink healthy, and I'll see you at your next appointment. One of my nurses will call you later today to check on you. Okay?"

Stella tried her best to smile, though it probably looked like a pitiful grimace. "Thank you, Dr. Ormond. That's what I intend to do."

After dressing, she waved goodbye to the front desk staff and walked down the street to her car. She wasn't surprised this had happened. The overwhelming surprise and sadness and disappointment she'd felt from David's reaction was almost unimaginable. Yes, she was upset, and, yes, all this devastated her. Her hopes were dashed to the ground; her anticipation of a positive reaction had evaporated.

She wanted to talk to Robert. But she held that thought at bay and headed home, her sanctuary, to wait for her family to get home. Her family… minus her husband, who would be moving away to a rehab center soon instead of to his home. But for how long? Weeks, months?

And then what?

Chapter Thirty-One

Stella passed St. Salvador's Church, glanced in the rearview mirror, saw the bell tower and stained glass windows, and decided to turn around, stop in for a quick chat with… well… she still felt on the fence about God's existence. Looking back on her life, she recalled the detritus of bad luck littering the path leading to where she found herself today.

Both parents killed in a boating accident when she was a kid, marrying Robert and suffering for more than ten years under his abusive hands, escaping her marriage by pure luck and the kindness of an unknown, long-haul trucker and her long-lost sister Kat. Her journey had ended where she'd landed today, with a husband she hoped to love and have more children with, who had lost his memory, leaving her stranded and alone with two children who would have no father and a bakery she didn't own that she ran in honor of her memory-less husband's dead wife.

Her mind whirled and jittered like a top at the end of its spin cycle. After parking the car in the back lot of St. Salvador's, she walked around to the front of the church, slowly ascended the steps to the huge front doors, passed through the foyer, and entered the empty cavern of St. Salvador's. Her body felt drained of all energy, but she managed to make her way to the alcove at the side of the altar, where a statue of Mary holding the baby Jesus stood behind a small table, on top of which sat numerous steepled rows of unlit tea lights.

Stella paused in front of the tiny candles, picked up the box of matches, lit one of the tea lights, then knelt on the padded kneeler in front of the table. She folded her hands in prayer-like fashion and bowed her head. "I'm not doing too well here… uh, Jesus… or God… or whatever I'm supposed to call you. I don't mean any disrespect. You remember me, I'm sure. I was here awhile ago, begging you to give David his memory back."

She paused, took a deep breath. "My life hasn't been all that bad, and I don't mean to complain. I think it's just… well, I'm depressed and I need your… well, *someone's* guidance and I don't know who to turn to."

She looked up at the baby in Mary's arms. "I was blessed, if that would be the right word, with two loving parents and, yes, they died. But then Fiona and Nason adopted Kat and me. They loved us as if they were our birth parents. Then I met Robert, and, well, he turned out to be pretty bad, but that led me to Monarch Bay, where I met David, and, oh, God, he's such a great man—kind, good-natured, handsome, and loving." She covered her face with her hands, and tears flowed down her fingers, dripping off her wrists onto the marble floor. "I love him so much. But he doesn't know who I am, and he's not interested in finding out. It hasn't been months or years, God. I know that. But how long am I supposed to wait? I'm too young to wait forever. What if he never gets his memory back?"

She reached into her pocket and found a crumpled-up tissue and dabbed at her cheeks. "And now Robert returns, and he's changed. I mean, really changed. And he loves me. He wants to be a father to my baby too. I don't want to do this whole parenting thing alone… uh… Mary. You surely can understand that. But I don't know what to do. Do you think you could give me a sign or something to show me the way? Anything you can do to guide me in the right direction."

She shrugged, swiped at her cheeks again. "That's all, I guess. I don't know what else to tell you, since… well, if you're God, then you know all this stuff anyway. But I could really use a sign. I'll take care of the rest, but I need help. Just a little bit, not too much. I'm not asking for a miracle or anything like that." She stopped and sighed. "Amen."

She stood, genuflected, nodded to Mary and her child, then turned around and walked down the center aisle. The church doors opened wide, and Robert walked in, head down.

She stood immobile for several seconds as he walked slowly, like an old man, several feet before glancing up.

"Stella!"

She squinted. "Are you following me?"

He shook his head. "Of course not. I came here to…"

"I didn't know you were… I don't know… religious?"

His face flushed. "Sounds cliché, but in prison a lot of guys find God." He shrugged. "I'm one of them."

Stella blinked, not believing what she was hearing or seeing. Robert in church? "Well, um, I think that's great. We need more people like that in the world, since it seems society is going down the drain, what with murders and rapes and the massacres in the Ukraine. I could go on and on, I guess, but—"

"My question is, what are you doing here, Stella? I didn't know you were religious either."

Stella shook her head, smiling. "You've got me there, Robert. I never really was. I mean, I wasn't an atheist. But I didn't belong to any church either. With everything that's happened with David and… well, with you coming back into my life… I need some guidance. I thought this was perhaps the place I'd find a sympathetic ear."

Robert pointed his finger at the altar. "Did He give you an answer?"

She blew out a stream of air. "I actually didn't ask for an answer specifically. I'd just like maybe… a sign? Not like I expect a bolt of lightning to hit me as I walk down the street or anything like that. I'd just like something, anything, to show me He's listening. I need to make a decision. You already know that."

"I'm not pressuring you."

"I know. But I hate living like this, in limbo. I'm married to a man who might never know who I am, but he may someday, when I'm too old and about to go to my grave. Or I can take advantage of the relationship you and I have and divorce him." She shook her head slowly. "Seems impossible to make such a decision."

"I agree with you. Totally. And I respect you, no matter what you decide, and, like I said, if it'll make it easier for you if I leave Monarch Bay so I'm not in your face all the time in such a small town, I'll get a house in San Luis Obispo. The twins can visit me there instead of here. I don't want to cause you any more stress and anguish than I already have when we were married, Stella." He laid his hand over his heart. "I'm not that type of man anymore. Whatever you need, I'll accommodate your wishes."

Stella's eyes filled with tears, and she tried her best to blink them away, but they slid down her cheeks anyway. "I'm sorry, Robert. I just don't know what to do."

He closed the distance between them and took her hands in his. "Please don't worry about this. I'm not going anywhere, unless you tell me to. Even if I buy a house and start my practice and you decide to stay with David, I can move. San Luis Obispo isn't that far away. Don't put added pressure on yourself. It's not good for you and the baby." He took her in his arms and rubbed her back, making shushing sounds as she sobbed into his shoulder.

When she pulled back, their eyes met and he took a handkerchief out of his back pocket and dabbed at her cheeks. "I love you, Stella. That's all I can say. Go home, take care of yourself. I've got some things I have to think about here too."

"Are you okay, Robert? Is there anything I can do?"

He smiled. "No, but thank you for offering. When I was in prison they had a tiny chapel. I'd frequently stop by and talk to God, but in the background there was always the constant noise of… well, a prison. But since you've never been there, you can't imagine the yelling and screaming and taunting. It goes on all day and all night, and it's enough to make you crazy. Sometimes I thought I *was* going crazy. Until I met a preacher there. He wasn't affiliated with any particular religion, but he believed in God, and he just had a way about him that was comforting and what he said made sense."

He looked around him. "Coming here is such a place of solace for me. It's quiet and calming and completely the opposite of the chaotic atmosphere in prison. I could hardly think coherently in there because of the noise, but praying and talking to God inside prison was the only way I kept my sanity. That's when I started anger management therapy, then I became interested in becoming a therapist and, well, you know the rest."

Stella kissed his cheek. "I'll leave you to have your private time. And thank you for talking to me. It helped."

He hugged her again and walked up the aisle to the altar.

Stella exited the church and drove home, feeling a bit less stressed, yet still confused, but with her eyes open and her mind ready to find that sign she asked for, to show her what path she should take. When she entered the house, the luscious scent of tomato sauce and garlic assaulted her senses, and her stomach growled. "Who's here?"

"It's me," Kat shouted.

When Stella rounded the corner to the kitchen, Kat twisted in Stella's direction and grinned. "I hope this is a good surprise and you weren't dreaming of an entire night alone, reading a book with your legs up on the coffee table in silence."

They hugged, and Stella pulled back, meeting Kat eye-to-eye.

"Thank you for coming over and fixing dinner. It's been one helluva day. This is fantastic."

Kat frowned. "One helluva day, huh? Tell me about it."

Stella looked around. "Who else is here?"

"The two boys are playing in Charlie's room. Loreen will be here as soon as the bakery closes. Marcus is still gone, probably in Kentucky or something by now. So it's pretty much just you and me. Wanna sit in the front room for a bit? I'll get you a glass of something to drink, and I'll have some wine. How's that sound?"

"Lovely. A cola would make my day. They're in the fridge."

Kat shooed her out of the kitchen, and Stella made her way to the front room, slumped onto the couch, took off her shoes, and placed her feet on top of the coffee table.

Kat joined her and set a glass of ice cubes and a can of cola on the table in front of Stella, then took a seat in an easy chair across from her. "Spill, Sis. We've got about thirty minutes."

Stella flicked open the can of cola, poured a stream over the ice cubes, then picked up the glass, letting out a huge breath as she leaned back into the cushions. "Do you remember going to church every Sunday with Momma Fiona and Papa Nason?"

"Sure do. Fiona made both of us wear floppy hats and patent leather shoes and fancy dresses. I hated that. The dresses were so itchy, and the shoes hurt my toes."

Stella laughed. "I know, right? But they both were such good people, weren't they?"

"As they say, salt of the earth, whatever that means." Kat chuckled. "But, yeah, they were good people. I miss 'em."

"Me too. The reason I bring them up is because I visited St. Salvador's church today. Actually, twice since David's accident."

Kat made a face. "Get outta here. Really? I don't picture it. I thought you gave up going to church a long time ago."

"I did. After Robert turned into a controlling monster, he wouldn't let me go to church anyway. It got to the point where I felt like, if there was a God, he or she wouldn't make me live with such a person and be abused for so many years. God would have intervened and helped me out, you know? Somehow. Some way. I thought, if there's a God then would He just stand by and watch what was going on? Especially since before the abuse began, I did believe in God." She paused. "Then I didn't."

Kat nodded. "I get you. I really do. It's hard to keep the faith when you're living a nightmare."

"What would you have done?"

"Oh, no. I can't tell you what you should or shouldn't have done, Stella. Believing in God is a very personal thing. It's your own private relationship with a being, or whatever you wanna call it, that you either do or you don't believe exists. It's all about faith, and faith is intangible. Just like God. I can totally see why you'd think God forgot about you, because He purposely didn't help you in your time of need.

"But, think about this, Stella. Did you ever read that book by Viktor Frankl, *Man's Search for Meaning*? The one where he tells his story when he was in one of the Nazi death camps?"

Stella shook her head.

"Well, it's worth reading. What he and thousands of Jews experienced is beyond our imaginations, for sure. But no matter what they did to him and no matter how he was treated, it was his mind they could never control. And that's essentially what, in my opinion, is the whole God thing. No matter what happens to you in your life, bad or good, doesn't prove or disprove the existence of God. In your mind, if you believe God exists, then nothing, no matter how wonderful or how horrible, can change what you believe or think about God's existence. God either exists for you or He doesn't, no matter the surrounding circumstances."

Stella chewed at her bottom lip. "I'll think about that. And I'll read the book too. That's some pretty heavy stuff."

"It is. But it's kept me sane for most of my life, Stell. I believe there's a God, and nothing and no one can change my mind about that. It gives me a sense of solidity and control over my own life and how I react to circumstances, both positive and negative. God is always there for me, through thick and thin, helping me work through my problems. Not doing the work *for* me, but being there *with* me when I'm struggling. Does that make sense to you?"

"Yes, it does."

"I know you're struggling. This David thing is incredibly confusing and difficult to know what to do. You've told me how he's acted, how he's treated you, and I can't imagine, knowing how happy you two were before the accident. And now he's a totally different person."

Stella started to cry again and swiped her tears away. "I showed him one of our photo albums today. He got angry. He didn't know who anyone was. And I get it. I really do. I can't expect him to look at pictures of me and the family, and just because it's true—that we're married and he has a family—doesn't automatically make him love all of us like he did before. That's ridiculous. I was just hoping to jar his memory or, I don't know. I thought he might be a bit interested. But that didn't happen, so I'm disappointed."

"But it could still happen, right?"

Stella breathed in deeply, trying to calm herself. "Yes, it could happen. So I went to church today and asked God for a sign. Any kind of sign to help me out. I just don't know what to do, Kat. Stay with David? Return to Robert?"

"It's been that good with Robert?"

Stella nodded. "I accidentally ran into him at church, as a matter of fact. He told me about his turning to God while he was in prison. I mean, we all know the stories of inmates finding God while doing time and on death row and all that. It's not unusual."

"You're right about that. I get it. I'm not going to fight you any more about it, Stella. I know people change. Obviously, Robert is one of them."

"And we've had some wonderful talks, and he's so great with Charlie, plus Loreen and Gabe really like him now." She chewed on her bottom lip while looking at the floor. "That's why I'm on the fence about this whole thing. All I'm looking for is something to help me make a decision either way."

"Take your time, Stell. That's all I ask."

Stella smiled. "I will. Pinkie promise."

They both laughed out loud, remembering their childhood habit of locking pinkie fingers and making life-long promises to each other.

Kat stood. "Dinner's ready. I'm starving, and I bet you are too."

"Thank you for everything you've done. Taking care of Charlie, bringing over casseroles and desserts. I love you, Sis."

"And I love you, Stell."

Stella's heart swelled, knowing she was lucky to have Kat in her life. And Loreen and Gabriel and Charlie and Peter and Marcus.

And now, she had to admit—Robert.

Chapter Thirty-Two

When Stella awoke the next morning, she dreaded going to the hospital. And she didn't anticipate David being any happier in his life after he was transferred to a rehab facility either. Every day turned into what Kat would term a "shit-show", with David unhappy or yelling at her. He'd gone from a mellow, happy, good-natured, loving, caring, empathetic, wonderful guy to a morose, sad, angry, self-centered man, who seemed not to care about anyone but himself. He'd morphed into a narcissist.

Having those thoughts not only scared Stella, but made her feel like a narcissist herself, because all she was thinking about was how negatively this affected *her* life. However, if David was the man she'd be living with for the rest of her days on this Earth, that frightened her. She wouldn't want Charlie and Loreen and Gabriel around him. Every time Stella visited David she left feeling like crap, a useless nobody who was bothering David by her mere existence.

And yet, wasn't she being selfish by thinking that way about David? The poor man had suffered a TBI and the horrible complications accompanying such an injury. And none of that was his fault. The trucker traveling too fast on the freeway who'd run smack into David's van was to blame for all of this. David was an innocent party, and she shouldn't be "dissing" him. She should be ashamed of herself.

But she had to think of Charlie and the baby she was carrying. They deserved not only a happy mom—which Stella most definitely was not these days—they deserved a father who loved them more than anything and took care of their every need. A father who read to them, played with them, took them on vacations. They deserved it all.

And it didn't look like David was going to be able to provide those things. Shouldn't Stella act? Shouldn't she "do" something before David ruined their young lives with his withdrawn and angry nature? Was it the right thing to do—subject them to David's behavior, hoping his memory would return, and he'd be the David they all knew and loved? Was it fair to the kids? Was it fair to her? If she lived for however long it took for his memory to return, hoping every day it would come back and they'd all live happily ever after, was it fair to live like that for what could be decades? Or should she play the realist and "man up", as people often said, act now or forever feel guilty for not doing something when she had the chance?

Where was the sign she longed for, that she'd prayed for in St. Salvador's Church? Was God ignoring her in her time of desperation, again? Stella longed for something… anything that would point her in the right direction. Or was that just her way of not deciding "on her own" what to do? Did she really need to "lean" on God for a sign? Couldn't she just think this through logically and come up with an answer that would benefit them all?

And what about David? He wouldn't be happy living with her and Charlie and a new baby. They all meant nothing to him. She could not picture him living with a group of strangers. Or should she just wait it out and live with him for a certain number of months or years before acting? That sounded like a bad idea to her, since David's actions and words impacted more people than just Stella. Just because she could "take it" didn't mean five-year old Charlie, the twins, and the baby would be immune to David's negativity, criticism, yelling, and angry nature.

Stella dragged herself through her morning routine until she couldn't wait any longer before visiting, not wanting to arrive at lunch time, since David did not like people watching him eat. He made that very clear to the nursing staff. He didn't want visitors at meal times. But what was he talking about? Stella was his only visitor, as far as she knew. So he obviously didn't want her around while he ate. Then again, he didn't want her around. Period.

She took extra care with her make-up and hair and slipped on a spring rayon dress with pink and yellow rose petals dripping across the material like a Monet painting. She hoped David would see she was trying her best to please him, that she wanted to be friends and make him happy.

When she entered his room she actually felt happy, sort of, hoping today he'd be in a better mood. Maybe she'd have the opportunity to tell him about the baby. That could be the key to opening his heart and maybe his memory bank. She could only hope.

"Good morning, David."

He glanced up from the fishing magazine he was looking through. Fishing magazine? David hated fishing and hunting of any kind and was (or had been) turning vegetarian before his accident. She was taken back by the sight of him turning the pages with interest before he acknowledged her. He lifted his eyes in her direction, then continued to peruse the magazine, ignoring her.

"How're you feeling today? Better?"

He shook his head, silent.

"I brought some of your favorite chocolates. The See's truffles with the ganache center. You love these. Actually Loreen and Gabriel bought them and asked me to give them to you." She held out the bag. "They said to tell you they love you and miss you and will come and visit whenever you're ready."

He turned his head toward the window, staring out at something, then looked back at her. "Who in God's name are Lorraine and Gabrialle?"

Stella painted a smile on her face, even though she wanted to scream with frustration, wondering how in the world people lived through this. "David, honey, it's Low-reen and Gab-ree-ell," she enunciated. "Our… I mean, my kids. They're twins. Remember me telling you about them?"

"Yes, I remember you telling me about them," he sing-songed back at her, making fun of her. "And don't call me honey, will you Sheila? It makes me uncomfortable."

Stella shut her eyes and counted to three, then opened them. "It's Stella, David." She placed her hand on her chest. "My name is Stella." She paused, trying not to let him get to her. He had a TBI. It wasn't his fault. "As far as Dr. Hamilton told me, the memory of part of your past has been either erased forever or just gone into hiding for awhile. He never said it was typical for TBI patients to have memory loss of current events happening right now. I tell you my name is Stella every single time I visit you, which is pretty much every day, David. And my two kids from a previous marriage are twins, Loreen and Gabriel. You can probably remember that, if you really try. And you could be a bit nicer when I come visit you and bring you a gift from Loreen and Gabriel, who love you, whether you remember them or not." She paused. "David, you have people who care about you. Me, the twins, your son, Charlie, and soon… "

"Soon what?" he mumbled.

"And soon you're going to have another son or daughter, because

I'm pregnant," she shouted, then covered her mouth with both hands and ran from the room, sobbing.

She made it to the car before vomiting in the bushes next to the back bumper. After finding her keys, she unlocked the car door and slipped into the seat, laid her forehead on the steering wheel and took huge gasping breaths, trying to get her emotions under control.

Why had she told him about the baby? She could blame her reaction on hormones raging in her blood stream. Or was she simply allowing her emotions, her anger, and her frustration get the better of her in the moment? Was she that out of control?

She twisted the key in the ignition and pulled out of the parking lot onto Main Street, headed for… where? Should she go back to church and beg one more time for a sign? Should she talk to Kat again? Should she call Robert and ask him to meet up with her to talk?

But she had already talked to Kat about this… and Robert as well. What good would it do, when ultimately it was her decision whether to stay with David and wait it out… or divorce him, leaving him alone with no one to care about him. Even to her own eyes, that made her seem like a mean, uncaring person, abandoning the poor man suffering with a TBI on his own, with no friends or relatives, since he didn't remember he had any. That wasn't Stella. She'd never been heartless. It was like bringing herself down to his level of negativity and narcissism. But David had an excuse and a reason for his current behavior.

She did not. She had a family and friends and a job and was looking forward to the birth of her unborn child. What did David have going for him, that he could remember, that is? Not much of anything. And she was comfortable abandoning him in his time of confusion and need?

Her mind whirled round and round on the same carousel of thoughts she'd been riding for weeks. A headache right behind her eyes lingered, waiting to make its appearance. She wanted to climb into bed with a good book and a hot latte and forget about everything. Forget this nightmare both she and her husband were living. Escape seemed like the most inviting alternative. But she knew that would solve nothing and was irresponsible.

She'd take a long nap then… then what?

She hadn't a clue. And there was no one she could ask for advice, because only she could make this decision. It was her responsibility to act and no one else's.

At least that was how she looked at it. She didn't see any signs pointing her in any particular direction. Thank you so very, very much, God.

Now who felt abandoned?

Chapter Thirty-Three

Stella took the night off, meaning she ordered a pizza for her and whomever was around that evening, then turned on the Netflix channel and watched *Out of Africa* for the millionth time.

She loved that movie. The sound of Meryl Streep's voice calmed her. Robert Redford's countenance screamed, "I love you, but I'm not a part of you". Streep played such an independent woman, especially for the time in which she lived, and yet Redford's opposition to marriage became a significant sticking point, and Streep ultimately kicked him out of the house. Yet, watching the movie Stella could just feel Redford coming around to Streep's side... then he died in a fiery plane crash.

What if David had died in the fiery car crash? Would he have been better off? Not that she wished that, because she unequivocally did not. The David she knew and loved had been her dream come true. But this David, the David in the hospital? Part of her wished she'd never met him, because the heartache invading her soul and her heart felt overwhelming.

Sometimes she just wanted it all to go away, because she couldn't take one more day of David's dislike of her and disinterest in his family. The way he looked at her, the way he spoke to her... was all so dynamically opposite to the relationship they had before the accident. Every single, damn day the words coming out of his mouth astounded her, the sneering contour of his lips when he spoke to her, the grating sound of his voice as he yelled at her.

He'd morphed into someone she no longer recognized. And actually that wasn't all of it. David had turned into someone she no longer liked... nor loved.

There! She'd finally said the words lingering in the back of her mind, lurking along the edges of her heart for weeks. She wondered how long she could withstand his verbal and emotional abuse before she exploded. Better yet, would there come a time when, *if* his memory returned, it would be too late? Stella wondered about that sometimes. Then again, if she could take Robert back after everything he'd done, why couldn't she take David back, in the event his memory returned?

But in the meantime? How long could she participate in David's recovery, which at this point was a physical recovery only, since his emotional recovery was at a stand-still? Soon he would walk out of the rehab facility, and then what? She had no clue. She didn't even want to think about it. She had another human being to think about these days, and she didn't want to compromise the baby's future by letting all of this get her down, not eating, not sleeping. She had to get control of her emotions before they harmed both her and her unborn child.

Stella tried her best to paste a positive look on her face before entering David's room. When she walked through the doorway, a small suitcase lay on the top of his bed. He threw various personal items like toothpaste and shampoo into it with a vengeance.

"What's going on, David? I didn't realize today was the day you're moving to the rehab facility." He remained silent, and she moved to the other side of his bed, so she could face him. "Can I help you? I'm pretty good at this sort of thing, especially after having two kids who don't know how to pick up after themselves." She smiled, but he wouldn't look at her.

"I can do this on my own, Sheila. I don't need your help."

Stella took a deep breath and counted to ten.

"What the hell are you doing?" David said in the tone of voice Stella was becoming all too familiar with, the one with an edge of irritation and dislike so obvious, it stung her like a bee… or more like the bite of a rattler in its intensity.

Stella gritted her teeth. "I'm trying to… I'm trying…" Suddenly she burst into tears, letting them flow down her face without trying to hold back or look for a tissue to swipe them away. Let him see what he did to her, how he made her feel. Why should she hide the ramifications of his actions?

After he re-entered the real world, he'd discover quite quickly, he couldn't speak to people like that and get away with it. And she was here to tell him, today was the day it all ended. He had to learn how to talk to her. He had to re-learn everything else in his life, didn't he? How to walk, talk, dress, and down the road, go back to work. And when he was at Patti's Pastries again, dealing with customers, he couldn't act this way either. What better time than now for a little lesson in propriety?

"Listen to me," she growled.

His head jerked back, and his eyes almost bulged out of their sockets.

"Don't say a goddam thing right now, David. Just shut your mouth and listen to me for a few minutes, then you can talk or I can just leave, whatever the hell you want. All right?"

His nostrils flared, and she knew he was holding his tongue, something he hadn't been able to do since he'd woken up from the coma.

Stella took the opportunity that had dropped into her lap, knowing it might not last, and she'd better make the best of it. "Whether you remember or not, and I totally understand you don't remember, because you've suffered a horrible TBI, and that's not your fault. But… you're going to walk out of that rehab facility, David, and you cannot act toward people the way you act with me. You're rude, and mean, and don't listen, and you're freaking alienating all the people who love you.

"I'm your fucking wife, David, whether you remember that or not. The truth is, I am. And I'm carrying your baby. When you get out of rehab, what're you going to do? Move in with me and Loreen and Charlie and Gabe and treat them like you treat me? Granted, I think Gabe and Loreen will both find their own apartments soon, but then it'll only be me and Charlie and the new baby, and you cannot treat little children like you treat me. I simply will not tolerate it.

"I understand you're mad, and the world has dealt you a shitty hand, and you resent having to listen to the crap I'm telling you. But you've gotta hear it, David. You're going to have to make some big decisions soon that involve me and your two children, and I cannot have you ruining their lives because you can't control your temper, nor what comes out of your mouth. Words matter, David. They do harm. But they can do good as well, and I'm assuming you have access to a therapist who can help you get through this very difficult period.

"You'll need help with the transition from being in rehab to regular society. The doctors and nurses say you're progressing quite quickly and excellently, and pretty soon you're going to be back in Monarch Bay amongst all the people who know you and love you. And you cannot treat them the same as you're treating me. And I'm your wife."

David zipped up the sides of the suitcase and threw it into the chair next to the bed, then turned to her. "Not for long."

Stella frowned. "Not for long? You mean you won't be in rehab for long? How do you know that?"

He opened the tiny closet next to the bed and grabbed the jacket she brought him, along with a pair of pants and a long-sleeve shirt, dumped them on top of the suitcase then leaned over the bed, hands fisted on top of the sheets and looked her in the eyes. "I've hired an attorney. He'll be filing papers with the court soon. I want a divorce."

Stella could actually feel her face drop downward like candle wax in front of a flame. "You did what?" she whispered.

"You heard me. I'm filing for divorce. I don't know you, and I don't want to be married to someone I don't know. And I don't know this Lauren person or Gabby or whoever they are."

Stella's lips trembled. How dare he throw her children under the bus like this. It was inconceivable. "Their names are Loreen and Gabriel. By now you know their names," she said through gritted teeth. "And you've conveniently forgotten your only son, whose name is Charlie. I know damn well you haven't forgotten about him. I've told you about him over and over." She placed a hand on her abdomen. "And remember something, David. I'm carrying your baby." Tears flooded her eyes. David's face shimmered in front of her like a sickly ghost. "You're going to abandon all of us? Just like that? How can you divorce me anyway? You're not mentally competent."

"My lawyer told me the law requires a person must have the capacity to understand the basic legal and financial consequences of entering into a divorce. I understand the consequences of my decision, and I'm able to make and communicate that decision too. I understand the benefits, risks, and alternatives. And to ensure that parties with mental health and competency issues are represented fairly in divorce proceedings, they've appointed a guardian ad litem to represent my best interests. Alongside my attorney, the woman who's been selected will make a wide range of legal decisions for me ranging from spousal support, property division… and, if I was interested, they'd take care of custody and visitation of the children, but I have no interest in that."

Stella felt as if she couldn't breathe. This was not happening. When had he done all of this? Why hadn't anyone told her about this before now? She took breath after breath, but it didn't seem as if she was getting any air into her lungs. It was as if a bowling ball lay on her chest. She grasped her throat in both hands and rubbed up and down, trying to ease the tightness there, so she could take in some air.

"Help me." The words came out sounding strangled and raspy.

"Nurse!" David shouted.

Nurse Ohara rounded the corner, and, right on her heels, Dr. Hamilton rushed toward her. Nurse Ohara pulled up a chair behind Stella's legs and forced Stella to sit and put her head between her knees, ordering her to take deep breaths and count in-one and out-one until she reached the number ten.

The pressure eased, and suddenly Stella gasped in a huge breath of air. Eyes watering, she coughed several times before the dizziness subsided, and she could clearly see Nurse Ohara and Dr. Hamilton standing over her.

"Better now?" the doctor asked, taking Stella's wrist and holding it between his fingers, taking her pulse. He placed a stethoscope on her chest for a few seconds then knelt down next to her. "You okay now?"

Stella nodded. "I'm much better. Thank you."

"I think you had a panic attack."

Stella nodded. "I think so too. Scary."

"You're pregnant, right, honey?" Nurse Ohara said.

Stella nodded again, then tried to stand, felt a bit wobbly on her feet, then looked around at the doctor, the nurse, then David. "I'll be okay. I have to get out of here."

"I think you should have a lie-down, sweetie," Nurse Ohara whispered. "Just for a few minutes."

Stella shook her head. "No, that's okay. I feel totally fine now." She glanced at the doctor, then back at Nurse Ohara. "Thank you for helping me get through that, but I have to go. I appreciate all your help." Stella walked solidly past them and out the doorway, then rushed to the stairwell and descended as fast as her legs would carry her to the bottom floor, out the exit door, and around the corner to her car, jamming her finger on the remote to open the car door. She jumped inside, where she lay her head against the steering wheel and closed her eyes.

"That son of a bitch," she whispered to the universe.

Then, as if she'd put her finger in a light socket, her head buzzed inside at the same time as a thought scrolled across her vision, like a ticker tape. "A sign. A sign. This is the sign: David's divorcing me."

She jerked her head up, and her mouth fell open... and she smiled. "Thank you, God," she whispered. "Thank you for answering my prayers."

Chapter Thirty-Four

The next day while Stella got ready to head out to Patti's Pastries to inform her two kids what was happening with David and their marriage, the doorbell rang. After looking through the peephole at a guy she'd never seen, she yelled through the door, "How can I help you?"

"I'm looking for Mrs. Stella Crockett. I have an envelope for you."

So… it was true. She was being served with divorce papers. David hadn't been making up a story to get Stella to stop visiting him. He actually got himself a lawyer. She opened the door, took the envelope the man handed her, thanked him, then closed the door.

After sitting on the couch, legs propped up on the ottoman, she unsealed the envelope and perused the legal documents. "So you really did it, David," she muttered. "And a guardian ad litem as well." She stared out the window at the lemon tree in the backyard and felt tears forming and let them flow. She loved David. Well, she loved the "old" David. The new David she could hardly stand to be near for more than a few minutes. For some reason, reading the divorce papers made her feel as if he'd died, as if she were reading his obituary.

She wiped the tears from her cheeks but couldn't stop sobbing. Why had this happened to such a wonderful, caring man? He was the epitome of a loving husband and father. He'd opened his heart to Loreen and Gabriel, treating them as if he was their father.

So now what? By California law, everything was split fifty-fifty, right down the middle. At least that's what she thought, but she guessed she better get her own attorney, so things would go smoothly and quickly. She wouldn't fight with David on anything. This had been his and Patti's house, and, if he wanted it, then so be it. He could take the whole shebang—the house and Patti's Pastries and whatever else he wanted. He was the one who'd been in such a horrific accident. He was the one with a TBI.

But it would be so difficult for Charlie, as well as Loreen and Gabe, to just forget David ever existed. That would be impossible. Had David turned so cold-hearted he'd actually dump all of them from his life like so much garbage? Her heart hurt. Beneath her chest bone she felt an ache so deep, she was afraid she might be having a heart attack. But she knew she wasn't, because she felt the same way when anything traumatic happened in her life. It was her body dealing with anxiety and stress.

She covered her face with her hands and cried and cried. Her eyes were so swollen, her nose so plugged, she ran to the bathroom for a box of tissues, then sat on her bed, thinking about what she should do next. She glanced out the window, saw a hummingbird flitting right outside the glass, wings flapping so fast, it was impossible for the human eye to see anything but a nebulous shadow on both sides of its tiny body.

Why was it so hard to live as a human? Right now, she'd much rather be a happy little hummingbird, visiting each blossom, sucking out the nectar to sustain the unbelievable amount of energy needed in order to just "be" a hummingbird. The effort must be insurmountable without replenishing its body every few minutes of every day. Yet, this little guy appeared happy. Or was that an illusion? No worries or cares in the world, unless the hummie had to feed a couple of babies sitting somewhere in a nest in the neighborhood. But, even then, there were so many flowers in Monarch Bay, Stella was sure the bird would have no difficulty feeding its young.

Which brought her back around to being a human. Stella's innate sense of motherhood put her in a position of caring for her young, just like the little hummingbird. She had to protect Charlie from David. David didn't want to see his son, and his behavior showed that. And what about the baby she was carrying who'd have no father to take care of him or her?

Stella jumped off the bed and ran into the front room, where she'd left the envelope. She hadn't read past the first page declaring David's request for a divorce. She flipped beyond the first page and read, slowly and carefully. When she got to the last page, she leaned her head back against the couch and held in another wave of tears. He didn't want to be part of their lives but realized that being married to Stella and having a son and another baby on the way were facts he could not ignore. Therefore, he'd given the entire house to Stella, no strings attached, as long as she signed over any interest in Patti's Pastries. He also agreed to any reasonable demand for child support for Charlie and the upcoming baby.

"So this is it," she whispered to no one. "My marriage is over." She rubbed her abdomen with her hand, round and round. "You poor baby… being raised by a single mom. It's just not fair."

Her cell phone rang, and she picked it up, staring at the name across the front. Robert. How could he possibly know this was the perfect time to call? Or was it the worst? She wasn't really sure. Should she answer it? Was it too soon to tell him the truth about David filing for divorce?

Robert would jump all over this, knowing Stella would soon be a single mom, with a baby on the way. He was still in love with her and wanted them to have a relationship, to try again. But she needed time to digest this whole divorce thing. With the paper still in her hands, she let the call go to voice mail. He said he wouldn't try to get in touch with her, that he'd wait for her to phone him. So why was he calling?

Stella waited to see if he left a message. Within seconds the tiny icon indicated he had, and she pressed on it.

"Stella, this is Robert. Don't be upset, but I'm in the hospital having some blood work done in the west wing, and I decided to visit David. I wanted to see what he's like. He and I have never met, of course. But I thought I'd like to formally meet him. I won't mention anything about being your ex-husband unless he already knows. But I won't be the one to bring it up. I was going to tell him I read about the accident he was involved in, and, as a friend of yours, I wanted to extend my condolences that he's having such a rough time. I hope you don't mind. Essentially it'll be two guys talking about the crash, and he'll probably tell me to get out or maybe he'll talk to me, and that'll be the end of it. I know he's been, uh, really negative with you when you see him. But I was thinking and hoping for your sake, that maybe my meeting him might jog his memory. Maybe he'll recognize I'm your ex-husband, and he'll recall something… anything. It can't hurt, right? Anyway, I just wanted to tell you beforehand, so if you visit him today and he mentions it, you'll understand why I'm going there. Talk to you sometime. No pressure. Whenever you're ready… or not. Hope you're doing well."

Stella breathed in and out slowly ten times before allowing this to sink in. How did she feel about Robert visiting her husband? Normally, the current husband would be upset meeting the ex-husband. However, David had no memory of being married to Stella. She hadn't envisioned Robert visiting David, ever. Though it made sense Robert would want to meet David, if he was hoping to have a future with Stella.

She, too, wondered if, when David saw Robert, that would jar his memory. All the horrible stories Stella told David about Robert were inside David's head somewhere. Wouldn't it be ironic, if those memories brought to light all the rest of David's past—being married to Stella, their son Charlie, Loreen and Gabriel, Marcus and Kat, Peter, Uje. Wow! Though Stella held out no false hopes seeing Robert would have such a huge impact. But it could.

Stella wrote a quick text to Robert stating it was okay with her he visited David and, if there was anything significant he wanted to tell her afterward, she'd be home for the rest of the day. She pressed "send" and sighed.

"I sure wish I was a hummingbird," she mumbled, then remembered, she had an appointment with her gynecologist that afternoon. She decided to put off informing Loreen and Gabe about the divorce papers, perhaps talk to them after they got home that evening. In the meantime, she'd treat herself to lunch before meeting her doctor.

Stella returned from her appointment, happy everything was going well and she'd soon be able to have an ultrasound to see how her baby was doing. She entered the house and remembered she'd received several calls while lying on the table in the doctor's office.

After clicking on the voicemail icon, she propped her feet up on the coffee table and pressed the speaker button, so she could listen to her messages.

"Hi, Stella. It's Robert. I just wanted to tell you that David and I had a nice visit. He had no idea who I was, other than I'm a fellow Monarch Bay resident who heard about his accident and wanted to extend my condolences for his injuries and such. No need to call me. I'm giving you the time you need to think about your and David's situation about the future. He told me a little about your visits and then he… well, for some reason he felt it was okay to share with me he's divorcing you. I don't know why he did that, since he didn't appear to know who I was or anything like that, and he and I aren't friends. Anyway… if you need to talk, I'm here for you. I have a meeting with my therapist this afternoon, but after that I'm free. Take care, Stella."

Her heart shifted, thoughts flying this way and that about her growing feelings for Robert and her waning feelings for David. She'd never been an impulsive person, always thought things over five or six times before making any decisions. But right now, she felt so low and so unwanted and so depressed, she shot off a text to Robert, asking him to swing by after his counseling appointment.

She needed to talk to someone who knew her well, who cared for her, unlike David, who couldn't stand the sight of her, who had dropped out of love for her, and didn't know who the hell she was anyway. She took a long, warm bath with lavender crystals, washed and dried her hair, put on a summery dress, and returned to the couch with a glass of cola. It was warm outside, so she opened the sliding glass doors leading to the deck and listened to the birds, a light breeze wafting through the tree branches, and breathed in the ocean's scent.

She was sick of feeling hurt, devastated her husband didn't love her any longer, longed to be cared for and loved as she deserved. She was alone now, with no one close but her young son and Loreen and Gabriel, who would be off on their own adventures soon. Then she'd be a single mom to a baby with no husband for support, no closeness with a man, no sex. Her world was now turned completely upside down since receiving the divorce papers.

And she knew damn well what would happen if Robert came over. She wasn't fooling anyone, least of all herself. She knew deep down what she was doing, but she was so angry with the world, at the fact David was divorcing her and had done a preemptive strike by wanting her out of his life before she was ready, if ever, to do the same to him. She thought she'd feel relieved, but that was more an intellectual thing. Emotionally, she felt put down, discarded, hated, and rejected.

So did she ask Robert to come by as way of getting back at David, like an "I'll show him" effort, when David wouldn't care anyway? But that made no sense, since David would never find out. David didn't believe he was her husband, so he didn't care about her or what she did with her life, or Charlie or their unborn child, so what did it matter what Stella did?

Any feeling of revenge was useless, because it was aimed at David, and he couldn't care less.

But she knew what she was doing, and she knew what would happen if Robert came over, and she knew why she'd gotten "ready" for his imminent arrival.

She was fooling no one.

The doorbell rang, and her heart thumped.

Chapter Thirty-Five

Stella looked through the peephole, took a deep breath, then opened the door. "Robert." Just saying his name, her insides turned into mush. Her thoughts went straight to the bedroom, and she had to literally stop herself from jumping his bones. She'd enjoyed their time together, when he spent the night and, she had to admit, she wanted a re-do.

But above and beyond that, they needed to talk, and this was a perfect time for that. No one was home but the two of them, and she needed to explain how she was feeling. Otherwise he might think she was just using him, as people always talked about men using women for sex. That's not what this was about.

Robert held his hands behind his back, and Stella frowned.

He pulled one hand around to the front. "You always loved roses." He pressed them toward her. "I hope you're not too depressed about David's, um… hasty action with the divorce. I think it's a crappy way of dealing with this situation."

Stella held her tongue, took the bouquet from Robert, and leaned toward him to kiss his cheek. He moved his head quickly to the side, and their lips met. At the same time, he wrapped his arms around her waist, bringing her closer, and deepened the kiss.

Stella melted into his embrace and felt the bouquet slip from her fingers, falling to the floor. Without thinking it through, since her mind wasn't on flowers, but rather how lonely she felt and how very disposable she was in David's eyes, she pressed Robert to the wall. Their bodies molded together like a puzzle that fit perfectly. She felt him respond instantly, and he twisted her around to press her back against the wall at the same time sliding the short sleeves of her dress down her arms, past her thighs, until it dropped to the floor.

Standing in front of him with only a thong and no bra, she felt vulnerable under his pointed gaze, which travelled from her face to her toes. His mouth dropped open in what could only be termed surprise mixed with awe.

Stella grasped his hand and pulled him behind her to her bedroom, where they did everything but talk about her situation with David, then they fell asleep, until Stella heard noises in the kitchen, just like the last time Robert spent the night.

"Mom!" Loreen called out.

Stella quickly drew the covers over their naked bodies just as Loreen rounded the corner.

"What the hell?" Loreen whispered. Her eyes widened when Robert turned his head in her direction.

"Hi!" Robert mumbled, half-asleep.

"Sorry," Loreen said, backing away from the bedroom door.

Stella opened her mouth to explain, though she had no idea what she was going to say. She'd tell Loreen what had happened later, after Robert left, since she imagined it looked like Stella was cheating on her husband, which technically she was. However, without knowing the story about the divorce, Loreen got the wrong idea, as anyone would have in her situation.

Robert bent over, picked up his clothes, and dressed immediately. Stella did the same. He turned to her. "Should I stay, while you explain what's going on?"

"That I attacked you after I found out David's divorcing me?"

"Is that what this was? So it meant nothing more than revenge against your husband because you're angry with him?"

Stella stared into his eyes. "Absolutely not. That's not what I was thinking. Can we talk about this when we're alone?"

"Of course, since I really need to know what this…" he waved his hand over the bedsheets, "… was all about. If I want to just have sex with someone, I don't need to come to you."

Stella's eyes teared up. "That's not what this is about, Robert."

"I'll be back in a couple of hours, Mom," Loreen called out. "Going over to Aunt Kat's to see Peter, and I'll pick up Charlie."

"Thanks, hon," Stella answered, then flopped down on the side of the bed, hands folded between her knees, eyes never leaving Robert's gaze.

"Last night had nothing to do with revenge, Robert. I swear to you. I'm not that type of person. I don't use people. And I wasn't using you."

She took a deep breath, let it out slowly. "Yes, I was completely taken by surprise when I was served divorce papers yesterday, but only because it happened so soon."

"I'm surprised it happened at all. I didn't know someone in David's condition could even do something like that."

"He told me all about it when I saw him last, so I had time to think about it, but not much time. I didn't really believe him. I thought maybe he was acting sort of delusional and lashing out in anger after I talked to him about Charlie and my pregnancy. It just really didn't set well with him. He was pissed off, because he doesn't feel anything for me or Charlie or his unborn child. Then out of the blue he tells me he's hired an attorney, and he's having a guardian ad litem assigned to his case, who'll act in his interests to make sure he understands all the legalities so he can divorce me and his kids.

"I was really not just surprised, to be honest with you, Robert. I felt discarded, like a piece of garbage, useless, worthless, misunderstood, and so, so alone." She shrugged. "David and I have been together for more than five years, and he was always my rock. We were good together. So good together. Then all of a sudden—poof! No more marriage, no more husband. I'm going to be a single mom. He wants to give me the house, but he'll keep Patti's Pastries for himself. Essentially I'll be out of a job. I wouldn't want to work with him. Not after this. But with two kids and soon an infant as well, I couldn't work much anyway."

She stood and took Robert's hands in hers. "I realize I pushed him to take action, because I wouldn't let up about us being married, that he had a family and a son and would soon have another baby. He didn't want to hear it. He refused to acknowledge what I was telling him was the truth. So, yes, I was really, really angry with him. But that's not why I wanted to talk with you. And it's not why I pretty much attacked you when you arrived here. I mean, I saw those beautiful flowers you brought me and the kind way you've treated me since you arrived in Monarch Bay, and I…"

Robert squeezed her hands and brought his face closer to hers. "And you what, Stella? Tell me how you're feeling."

Her eyes filled with tears and she swallowed, trying not to break out in sobs. "I love you, Robert. I feel the same as I did when I met you long ago, before we were married. But actually I feel better than that. You've grown and changed so much, I no longer think it's a ruse or that you're pretending. People can change and, I think I believe you've changed too."

His brows furrowed. "You think I've changed. You're still not sure?"

She tilted her head and stared at his face. "It's hard to believe that the man you were in Oregon when we were married is the same man who's standing with me right now… more gentle and more understanding than I've ever seen you. You're no longer a narcissist. You're kind and loving. Can't you understand that I, of all the people close to you, would be highly skeptical such a metamorphosis could happen?"

He reached his arms around her and hugged her tightly. "Of course, I understand." He pulled back. "I'd be an idiot, if I thought I could come here and convince you in a short period of time. But I'm willing to take as much time as you need to prove myself, Stella. You're the love of my life, and I ruined everything when we were married for all the reasons I explained to you when I arrived in Monarch Bay. It will take time. I get that. And I want you to take all the time you need. I just don't want our relationship to be happening just so you can, underneath it all, get back at David for the way he's treating you. I don't want to be a revenge fuck. I want you to love me for who I am… today. I want to marry you again, Stella. I want to prove to you I can be the best husband you've ever had. I want to be a stepdad to Charlie and to your unborn child. I want it all… with you, Stella. And only with you."

Stella nodded. "I loved you once, Robert. And that same feeling I had for you long ago came back. Slowly but surely the old Robert blossomed in front of me, and you captured my heart once again. Would we be a couple if David's accident never happened and if you just showed up here out of the blue? Of course not. The old David was everything I ever wanted in a husband. We were happy. But that's in the past now. And… I think now… you're my future."

Robert kissed her gently on the lips. "I've been waiting to hear this for years. I dreamed about having this happen while I was in prison. I fantasized about making slow, passionate love to you the way you always deserved when we were married. You deserved everything I wasn't giving you, and I dreamed of getting the chance to show you I truly loved you but was so messed up in my head, I screwed everything up. But after getting counseling, it was like a light bulb went off inside me and lit up my life. The way I thought, what I wanted out of a relationship, all of that changed. And it's a totally new feeling for me too.

"And I prayed, Stella. I prayed to God I'd get one more chance to prove to you I could be what you needed and wanted. And what happened to David… well, it accidentally gave me that opportunity. Of course, it's a terrible thing what happened to him, but it was like… I don't know… like a sign or something. So I grabbed the opportunity and thought, this is my chance. Don't blow it, Robert. Show her. Prove to her you're the man she wants to be with forever."

Stella brought her lips to his, and they kissed. She pulled away and smiled. "Thank you, Robert. For understanding me."

"And thank you for letting me into your life again."

She nodded, then plopped back down on the bed. "So what now?"

He sat next to her and took hold of her hand. "It's your call, Stella. I'm not going anywhere. You're the driver. I'm the passenger. And I'll go anywhere and do anything you want and need right now."

Stella nodded and nodded, thinking about her next move. "I need to get myself an attorney. Find out how long this will take, since I'm not going to contest anything. Letting me have this house—which was his and Patti's—is very generous. And I don't want any part of Patti's Pastries. I can walk away from that. But I need to figure out my financial position. I have to be careful about how many hours I work, because I'm pregnant and not twenty years old any longer. My doctor talked about putting me on disability just to be on the safe side. I have a mortgage payment, I—"

He placed his finger under her chin and turned her face toward him. "Stella, you don't have to worry about money, if you and I are together. I have plenty. You could sell this house and move into the house I'm buying. There's enough room for both of us and Charlie and the new baby and Loreen and Gabe, if they want to stay there. I'll take care of you, just like I did when we were married. But this time, I'll take care of you and the family like I should have. It won't be just a financial thing. I want to care for everyone emotionally, like a real father and husband."

"Oh, Robert. Thank you for being here. You've been so kind. And I appreciate your offer. Just let me talk to an attorney first and also talk to the kids and explain to Charlie what's going on with his father."

"Of course. Then we can… maybe discuss getting married again, and we can move in together, and you can have the baby. It'll be good this time, Stella. I promise you."

"I want to believe you, Robert. And I don't want to hurt your feelings, but I'm not quite there yet. There's still that part of me that can't believe the person sitting here with me today is the same person who once treated me so bad. My mind literally reels sometimes, just thinking how much you've changed. It's hard to swallow, you know?"

"Yes, I do know. Most days, I marvel at how much I've grown and learned and changed, since I went to prison and all that happened to me while I was there. In all ways that are important, it was the best thing that ever happened to me… besides getting another chance with you, Stella. It's a dream come true."

"I love you, Robert," she whispered.

"And I love you, Stella."

They sat looking at each other for several minutes before Stella stood. "I have things I have to do. Today. I don't want to wait around any longer for David, for a court date. All of it, I wish would just happen in an instant because it's so stressful. And that's bad for me. And bad for the baby."

"I agree. Do you want me to look into finding an attorney for you? I can research that. Take that burden from you. Talk to some people."

"Okay. Thank you. I'll talk to the twins about us, then I'll tell Charlie. That will be the hardest thing for me to do. I'm dreading it."

"I can't imagine, Stell. And if there's anything I can do—"

"Just the attorney thing is enough, Robert. I have to do the rest all by myself. It'll be okay."

They parted ways, and Stella picked up her cell phone to call Loreen and Gabriel. She wanted to meet with them this evening and then talk to Charlie at some point.

She thought the twins would be fine, once they found out David wanted a divorce, especially since she already shared with them how David had reacted to her since day one. But the thought of explaining all this to a five year-old was another matter entirely. Stella wondered if it would almost be better to tell him his daddy died. Except in such a small town like Monarch Bay, that was a secret that would be impossible to keep hidden.

But this would break Charlie's heart. Recently he quit asking to visit David, but Stella knew he hadn't forgotten about his father. Kat told Stella she overheard Charlie and Peter talking almost every day about when David would come home and what Charlie planned to do with his daddy in the future. If she had a family therapist, perhaps she or he could help Stella figure out how to explain such a devastating fact to a five-year-old.

Stella blinked several times as a thought appeared in the back of her mind like a memory repressed. She knew a family therapist quite well.

Robert.

Chapter Thirty-Six

That evening Loreen and Gabriel and Stella went out to dinner together, while Charlie spent the night with Peter at Kat's place. Stella really didn't have to explain much about her relationship with Robert, since the twins already knew. Stella and Robert had talked with them all the time since David's accident.

They were both gobsmacked David went so far as to hire an attorney to divorce Stella. They were hurt that their relationship with David was at an end. However, they understood David's memory might never return, and, if they put themselves in David's shoes, it was understandable why he'd want a divorce. They were all strangers to him, so what was he supposed to do? Live with them in the house and pretend? That sounded weird to all of them.

The part that was hard to swallow was the fact David knew he was married to Stella, had a son, a baby on the way, and an extended family, but he still didn't want to get to know them, didn't even want them to visit him. His personality had completely changed. He was unrecognizable to Stella and would be to the rest of them as well, except they just had to take her word for it, because he didn't want them to visit him.

But Dr. Hamilton explained all this to Stella from the beginning, so it was no surprise. However, knowing it did not lessen the impact it had on all of them. Stella missed the "old" David and the kids missed him as well, though they hadn't interacted with him after the accident, so they had been spared that debacle. Stella was not only sad for herself, having lost her husband, she was devastated for Charlie and the twins, too, of course. But the twins were adults and could compartmentalize and deal with it. Charlie would be heartbroken. And, on top of that, Stella would eventually have to deal with the child she was carrying and explain all this to him or her as well. What a nightmare!

Before going to bed that night, Stella texted Robert, asking if they could meet up the next day and talk. She wanted to get his views and suggestions on how best to speak with Charlie about David's decision to divorce all of them. Naturally, Robert texted he was more than happy to help her and the family, in whatever way he could. They agreed to meet at his temporary office off Main Street. Until the house he was buying closed escrow, he was practicing on the third floor of a quaint Victorian with a view of the ocean and the trees lining Main Street.

Stella bought two coffees from Patti's Pastries and sat on the couch across from Robert, who took an easy chair next to the bay view window.

"Thanks for this," he said after taking a sip. "I had an early appointment and didn't have time for my morning java." He set the cup on the table between them. "So I'm glad you gave me a head's up about what you wanted to talk about. I took some time to really think about this."

Stella held her coffee cup in both hands and gazed into the foam, mesmerized by the way it looked like a small cloud.

"Stella?"

Realizing her mind had wandered from the topic she wished to discuss, she shook her head. "Sorry, Robert. I'm finding it hard to concentrate these days."

"How are you feeling? I mean, the pregnancy."

She smiled. "It's sure been different than when I was carrying the twins. The morning sickness has passed, but I'm just really tired, and that started last week."

"Perhaps it's not the pregnancy at all. It could be the stress of all that's going on. David's behavior toward you, his filing for divorce."

She nodded. "You're right. I'm so worried about Charlie." She took a deep breath, trying her best to hold back the imminent tears. "He's just a little boy. He won't understand why his father doesn't want anything to do with him. It seems impossible this won't screw him up for the rest of his life." Her bottom lip quivered and she placed the cup on the table and leaned back into the couch cushions.

Robert bent forward, hands dangling between his knees. "I'm not going to be able to tell you exactly what to say to Charlie. I'm sure you already know that, Stella. But I do have some advice on how to deal with a child whose father is going to be absent in his life." He cleared his throat and looked in her eyes. "You have to be proactive about this, which you're already being in the sense that you just found out David's divorcing you, and before Charlie finds out through the grapevine, you plan to talk to him about it right away.

"The best way to present this to someone who's only five years old is to be honest. Don't lie. Once you jump on a train of deceit and falsity, it's going to backfire on you. Maybe not right away, but down the road when Charlie's a little older, someone is going to say something, and he'll be angry that you didn't tell him the truth. Also, a child's worries and thoughts are much simpler than ours, and the last thing you want to do is start projecting your own worries and negative thoughts onto him. When he tells you his feelings, don't try to minimize them or take them away. Make sure you tell Charlie it's okay for him to feel sad or mad.

"Reassure him his dad's absence has nothing, and I mean absolutely nothing, to do with him. Now…" He paused. "That doesn't mean you should speak negatively about David. That's not what I'm suggesting. If you just tell Charlie the truth. David was in a horrible car accident and with the TBI, he's lost all memory of you and Charlie and the rest of the family. David isn't doing this to be mean or revengeful or anything like that. In David's mind, none of you exist. He doesn't remember you.

"Talk positively about David. You can explain… and this is the truth… that one day David may indeed get his memory back. That is a possibility. But until, or if, that ever happens, David will be on his own, not living with you any longer, because you are all strangers to him. That's a scary situation for anyone. And one that I think, at five years old, Charlie will be able to understand, if you come at it from that point of view.

"You should, of course, go at his speed. You know him better than I, and you'll be able to tell from the questions he may ask, or the responses you get while talking with him, what he's old enough to process and what he just cannot understand… yet. You can keep revisiting the story as he gets older too."

Stella glanced at the ceiling, trying to take it all in, then gazed out the window behind David's chair. "What are the ramifications of something like this on a boy his age, Robert? Should I expect this to just blow over and life returns to normal… just without David's presence in Charlie's life?"

Robert stared at his hands for a few minutes before replying. "I'm not going to sugarcoat this, Stella, but what I'm going to tell you doesn't mean it will happen with Charlie." He looked up at her. "When children feel rejected by a parent, they can tend to become anxious and insecure and over time they start to have low self-esteem, chronic self-doubt, and depression. They may even develop hostility and aggression toward others. This doesn't necessarily end in childhood either. The emotional pain can linger into adulthood.

"This is a long uphill process, Stella. So… always answer his questions simply and truthfully. Validate his feelings, reiterating it's not his fault this happened. Make sure he knows about his dad's good qualities, because you never know what might happen with David down the road. You don't want to ruin any future relationship between the two of them, if that's ever possible.

"And, finally, be sure Charlie's surrounded by at least one father-figure you can call upon in times of need, such as Father's Day, or a dad-day at school, or a time when you think a father-figure might be most appropriate for working through a problem. Sometimes sons in particular don't want to talk to their moms about certain things, so having someone on call to take him out for ice cream for some dude-time can help provide him with an outlet."

Stella tilted her head. "All great points for me to think about. Thank you." She paused. "The last suggestion… you know, the one about having a significant father figure?" She looked him straight in the eyes. "I'm imagining that could be you, Robert."

He laid a hand flat on each of his knees and took in a deep breath. "I was hoping you'd say that, Stell. I would not purport to replace your husband. David will always be Charlie's father. But… I don't know… it's almost like this is my second chance to get it right from the get-go, you know?"

"Because of how you treated the twins when they were growing up?"

He nodded. His cheeks tightened, and his eyes glassed over.

Stella actually felt sorry for him. "I understand. You probably carry a lot of guilt over that."

He inhaled deeply. "You cannot imagine how much. But my therapist tells me to look forward, not backward. Try my best to have a positive future, whatever that is. And I have control of my future behavior. I never had to be a controlling and abusive husband and father. That was an option I decided on. And it was wrong. I don't have to control others… just my own actions. It's been hard working on myself. But I understand why I acted the way I did, and it's unforgivable, and I'm not asking for absolution. But I'd love a second chance, not only with my own kids, which you've allowed me to have, but also with you, as your husband, and as a stepfather to Charlie and your new baby."

Stella smiled. "Is this your not-so-subtle way of asking me to marry you, Robert?"

He chuckled, stood, and knelt on one knee in front of her. "Stella Crockett, will you do me the absolutely incredible and miraculous honor of being my wife for the second time. I swear before you and God and everything that's good in the world to do my utmost to make you and the family as happy as they can possibly be." He took her hands in his. "I promise to be the best husband this time, so that one day perhaps you'll forget I was any other way."

Stella felt a tear glide down her cheek and slip off her chin onto their clasped hands. "Yes, Robert. I do."

"You've made me the happiest man on this earth, Stell." He sat on the couch next to her. "What do you think about me joining you when you talk to Charlie? I could help. But I understand, I may be overstepping."

Stella took a few moments to mull it over. "I think I'll need the help, Robert. I understand all the salient points I have to touch on when I talk to him, but maybe if you could act as a quiet back-up?"

He nodded. "Of course. You will be the leader of the discussion, and if you need anything from me, all you have to do is give me a look or a hint that you want me to add something. This is your son, not mine. But I can do my best to make it easier for the two of you."

"I agree. I think it's a great idea. And thank you for offering."

He stood, grasped Stella's hands and helped her up. "As far as the rest of it… you know, the wedding, and such… that ball is in your court, Stell. Whenever you feel ready and however you want to do it. I'm not going anywhere."

"And neither am I. Let's talk about it later. For now, the most important thing is explaining all of this to Charlie."

"I don't think we need to tell him we're going to get married."

"Neither do I. We can take it slow. We'll know when it's time."

He kissed her chastely on the lips. "I believe we will."

Chapter Thirty-Seven

Three Months Later

Stella invited the family to the house for dinner. She and Robert decided to announce they were getting married in two months. Loreen and Gabe had both moved out of the house. Loreen was living in an apartment off Main Street with a girlfriend who'd been a long-time customer at Patti's Pastries. After David returned to the bakery, Loreen graciously removed herself from that venue, finding it awkward to be working with David, who had no clue who she was.

Gabriel decided to tour Europe with a woman, Sandy, a customer he met at the bakery as well. He didn't feel comfortable working with David either. Plus he was thinking of returning to the university for a Master's degree. Sandy had just graduated with a nursing degree, but hadn't applied for jobs yet. They both decided to take advantage of their unemployment status and travel abroad while they had no commitments. In the meantime, they rented an apartment and were working at a restaurant on Main Street to earn their travel dollars.

Charlie became super-close with Robert. They played catch in the backyard almost every day before dinner. Charlie still asked about David. Stella and Robert always took extra time and care to explain how David was doing. They never visited Patti's Pastries. Robert and Stella agreed, it would be emotionally abusive to force Charlie to see David up front and personal since, although he knew David had a medical condition that had ripped him of all memory of Charlie and the rest of the family, a little boy who'd just celebrated his sixth birthday was still too young to make complete sense of the situation.

Robert wanted to formally adopt Charlie after he and Stella were married. They both wanted to solidify Robert's position as a father figure to Charlie. David had signed the necessary papers during the divorce in which he also divorced himself from Charlie, allowing Stella to have full custody, totally disengaging himself from any relationship with his son as well as the child Stella was carrying.

Stella was due to give birth to their little girl or boy in a month. Neither Stella nor Robert wanted to know the sex of the baby until the birth, both loving surprises. At this point, Stella and Robert were accustomed to surprises in their lives, never expecting to get back together nor that Robert would have his own family practice or that Stella would be carrying David's baby and Robert would adopt him or her.

Life was one big, unexpected surprise, and the two of them embraced it with open arms and gratitude. They were excited about getting married again and having a baby together, and Robert was elated to have the opportunity to help raise a new baby, whether it was his or not. Charlie and Robert's relationship blossomed to completely unexpected heights, especially since Charlie had been so close to David. Robert assumed Charlie would reject him, if anything. But, surprisingly enough, Charlie began to call Robert "Daddy".

Robert's relationship with Loreen and Gabriel was tighter now than it had ever been. They were planning a camping trip together, just the three of them, before Gabe and Sandy flew off to Europe. Stella was looking forward to staying home to rest, relax, and have one-on-one time with Charlie. Camping might not be the most comfortable venue for her now anyway since her due date was looming, and her doctor advised her to take it easy, given her age.

They were taking this evening to talk about all their future plans and set dates for camping for the three of them, Europe for Gabe, as well as Stella and Robert's marriage ceremony. Robert suggested a barbecue and was taking care of all the planning, cooking, menu, and set-up. He told Stella and the kids all they had to do was "show up" at seven o'clock and have a good time.

Gabe and Loreen arrived together, and Charlie greeted them at the door, announcing Robert had allowed him to use the hand-held lighter to ignite the coals, and they had marinated the chicken together as well as chopped the vegetables for a salad. Everything was almost ready, and, after grabbing cold drinks, they all sat outside on the back deck at the picnic table, waiting for dinner to be served.

"Where do you and Sandy want to go when you visit Europe, Gabe?" Robert said while cutting into a piece of chicken on the grill to test if it was ready.

Gabe grabbed a piece of French bread and buttered it, took a bite. "I'd like to go to some of the more unusual places, but Sandy is all for the touristy spots, like Paris and Rome and Madrid."

Stella laid a paper napkin across her big belly. "So what are the non-touristy spots you'd like to visit, Gabriel?"

Gabe grinned. "Transylvania, for starters."

Robert set the plate of chicken in the middle of the picnic table and took a seat next to Stella. "Is that really a place?"

Loreen laughed out loud. "I know, right? I thought that was just something vampires talked about in the movies."

Charlie wiggled in his seat. "Vampires. I love those. Daddy and I watched *Twilight* last night together."

"I did, too, young man," Stella said, fluffing up her son's hair with her hand.

Charlie shook his head. "You fell asleep before Edward Cullen even showed up, Mommy."

Stella grinned. "Well, you're right. There is that. But I've seen it before. I enjoyed it the first time, though."

Robert winked at Charlie. "I'd never actually seen it. I enjoyed it, too. In fact, I'd like to see the rest of the series."

"That was my favorite movie of all time," Gabe added. "Let's watch the second one. What's the name of that one, Charlie?"

Charlie bounced up and down. "First there's *Twilight*, then *New Moon*, then *Eclipse,* then there's, uh… *Breaking Dawn Part One* and *Part Two*."

Gabe nodded. "You got it, Charlie. You really do like vampire stuff."

Charlie nodded enthusiastically and turned to Robert. "Wanna watch all of them this week?"

Robert reached over and high-fived Charlie. "You're on."

Stella and Loreen glanced at each other.

Stella smiled. "Not exactly a rom-com or a chick flick, are they, Lo?"

Loreen shook her head. "You and I can watch that Netflix series *Dead to Me* with Christina Applegate. She's hysterical."

Stella high-fived her daughter. "I'm in, Lo."

The doorbell rang, and Stella caught Robert's eye. "We didn't invite anyone else, did we? I know I have a bit of forgetfulness going on, with the pregnancy and all."

"It could be Kat and Marcus and Peter dropping by, but I didn't invite them to dinner," Robert said, "since this is supposed to be a planning session for all of us."

Stella stood. "I'll get it. I need to go to the bathroom again anyway." She laughed. "Seems like that's where I spend most of my time these days."

Robert scooted the bench back, making it easier for Stella to get up. "Need help?"

Stella rolled her eyes. "I think I can handle it from here." She walked through the kitchen to the front door and opened it.

"Hi, Stella," David said.

Chapter Thirty-Eight

Stella took a step back, eyes wide. She felt her face flush and opened her mouth to speak but didn't have a clue what to say. She hadn't seen or talked to David in months.

"I really wasn't going to just drop by but… I just had to tell you, and I thought texting or calling was inappropriate and—"

Stella swallowed. "Why are you here, David?"

He glanced down and shook his head, then looked her straight in the eyes. "I remember, Stella. I know who you are." He smiled. "And Charlie and Loreen and Gabriel and Marcus and Kat and Peter." He threw his arms into the air. "My memory came back!" he shouted.

Stella felt a stirring behind her and turned to find Robert walking up to join her.

"David," Robert said in a whisper. "What's going on?"

David's smile disappeared instantly. "You're Stella's ex-husband."

Robert nodded. "Yes, I am. What are you doing here?"

David stared into Stella's eyes. "That's between me and Stella."

Stella placed her hand on Robert's shoulder. "Honey, why don't you join the others at the dinner table. I'll be right there. It'll be just a moment or two."

Robert nodded. "If that's what you want, Stell." He caught David's eye for a second, then walked away.

Stella stepped over the threshold and closed the door behind her. "I don't know what to say, David. That's fantastic your memory returned. I—"

David put up both hands. "You don't have to say anything, Stella. I know this is coming at you totally out of the blue. And I know you and Robert are back together and that you're planning a wedding and that you're…" He paused. "I know you're pregnant with my child."

Stella nodded, tears coming to the edges of her eyelids. She tried hard to hold them at bay, but they slid down her cheeks. "That's all true," she whispered.

"I love you, Stella. And I'm sorry for the way people said I treated you after the accident. But you've gotta know that wasn't the real me. Dr. Hamilton said my memory might never have come back, but there was always the possibility it could. And it has, Stella." He placed his hand over his heart. "This is me, Stella. David. Your husband. Charlie's father. And the father of our unborn child. And I love you."

Stella covered her mouth with her fingers, lips quivering. "And I loved you, too, David."

He took hold of her hand, pulled it up to his lips and kissed her palm. "Loved me? As in past tense? You don't love me anymore, Stella?"

She closed her eyes and pulled her hand away, his kiss lingering on her palm, memories of his kisses on her lips and her face and making love with him for the years they were together. When she opened her eyes, the look on his face brought him back into her life, into her heart, into her soul. "I… I… this is just so unexpected, David. I don't even know what to say."

"And I don't expect you to give me any kind of answer, Stella. I am just so excited, I had to share it. And I spoke at length with Dr. Hamilton. He advised me to share it with you, when I was ready and felt stable enough to do so. And I wanted to share it with the only person who would understand.

"I love you. So much. And I am so, so very sorry about the way I treated you. Dr. Hamilton and the nurses explained it all to me, and I… I apologize, Stella. But that wasn't me. The real me is here." He placed his hand over his heart. "I'm here, Stella. Really and truly here. The David you know. The David who's your husband. The David who loves you more than life itself. Please don't marry Robert. Please think about this for more than a few moments before telling me no. I'm begging you."

Stella swiped at the tears covering her cheeks. "I will, David. I will."

"Thank you. That means everything to me." He took a step back, his eyes never leaving hers. "Call me or text me anytime, day or night. I'll be waiting."

She nodded slowly, up and down and up and down.

David turned and walked across the street toward the ocean.

Stella watched his figure recede until the street crested, then sloped downward toward the water. When he disappeared, she grabbed the railing and slowly slumped to the top step, staring at the exact spot where she'd seen David on the crest before he vanished from sight.

From somewhere far away she heard the click of the front door, then Robert sat next to her and put his arm around her shoulders.

"His memory returned, didn't it?" he said.

"It did," she whispered.

"What are you thinking?"

She stared straight ahead, seeing nothing, yet, at the same time, seeing in her mind's eye David's back as he walked away. "There are no words, Robert. I—"

"Don't tell me you've already told him you'll go back to him. Just please tell me you'll at least think about staying with me, Stella. Please."

She felt her head go up and down, though she wasn't sure if she'd imagined it or not.

"Thank you," he said.

It was impossible to grasp David's words, to understand that David, her David—the man she loved more than she'd loved anyone in her entire life—remembered her. The real David she'd married had returned to her. The father of her child had come back to her. They could continue their life together. They could go back to being the family they'd been, to the time she'd been the happiest in her life. To being Stella Crockett once more. The love of her life had come back to her.

She shook her head, ever so slowly, back and forth, back and forth, as she felt deep inside of her gut and chest a swelling or a wave of heat crawling from her toes to her knees, across her stomach through her breasts up to her throat, making its way to the roots of her hair.

And that feeling was fear.

How could she know the "old" David had returned forever? Would he relapse to the mean, post-TBI David? Could such a thing happen? Since it seemed his "coming back" was so sudden, could he just as suddenly go back to acting like the asshole David he'd become after the accident?

These questions filled up the inside of her head like a bucket under a spigot of water. She literally felt deep, black fear inside her chest, as if she'd come face to face with an imposter, and she wanted to run as far away as possible to get away from him. Because maybe he was lying. The real David was the David she'd decided to leave forever. For God's sake, they were divorced.

But was the David she'd divorced the new and real David? Well, she'd assumed so, since she'd experienced his cruelty and mean spirit enough times to think it was a permanent state. However, she needed to remember, she was not the one who wanted the divorce in the first place. It was David who had divorced her. But, in truth, how long would she have stuck around? She knew inside her heart, if the new David had continued to be aggressive and cruel, she would have eventually stopped visiting him, and she probably would have asked him for a divorce in the near future.

But now what should she do?

Should she believe him? If anything, he definitely deserved a chance to prove to her he was a changed man, that he'd become the old David, the one she knew and would have loved forever and never would have thought of leaving for another man.

She'd give him that chance. He deserved it, because what had happened to him wasn't his fault. It was the TBI talking meanly to her, not the David she'd married. And if he was now the David she'd married, he most assuredly had her heart and her love, forever. But she'd have to see him one-on-one first. Talk to him about how this "change" had occurred, what had brought it on, listen to him explain what he was feeling right now. She couldn't just fall back into his arms after the short conversation they'd just had. Just because he said his memory came back wasn't enough to prove that her David, the love of her life, had returned. They needed to talk at length. She needed a thorough explanation of the facts.

"I'm sorry, Robert." She wasn't sure if she said the words out loud or just thought them.

"You're sorry about what, Stell?"

She turned her head, though it felt as though it swiveled on its own in Robert's direction. And she spoke words she wasn't positive were exiting her lips. "I can't marry you."

Robert gently took her face in the palms of his hands and stared at her. "You said you'd think about it, Stella. Just take at least a few hours or days or however long you want or need to give us some thought. We deserve at least that much."

Stella slowly raised both arms and took hold of Robert's wrists, easing them down. "I should have said, I can't continue with us, with you and me, and all the plans we're working on for our wedding, until I give David a chance to show me he's the David I loved before the accident."

She closed her eyes and bent her head, facing her knees and whispered, "He deserves a second chance, Robert." She lifted her head. "You know he does."

She took a long intake of breath. "I never stopped loving him, Robert. I loved him more than I ever thought I'd love any man. You know that. I told you that." Robert nodded. "I can't leave him. A huge part of my heart belongs to him. That never went away. I pushed it down and squashed it, because I had no choice. But now I've been given…" She touched Robert's cheek with her hand. ". . . I've been given a second chance. This is the miracle I prayed for every day. Then I stopped praying, because I felt God was ignoring me. That perhaps finding you again was His way of giving us… you and me… a second chance.

"But now He's given David back to me. And if this truly is the forever David, then… all my prayers and my begging and pleading… it's all come true. David remembers how much we were in love. He loves me again, just like he did before the accident. He truly wants to go back in time and start from where he and I left off. To begin again. God answered my prayers, Robert. And I'm so thankful for that."

Several tears slid slowly down Robert's cheeks and his mouth opened to speak. He inhaled a deep breath before answering. "In all fairness, as much as this is totally breaking my heart to pieces, Stella… you're right. He was your husband. You didn't ask for the divorce. He did. And you divorced the new David, not the David you married. So, if he's truly the David you know and loved all along, then I understand. Of course, I understand."

He once again gently cupped her face between his hands and kissed her, like a butterfly fluttering over a blossom, just for a second, then whispered, "I'll always love you, Stella. And if he'll make you happy, then I want that for you." He slowly stood and pulled her up with him. He faced her full-on. "But if this is something temporary… if he reverts to the David he was right after the accident… I'll take you back, baby. I love you that much." He took a step back. "But I love you enough to let you go, because I know he was the love of your life."

Stella's tears blurred her vision, and Robert's face shimmered like an apparition before her eyes. "I'm sorry, Robert. So very, very sorry. But I wanted David to come back to me, and now he has. He has my heart, and now I don't want it back. It's where it's supposed to be. With David. Where it's been for a long time… and was supposed to be forever.

And now, forever can come to be. It's a miracle. And I want to give him the chance to explain everything to me… everything he's thinking and feeling. I love him, Robert. This was meant to be. And I believe it's actually God's will, so I can't say no."

Robert looked down, seeming to focus on the concrete of the porch beneath his feet. He swiped at his eyes with the back of his hand, took one last look at Stella. "I would do the same thing, if I were in your place, Stella." He turned and walked down the stairway to his car.

Stella watched him open the car door, slide into the driver's seat, heard the engine turn over, then stared at the back of his head as the car crested the hill at the end of the street and slipped away, leaving only the pink and orange colors of the horizon in the distance.

She bent her head back and stared at a cluster of white puffy clouds making their way toward the beach. "If this is real… thank you."

She turned her heavy body toward the door and grasped the knob, turned it slowly, then paused and glanced over her shoulder. "I love you, Robert. But my heart belongs to David."

She pushed the front door open and closed it gently behind her, then walked to the back deck to join her family.

She paused, watching them talking and laughing at the picnic table. Her lips slid upward into a smile, and her breathing calmed. Her heart was full, her mind centered, her spirit warm, almost sunny, eager beyond measure at the opportunity before her—to find out what had happened to David to bring him back to her.

She had to know that first. Before she picked up where they'd left off, before his head injury.

She slid her cell phone out of her front pocket, scrolled through her contacts and pressed the icon for David Crockett.

"Hello? Stella?"

"David? Let's meet soon, so we can talk."

Chapter Thirty-Nine

David invited Stella to his place for coffee several days after he'd come to her house with his huge revelation about getting his memory back. He'd moved into the apartment above Patti's Pastries. It had been used for storage space, but only a few things had been scattered here and there along the sides of the walls, leaving it fairly empty for years. David said he'd redecorated it and it gave him easy access to come and go as he pleased throughout the long hours he needed to be at the bakery.

Stella's stomach, already in knots from anticipation of the baby's arrival, felt as if a vise were gripping her entire abdomen, squeezing so tightly, she wondered if the baby was arriving early. But after she had meditated for almost an hour, the tightness in her abdomen had subsided enough. She took the short walk to the bakery and slowly ascended the stairs on the side of the bakery building to David's apartment. She felt such anxiety about their upcoming conversation, she wondered why she'd bothered meditating at all.

She took a deep breath, let it out slowly, and knocked on the door.

Footsteps echoed from within, and David opened the door wide, then stood stock still, staring into her face.

"It's really you, Stella." He stepped toward her slowly. "Baby, it's really you."

Stella held his gaze for second after second after second until she opened her arms and fell into his embrace.

They swayed back and forth, as she wept tears she thought would never stop. He kissed the top of her head, nuzzled above her ears with his lips and chin, saying over and over how much he loved her.

Stella lifted her face to his, and they devoured each other with kisses and tongues and gasps and words of love. It was exactly like in the movies, but it was real life.

When Stella began to cry, David lifted her chin with his fingers. "Let's sit down, catch our breath."

She nodded.

David grasped her hand and guided her to the couch facing a huge bay window with an unadulterated view of the Pacific Ocean, palm trees swaying in the breeze.

They sat on the couch, and Stella turned toward him. "Tell me what happened, David. When did it happen? When did you realize you were the David before the accident? How long has it been? Tell me everything."

David took her hand and rubbed his thumb along her knuckles, quiet for what seemed like minutes before he spoke.

"I went back to work at the bakery, of course. I'm sure Loreen and Gabe told you that."

Stella nodded.

"I totally immersed myself in my work. You know how much I loved creating new pastries, working with Sunny on ways to entice people to return to the bakery again and again, knowing they were getting the chance to taste and enjoy the very best creations we could come up with to engage them in an eating experience they'd never forget." He paused. "What're you smiling about?"

Stella squeezed his hand. "I remember how you would wax on and on about your ideas and Sunny's about the new croissant or bread or cookie you had imagined. The look on your face after you baked it and discovered it turned out to be exactly how you dreamed it would be. The absolute—excuse the expression—orgasmic look on your face when you realized you'd done it. Seeing your imagination come to fruition… like after a painting is complete and the artist steps back and feels that 'voila, I've done it', you know?"

David brought her hand to his lips and kissed her hand, from her fingertips to her wrist. "You know me so well."

"And this… this is how we used to talk to each other."

He nodded. "You always understood."

"And you always 'got' me too." She straightened. "Tell me more."

"I began to remember our customers' names. All of them. Marjorie and Sam and Debi and… and all the people who'd been coming to the bakery for years. I remembered where they worked and the names of their kids. I recalled all the recipes I ever worked on for the pastries we served, what coffees people drank. I remembered it all.

"Then after a few days, I started to recollect episodes of you and me together. The day we met at the Monarch Bay Faire when Patti was still alive. Her battle with breast cancer. How you helped me with her memorial service. The night we made love for the first time. Loreen and Gabriel… and Charlie's birth. When you both came home from the hospital."

He moved a little closer until their gazes locked. "But most of all, I remembered… no, that's not correct… I felt, deep inside me, the longing for you in my heart. How much I loved you. How much we loved each other. How much we shared and how very, very much you mean to me, Stella."

He glanced down at their hands then back up at her. "I missed you so much. But I waited. I waited for four weeks… an entire month… before I went in to see Dr. Hamilton." He smiled. "That guy. He's always so serious and reserved. He literally lit up like a Christmas candle. You should have seen his face. He was so happy for me. Nurse Ohara came in and all the other nurses who, I guess, worked with me during my time in the hospital. They all shook my hand and hugged me, and some of them were crying." He laughed. "I was crying too."

Stella felt tears forming in her eyes, and David's face swam in front of her. "Did Dr. Hamilton say anything about this possibly being a transitory condition? You know, that you might forget again?"

"He said a full and functional TBI recovery is almost always possible, even though it might take a long time, sometimes years of dedication. But he said I have to take the initiative and that, in fact, without consistent work, brain injury recovery can stall and even regress and that I could still have occasional memory loss.

"But he also said that if I work hard at it and develop certain skills, which a therapist can help me with, there's no reason to think my recovery isn't permanent. I'm willing to put in the work, Stella. But are you willing to do that with me?"

Stella leaned forward and kissed him, a lingering kiss, transmitting all the love she'd ever had for him through her lips to his, with extra fervor and emotion. She pulled back, opened her eyes, and met his, memorizing every fleck, every nuance of color, every detail of his gaze meeting hers. "Yes, I am, David. Yes, I am."

His eyes overflowed with tears, and they fell down his face, one tear after another, onto their clasped hands. "Thank you, Stella. Thank you." He took a deep breath. "Can I meet up with Charlie? I've missed him so much. We were always so close."

Stella nodded. "I think that's a fantastic idea. I can bring him here after school. Today, if you wish."

"Yes. Yes. I'll grab some of his favorite chocolate chip cookies and—" he lifted his index finger—"along with some ice-cold milk in the special Patti's Pastries glass he always liked." He stood. "You'll stay here while he and I visit, right?"

"If you want me to, sure. It might make it a little easier… for both of you." She paused. "I'll be honest with you, David. He calls Robert 'Daddy' now. Robert had all the intentions of adopting him too. They're quite close."

David blew out a breath. "I understand. I really do. It's not like I'm surprised he'd bond with whoever you ended up with after our divorce. But, God, Stella, I never thought it would be Robert."

"Well, that's a story for another time. And I'd rather not spoil today with tales of Robert and my renewed relationship."

"Not a problem." He stood. "What time will you and Charlie be here?"

Stella followed him to the front door. "Soon after school gets out. I'll want to talk to him first. Prepare him before we get here. How's three o'clock?"

Chapter Forty

Before picking up Charlie, Stella took a short nap, showered, then selected a dress with colors David always favored. Then she drove to the school to pick up her son. She had to prepare him for what was to happen. She couldn't just drive over to David's apartment without giving Charlie an explanation. She wasn't sure how he'd handle this unexpected surprise.

Charlie and Robert had bonded. And now, what would Charlie think about Robert? What would he want to do with the relationship the two of them had formed? Would he want both Robert and David in his life? Robert had a relationship with Loreen and Gabe, so Robert, of course, would be coming around the house often. How would that affect Charlie?

But wait. What did Stella want? Could she leave Robert? Again? For the second time? But this time would be hugely different from the first time. Back then, she'd actually escaped. Ran away, as fast as she could. This time would be totally different. She loved Robert. She had been planning on marrying him.

Now what?

Again… what did she want?

Stella pulled up in front of the school, and Charlie rushed to the car, slamming the door behind him then buckling his seatbelt. He immediately began a detailed explanation of his day, to which Stella commented enthusiastically, as always, while she drove to the beach. She intended to park in a secluded spot overlooking the ocean where they could talk.

"Where're we going, Mommy?"

"I thought we'd park at that cool spot next to the beach. I have something I'd like to talk to you about."

"Did I do something bad? Did the principal call you? 'Cause I haven't done anything wrong, Mommy. I swear it."

Stella drove through the parking lot to the very end, where windswept trees hung over the sides of the parking spaces, shading the car from the sun's rays. It was out of the way and quiet. She parked and asked Charlie to join her in the front seat.

After settling into the passenger seat and turning toward her, Charlie looked at Stella with fear in his eyes. She knew by the expression on his face, he believed he was going to get in trouble. She felt sorry for the poor little guy, knowing what she had to tell him would, in some ways, be a double-edged sword. She would be giving him back his father, and, at the same time, taking away the father he was planning to have instead of his birth dad.

Stella reached out and took Charlie's hand in hers and smiled. "Honey, you remember your Daddy, of course."

Charlie nodded.

"That he got into a bad accident and had a serious injury to his brain."

Charlie nodded again. "And he doesn't remember any of us, so he got a divorce with you and you're gonna marry Robert instead, and we're all gonna live together and be a new family. That's what you said."

Stella nodded. "You're right, honey. That's what I told you. But things have changed, and I want to explain to you what happened, so you'll understand what's going on now."

Charlie's sweet little face clouded over. "Did Robert and you get in a fight? Aren't you gonna marry him anymore?"

"No, baby, Robert and I didn't get in a fight. He and I are really close friends. But, Charlie… um… David… I mean, your daddy… well, his brain healed. I went to visit him this morning, and we talked for a long time. He remembers everything now. He remembers that you're his son, that he's your daddy. He knows who I am and who Gabe is and Loreen and everything."

Stella had no idea what she had expected, because she had no expectations. This was one of the weirdest situations she'd ever experienced. But she wasn't expecting the tears sprinkling her son's cheeks and chin while his bottom lip trembled. Why exactly was he crying?

She cupped his face between her palms and bent toward him. "Honey… Charlie… tell me what you're thinking. Tell Mommy what you're feeling."

He sniffled and wiped under his nose with his sleeve, then looked up at her. "I prayed to the baby Jesus to make Daddy's memory come back. Every night after you read me my story? I waited for you to leave the room, then I sneaked out of bed and stood in front of the window and knelt on the floor and… and I cried… every night… I wanted Daddy to come back to us, and I tried to be good. Every day I tried not to get into any trouble at school, to not call Gabe and Loreen stupid, and I ate all my vegetables and salad. I wanted to be the best boy I could be, 'cause I wanted Jesus to know that I wanted Daddy to remember me and come back home to us." He leaned over and laid his head on his knees and sobbed.

Stella's heart felt as if it had cracked in two. Her son was such a gift, always had been. And she loved him more than she ever imagined possible. He was a good kid, a good person, with a kind and gentle heart. She had no idea he'd been praying for his father's memory to return. He was always so happy when he and Robert were playing together, throwing the baseball back and forth in the yard, going to the park, and to the movies. She hadn't a freaking clue his heart was breaking every single day over the loss of his daddy. And that he'd hidden it so well. She'd been clueless.

Stella rubbed his back and kissed the side of his silky-soft hair then laid her hand on his neck and waited for his crying to subside.

After a few moments, his sobs turned to sniffles until he sat up and turned his head toward her. "Can I see him?"

Stella smiled and grasped his hand once again. "Of course, you can. He's waiting for us right now. He lives in the apartment above the bakery. He's so excited to see you, Charlie. He was hoping you'd want to visit with him today."

"I do. I do. I don't wanna wait. Can I see him right now?"

Stella reached for the keys dangling from the ignition. "Let's go!"

She drove the few blocks to Patti's Pastries, parked in the back then climbed the stairs to David's apartment with Charlie in tow, his hand wrapped around hers. She could tell he was excited and nervous, because his grip was so tight, her knuckles ached. Yet she couldn't hide her smile. This was a day she never thought would come.

Was it an accident, or had Charlie's prayers and her prayers too been answered? After all was said and done and after Stella's many visits to the church, she believed it wasn't fate. Nope. This was a miracle.

Stella knocked on the door and held her breath.

The door knob turned, and David opened the door wide until it reached the wall. He stared down at Charlie, eyes glistening. "Charlie," he whispered, opening his arms.

Charlie rushed into his embrace, smashing his face into David's stomach, reaching his arms around David's waist and squeezing, his sobs muffled.

David wrapped his arms around Charlie's back and patted him over and over then gently pulled away and knelt down in front of him. "I've missed you so much, Charlie. And I'm so sorry I didn't remember you. Please forgive me."

Charlie hiccuped, tears gliding one after the other down his bright red cheeks. "I love you, Daddy. I prayed to the baby Jesus every night that you would come back home."

David smiled through the tears running down his face, dripping off his chin. "I guess your prayers were answered then, buddy, because I remember everything about you… and Mommy and Gabe and Loreen."

Charlie nodded. "And I'm gonna have a baby brother or sister soon too. And it's not Robert and Mommy's baby, she said. She told me it's you guys' baby, but she doesn't have a name for it, 'cause it might be a boy, but she's not sure, 'cause the nanogram lady didn't tell her what the baby is."

David chuckled. "The nanogram lady, huh? Well, I guess it's going to be a big surprise for all of us now, isn't it?"

Charlie nodded. "Can you come home with us now, Daddy?"

David glanced over Charlie's head at Stella and lifted his eyebrows.

Charlie turned to Stella. "Can he, Mommy? Can he?"

Stella knelt down, placed her hands on Charlie's shoulders, looked into his eyes. "I think that sounds like a great idea, honey." She bent her head back to see David's face. "What do you think, David?"

David pulled Stella and Charlie into an enthusiastic hug. "I want to go home."

THE END

BOOKS BY PATRICIA YAGER DELAGRANGE

A Heart Life
Mending Fences
Moon Over Alcatraz
Maddy's Phoenix
Taken Away
Passing Through Brandiss

ABOUT THE AUTHOR

Born and raised in the San Francisco Bay Area, Patricia attended St. Mary's College, studied her junior year at the University of Madrid, received a B.A. in Spanish at UC Santa Barbara then went on to get a Master's degree in Education at Oregon State University. She lives with her husband and two children in Alameda, across the bay from San Francisco, along with two chocolate labs, UJE and Remy. Her horse Zemra, a Gypsy Vanner, lives in the Oakland hills. He's now the new equine love of her life.